MW00830650

The Feminine Future

DOVER · THRIFT · EDITIONS

The Feminine Future

EARLY SCIENCE FICTION
BY WOMEN WRITERS

EDITED BY
MIKE ASHLEY

DOVER PUBLICATIONS, INC.
Mineola, New York

DOVER THRIFT EDITIONS

GENERAL EDITOR: MARY CAROLYN WALDREP
EDITOR OF THIS VOLUME: JIM MILLER

Copyright

Copyright © 2015 by Dover Publications, Inc.
All rights reserved.

Bibliographical Note

This Dover edition, first published in 2015, is a new compilation of early science fiction stories by women writers, selected and edited by Mike Ashley. For information on the sources of the texts, see page 227.

International Standard Book Number
ISBN-13: 978-0-486-79023-7
ISBN-10: 0-486-79023-1

Manufactured in the United States by RR Donnelley
79023102   2015
www.doverpublications.com

Contents

INTRODUCTION:
FORGOTTEN PIONEERS

THERE HAVE LONG been two misconceptions which I like to think are changing, but I'm not always entirely convinced. The first is that science fiction is only about adventures in space and time, with alien monsters or mad scientists or superheroes. Many critics of science fiction are set in their beliefs and aren't about to change overnight, but over the last twenty years or so there does seem to have been a mood swing, albeit begrudging at times, to recognize that some works of "literature" might also be science fiction; works like George Orwell's *Nineteen Eighty-Four* or Thomas Pynchon's *Gravity's Rainbow*.

The second misconception is that until recently few women wrote science fiction. This even though one of the very first works regarded as science fiction was by a woman, *Frankenstein* by Mary W. Shelley. It is recognized that considerably more women are writing science fiction today and, indeed, the two misconceptions can be brought together because so many women are writing science fiction "literature"—Margaret Atwood, Doris Lessing, P. D. James, Ursula K. Le Guin, and so on.

Yet the early contribution of women to the field continues to be overlooked. We have certain milestones, such as Clare Winger Harris being the first woman to contribute to the science fiction magazines, and Anne McCaffrey being the first woman to win the science fiction achievement award, the Hugo.

But if we were to only look back and consider what many women were writing, we will see that they were producing science fiction from time to time, and often helping develop new ideas and define the nature of what science fiction is.

And that's what this anthology is all about. I've brought together a selection of early stories, most, but not all, pre-1920s, all of which are science fiction, though some may come as a surprise. The fact that not all of the writers are household names is itself a sad reflection on our understanding of our literary roots. Some were well known in their day: Alice Brown, Harriet Prescott Spofford, Clotilde Graves, but over time their stars have faded. And because so many are forgotten, so is their contribution to science fiction. Which is one reason why we say so few women wrote science fiction in the early days: it's because we've simply forgotten them.

This anthology hopes to redress this situation.

Here are stories that help develop many of the basic ideas of science fiction—alternate worlds, other dimensions, invisibility, super-powers, shifts in time, automatons and cyborgs, thought-reading, immortality—in some cases amongst the earliest treatment of that theme, making them of historical significance. I was also keen to present stories that showed the human side of life—what the impact of technological progress was likely to be on us as human beings, and how we might cope.

I've looked for a diversity of treatment as well as ideas. Some stories are humorous, others serious and even shocking in their outlook on life and society. As well as being enjoyable, they cast a light back into those dark corners of science fiction history and hopefully provide at least some idea of what women were writing.

Mike Ashley

WHEN TIME TURNED

Ethel Watts Mumford
(1876–1940)

There's a good chance you've heard of Ethel Watts Mumford without realizing it, or at least one of her quotations: "God gives us our relatives—thank God we can choose our friends." It comes from The Cynic's Calendar *which she compiled with her friend Addison Mizner. Starting in 1903 the two of them produced a calendar where each week there was a new epigram or aphorism casting a cynical eye over the human condition. They added the name of Oliver Herford to the book as a joke, but it proved a good sales pitch because Herford, regarded as the American Oscar Wilde, was known for his wit. It was Herford who encouraged Mumford to write.*

Born Ethel Watts, in New York, she was the daughter of a wealthy business-man and had a good education. She travelled extensively in her youth but married young, in 1894, to the lawyer George Mumford. It was an unhappy marriage, as he disapproved of her writing and painting. At this time she was becoming not only an accomplished artist but a decent poet and a fledgling playwright, penning a number of farces. She tired of her husband's controlling arrogance and in 1899 ran away to San Francisco with their son and sued for divorce.

It was then Mumford turned to writing fiction in earnest. She entered the fol-lowing story in a contest run by The Black Cat *magazine. This magazine was famous in its day for discovering new authors, perhaps the best known being Jack London. It published what it called "clever" stories, which used unusual ideas in an original way. Her story "was a genuine brand-new idea," she later wrote. It was indeed—that we might start living our lives in reverse. This concept is probably best known from F. Scott Fitzgerald's story "The Curious Case of Benjamin Button" (1922), but here it is, twenty years earlier.*

Mumford later returned to New York and remarried, this time to a man who appreciated her literary and artistic talents. Thankfully we can still appreciate her ingenious prize-winning story.

I DROPPED IN at my friend Dr, Lamison's rooms, for I had been dull and bored all day, and Lamison, partly by reason of his profession, partly because of his own odd humor and keen insight, is a delightful companion.

To my disgust he was not alone, but deep in an animated discussion with an elderly gentleman of pleasant appearance. Being in no mood to talk to strangers, I was about to make my excuses and retire, but Lamison signed to me to remain. "Let me present my friend Robertson, Mr Gage," he said politely, as we both bowed with due formality. "Robertson," he continued, addressing me, "you will be interested in what this gentleman has to say on the Philippines—he has spent some years out there."

Mr Gage smiled reminiscently. "Yes, I spent some little time in the Islands. In fact, I am just on the point of going there now, and am very sorry I shall not see them again."

"What?" I asked. "If you're going, why do you say you will never see the place again?"

Lamison broke in abruptly. "That is a long story. Let's go on with the question we had in hand. You were saying that the Malays are singularly shrewd and cunning."

Mr Gage brightened visibly. "They are, indeed. Now, when I was in Manila,"—and he launched into a highly instructive lecture on the Malay and all his works, talking rapidly and tersely; his phrases full of vigour and originality, his descriptions vivid and picturesque; in fact, it has rarely been my good fortune to listen to so brilliant a conversationalist—though conversation it could hardly be called, for by common consent he had the floor to himself. Occasionally I asked a question, or Lamison punctuated the discourse with nods of approval as he flicked his cigar ashes on the floor.

From the Philippines we wandered to the Chinese empire and its destiny. Gage had spent two years in Tientsin and Hong Kong and was as well informed and interesting as a man could be. His observation was phenomenal, and his memory likewise, and he had a way of presenting his facts that was positively evocative. I felt, after listening to him, that the recollections were my own, so distinctly did he force his mental pictures into my consciousness. He was eminently moderate in all his views, avoiding extremes and holding a mean of charity and common sense that is, to say the least, unusual.

A flash of lightning that stared suddenly through the windows, and was followed by a terrific thunder clap, made us start and pause. Mr Gage arose and, going to the window, looked out into the murky night, remarking as he did so on the suddenness and violence of storms in the tropics.

I seized the occasion to nod to Lamison. "What a brilliant chap," I said. "I never heard a man express himself so well and sanely—who is he, anyway?"

"A gentleman and a scholar, also my guest for the present," my host answered. "So you think him well balanced?"

"Eminently so," I said heartily. "Not many men could state the facts of an international feud with such moderation."

Dr. Lamison smiled a strange, grave smile.

Our companion came back from the window whereon the heavy wash of the rain was now playing, and refilled his glass from the pitcher of shandygaff.

"So you are just on the point of making your first trip to the East?" Lamison asked, to my unutterable amazement.

Gage nodded. "Yes. In a few days I shall have decided."

I looked blankly at him.

"Then I suppose you will have, your quarrel with the family by next week?" my friend went on.

Gage sighed deeply. "Yes, I shall have to go through with it again. Fortunately the worst stages come first, and I have been feeling the after effect for some days already."

Lamison looked at my confusion with amusement.

"Tell Robertson about it all, old man," he said. "He is perfectly trustworthy, and yours is such an interesting story. To begin with, tell him how old you are."

Gage laughed, a quick boyish chuckle, and sprang up gaily, stretching himself before the sparkling fire. "Just three and twenty," he answered hilariously.

I looked at him carefully. His iron-gray hair, the infinitesimal tracery of lines that covered his face and hand like a fine-spun web, and the slight stiffness of his joints, in spite of his quick and rather graceful movements, bespoke a man in the later fifties. I understood now. He was doubtless one of the curious cases of mania which the doctor was constantly picking up and studying.

"Tell him how it happened," Lamison suggested.

Gage's face grew grave. "It's very sad, part of it—but on the whole I have been blest above all men, for I have lived my life twice over. It was this way"—he sat down once more in the easy chair from which he had risen; "I was devotedly fond of my

wife—one of the most charming women in the world, Mr
Robertson; but I lost her. She died, very suddenly, under singularly
painful circumstances." His mouth twitched, but he controlled
himself. "I was away on business in Washington when the news of
her sudden illness reached me. I waited for nothing, but left by the
first train. I remember giving ten dollars to the driver of the cab I
hailed on my arrival, if he would reach my house in ten minutes.
Aside from that the journey is only a blur of strain and horror. My
memory becomes clear again with the moment when I saw my
doorstep, wet and shining in the rain. I noted the reflected carriage
lamp on the streaming pavement. The servant who opened the
door at the sound of the stopping of my cab was crying.

"The house was brilliantly lit and I could hear hurried footsteps
on the floor above and catch a glimpse of the blue-clad figure of a
trained nurse. I rushed upstairs and into my wife's room. She raised
one hand feebly towards me, and a flash of recognition lit up her
face for an instant and then faded into waxen blankness. I can't
describe that hour—it is too keenly terrible for me to repeat and it
is not necessary to the story.

"At last it was all over, and her dear eyes closed forever, as I
thought then. A great emptiness settled upon my brain and heart.
Then came a slow tightening and straining sensation, somewhere
inside the dome of my skull, that seemed as fast as St. Peter's. A *snap*,
sharp as a broken banjo string and as perfectly audible, was its climax.
Then I steadied myself and looked about. Nothing had changed.
The room was still, for the others had gone and we were left alone
together—my wife and I. The silence was awful. Only the clock
ticked louder and louder and louder, till it beat like a drum.

"Then I glanced at the timepiece, an ordinary little porcelain
thing that my wife kept by her on the medicine table, and a cold
fear gripped me as I looked, for I realised that something wonderful and terrible was happening. With each tick the second hand
jerked one second backwards—the hands were moving around the
clock face from right to left. I started, and almost at the same
instant I felt the hand I held in mine grow relaxed and warm. I
gave a cry. The door opened. The nurse, who had been the last to
leave the chamber of death, came in. I saw her do exactly what she
had done before—but reversed. Then my sister backed in from the
opposite side, exactly as she had walked out, and turning, showed
me her tear-stained, convulsed face with the very movement with
which she had left us. The others came in; it was a strange

phenomenon. The doctor was there now, standing at the head of the bed. I looked at the clock. It was ticking and the hands slowly turning backwards. All at once I realised what had happened. Time had turned.

"I gasped when the thing dawned on me, it was so stupendous. But I saw my sweet wife's eyelids flutter, I saw her breath coming with difficulty, and I suffered once more with all my soul that terrible death agony. She turned toward me and lifted her hand with the gesture I had seen as I entered the room. In spite of myself I rose, and left her. I went down the stairs—the servant was there—I passed out into the street, to find the cab that had brought me standing before the door. I backed in. The horse trotted backward all the way to the station and I found myself on the train speeding backwards to the city I had left to come post haste to my darling's bedside.

"My reason shivered in my skull. If I could not sift this matter I knew I should go mad. The thing was strange past all endurance. So I sat in the train that was carrying me over the miles so recently covered, and considered. A dawn of delight came to me. It would not be so long before all this horror would have doubly passed. I would have to go to the hotel and receive that terrifying, crushing telegram announcing Isabelle's illness once more. Then I should go over the business that had called me on to Washington, but after that I should go back to my wife to find her strong and well, to live over again the happy years of our married life, to watch her growing daily younger, while I grew young with her.

"What matter that little tiffs re-occurred—they were so few, and the joy of those years so infinitely great. And that, Mr Robertson, is just, what happened."

He went on, after a pause, in which he seemed lost in happy reverie. "In a week I had grown somewhat accustomed to doing over again the things I had done, only reversed; it seemed almost a matter of course; and, after all, I cared little, for I knew I was soon going to find Isabelle, to be greeted by her good-bye kiss, the same with which she had bid me Godspeed on the fatal journey. I could hardly hold my impatience as, at last, I backed up to the house, and when I saw her standing on the porch as I had last seen her, well and strong, dressed in the pretty gray cloth, so becoming to her bright complexion and copper-coloured hair, I could have cried with joy. She greeted me as I expected, with good-byes, but my heart sang with delight as we went into the house together. I put down my dress suit case, and we ate luncheon together, beginning with dessert, and ending with the delicate omelette she had prepared herself, in honour of my unusual freedom to lunch with her. We went over our old conversations. I was longing to tell her of my delight in her presence, of my gratitude for the extraordinary reversal of nature that gave her back to me, but I could not. I was under bondage of the past. I could only say what I had said, do what I had done.

"Luncheon over—or, rather, correctly speaking, before it had begun—I bade her goodbye in my heart, but greeted her in my speech and went down to the treadmill round of my office work. My recent bereavement made me so tender of her presence, so hungry for the sight of her, that my very soul longed to expand itself in loving words and acts; I yearned to do and say a thousand affectionate things, but I could only do as I had done. I began to appreciate how I had let our relations become commonplace, and I hated myself for it. I saw a thousand ways in which I could have made her happier, or spared her pain, yet I could not take advantage of my new realisation of my love of her. Ah, it takes such an experience as mine to make a man understand what he has missed and what he might have been. But even if I could not be to her what I so dearly longed to show myself, yet in my heart no gesture of hers went unnoted, no tone of her voice unloved. She delighted me wholly and completely, and the caresses that I gave her in seeming perfunctoriness, and the words seemingly mere habits of expression, were really the outlet of my soul's yearning to her. We were very happy. For years we were constantly together, and never was wife so appreciated.

"Then a great fear began to grip my heart. I remember it came suddenly, in the very midst of the little feast we were having to celebrate the first year of our wedded life—our first anniversary. I realised that soon, in the very joy of our honeymoon I must anticipate our separation—the wedding would take place, next we would be engaged, then mere acquaintances, and, after that—oh, desolation—it would be before I met her, and I should never see her again. I lived that year, our second honeymoon, and the last of our life together, torn between the joy of my returned happiness and the terrible knowledge of my coming loss. The wedding day came and I could have cried out in my agony, but I could give my pain no voice. I had no tears, only smiles and laughter that must be gone through with, though my heart was breaking. Imagine it if you can, sirs. Was ever a man so tried?

"Then came the period of our engagement, when I knew we were drifting slowly and surely apart—and the happiness and misery of that time was, perhaps, the hardest of all to bear, even worse than the actual slow separation, though after my declaration, when our relations were formal and distant, it broke my heart to see her, whom I had loved so long, treat me as a mere acquaintance; and with it was the awful knowledge that there was no future hope, no possibility of our meeting—on this earth at least.

"The poignant day of my first meeting with her arrived at last. I saw her, as I had seen her then, so many years before, lighting that conventional ballroom with her presence, a radiant vision, all gold and rose, her tall, graceful figure gowned in soft, filmy drapery. I saw her with all my heart and soul, with all the pent-up memories of my twice-lived life, for I remembered it was the first, and I knew it was the last time I should see her. She vanished and I was left alone. For some time afterwards, although I was living over my cheerful, happy-go-lucky bachelor days, I was internally of a suicidal turn of mind, even on my return journeys in the East. I could not resign myself to losing this girl that, according to reversed time, I had never met. But youth is gay, and its recuperative powers strong, and I am growing steadily younger, you see. Then, too, other loves came and went, or rather went and came, and in spite of myself I am able to contemplate my double past with the buoyancy of my second youth.

"Yet it is all very strange, and recently unaccountable intervals have intruded into my life, such as this evening, for instance. You, gentlemen, are not a part of my boyish past, and yet you seem to be interpolated into my otherwise coherently backward existence. This has been happening for some time, and grows more marked. You may be dreams of my old life that I had forgotten, but I am at a loss to account for it fully. For instance—how could I have foretold then what the future had in store? And yet, in one sense that is what I am doing now, in telling you of my experience. You must admit that it is confusing."

Gage's story had fairly made me dizzy. I admitted that it was confusing. I hardly knew what to think. I even turned an anxious eye on the clock over the fireplace to assure myself that its hands still moved from left to right. As I faced it, Lamison regarded me with his amused but sympathetic eye.

"I hope to interpolate myself a great deal into your world, Gage," he said. "It's time you stopped in your mad career of growing younger. I don't want you on my hands when you become a troublesome stripling, or even when you have to unlearn your college education."

Gage laughed. "It will be rather hard, but I did enjoy my Harvard days, before I had that row with the family. Whew! How the old man did blow me up! And when I think I have to hear all that over again, it makes me sick."

He paused again and assisted his courage from the cheering pitcher.

"Another thing that worries me," he went on, "is this: Have you noticed that although all the happenings of my life seem to follow in well ordered reverse sequence, what I say does not? For instance, by all rights I should repeat my sentences verbatim backwards. 'I am glad to see you,' in reversed language would be, 'You see to glad am I.' Now, in all my years of reversed experiences, although the order of conversation progresses backwards, the sentences themselves make perfect forward sense. This drives me to distraction."

The whole impossible proposition danced before me, but Lamison was evidently delighted.

"Good, Gage, splendid! You are making progress—your logic is returning. I am unspeakably glad."

Gage looked at him wonderingly, "Why should you? It is only more confusing. Ah, well. I should not be unhappy if it were not the awful prospect of being a baby again. That revolts me, like becoming senile. It is such a horrible thing to become a squirming. senseless infant—it makes me shiver; it keeps me from sleeping, it is a menace too ugly and loathsome to be endured. Fancy it, gentlemen, the ignominy of it—the hideous helplessness."

"We'll find a way to prevent that," Lamison said soothingly. "You are better already. It won't be long before we set it all straight. Come, come, be a man—" for Gage suddenly flung himself on the table, his face buried in his hands, moaning slowly, "I don't want to be a baby—I don't want to be a baby."

This exhibition was so pitiful that I turned to Lamison, almost with tears in my eyes. "Is there any hope for him?" I asked.

Lamison nodded. "Yes, he'll pull through. A condition brought on by overwork and the sudden death of his wife, of whom he was devotedly fond. You see how he is beginning to realise the discrepancies of his imaginary life. He will come out all right—in time."

Gage now had himself under control and sat up shamefacedly. "Don't mind me, Mr Robertson," he said. "I don't often break down this way, and I wouldn't have you imagine for one instant that I regret my life. I could not have asked a greater boon of Fate than those happy years restored to me, when time had turned."

He rose gravely, excused himself, and left us, and we sat silent and deeply thoughtful, staring into the red embers of the fire.

THE PAINTER OF DEAD WOMEN

Edna W. Underwood
(1873–1961)

The following is usually regarded as a horror story, inasmuch as it is remembered at all. But it is based on a central scientific idea—that of suspended animation. The idea that you might fall into a coma and sleep for decades, even centuries, had long been a literary device, best known from Washington Irving's story "Rip Van Winkle" (1819), and Mary Griffith had used it as a way to travel to her future utopia in Three Hundred Years Hence *(1836). In these and other stories, though, no explanation was given for the prolonged sleep. The growth in the use of anaesthetics provided a scientific basis and steadily authors adopted the idea of the use of drugs to prolong sleep, as H. G. Wells did in* When the Sleeper Wakes *(1899). However, in the following story the idea is that the sleeper doesn't wake, that the body is somehow preserved in a comatose state, with the mind still functioning! That's why it's treated as a horror story.*

Edna Worthley was born in Maine, but settled in New York after her marriage in 1897 to jeweller Earl Underwood. It was the atmosphere of New York that spurred her into writing, but it was a while before any of her work was published other than a translation from the Russian of a work by Nikolai Gogol in 1903. But by the end of that decade she had enough short stories to assemble a volume, A Book of Dear Dead Women, *published in 1911 by Little, Brown of Boston. Curiously, apart from one further novelette, 'An Orchid of Asia' (1920), Underwood wrote no more short stories. She turned instead to poetry and then novels, her books reflecting her passion for Russian literature and history.*

A Book of Dear Dead Women is unusual in that its author reflected upon the possibility that various scientific breakthroughs had been made in the early Renaissance but subsequently lost or kept secret. Another story, "The Mirror of La Granja" suggests that a medieval chemist had created a glass that could trap the essence of the human spirit. It was perhaps a loss to the early years of science fiction that Underwood was drawn away to her other interests as who knows what else she might have imagined.

WE WERE LINGERING over one of our honeymoon breakfasts in Naples, my husband dividing his attention between *Il Corriere di Napoli* and his coffee, and I planning for my favorite pastime, swimming, in that sea which looks like a liquid sapphire.

"'No clue to the mysterious disappearance of the Contessa Fabriani,'" he read. "'After a month's search, the police are baffled.'"

"That does not sound particularly remarkable to you, I suppose. Women and men, too, for that matter have disappeared from other cities. But this adds another chapter to a mysterious story of crime. For twenty-five years not only native Italian women, but visiting women of other nations have disappeared from Naples, and nothing has afterward been heard of them. The peculiar part about it is that they have all been young and beautiful, and women of the upper class."

I paid little heed to his words. I was thinking of other things. Besides, Luigi was a Neapolitan and interested in all the happenings of his native city. On my first visit to Naples I did not have time to interest myself in a sensational story such as I could read any morning in the London papers.

"You have not forgotten that to-night is the ball?" said my husband, consulting his watch and jumping up. "I want you to look particularly lovely. All my friends and your old rivals will be there. Business takes me from the city for the day, and in case I should not return in time to accompany you, I have arranged for Cousin Lucia to meet you at ten at the door of the Cinascalchi Palace. I shall come later in time for part of the dancing. Tell Pietro to get you there at exactly ten," he called, after he had kissed me good-bye.

When I took a last look at myself in the glass that night, I felt that I had obeyed my husband's instructions. I was looking particularly lovely. I had dressed with the purpose of appearing as unlike Italian women as possible.

My slim six feet of stature was arrayed in a plain white satin princess, from which the shoulders rose scarcely less white and satiny. My hair was the color of the upland furze, and my cheeks glowed like the roses of an English garden.

"Pietro!" I called, after we had driven what seemed to me a very long time. "Are you sure that you are going in the right direction? I did not suppose that it was outside the city." He reassured me and drove on.

We entered the courtyard of a country estate. As I stepped from the carriage, I saw in the distance the grouped lights of Naples. Pietro whipped the horses and drove off before I had time to speak.

There were no other carriages in the yard. Could I have mistaken the time? Lucia was not there to meet me, either. "She is probably within," I reflected, "since the palace is bright with light."

Doors swung back softly and, as if by magic, I entered. The blaze of light that rushed out all but blinded me. Words cannot express the horror of it nor the silence that accompanied it. There were no servants moving about. No one was in sight. I was alone.

Imagine a sweep of majestic rooms whose floors were polished to the surface consistency of stone; straight white walls of mirrored marble, and, blazing from walls and ceiling, prisms of cut crystal. Wherever you looked the glitter of light flashed back at you, confusing your eyes and dazing your brain. I did not suppose that light could hold such terror.

"There is surely some mistake," I whispered. "This is no place for dancing or merriment. It is more like a white and shining sepulchre. I would rather trust myself to the night outside," and I turned toward the door with the purpose of leaving. But the space behind, where I knew that I had entered, presented a smooth and evenly paneled surface. There was no door. Nor was there place for lock or knob. As I stood confused and hesitating, I learned to the full the demoniac power of light. The slightest motion of my body, my head, my breathing, even, sent from polished corners and cornice quivering arrows into my eyes. The mirrors and the shining marble reflected floor and ceiling until it was impossible to tell where one left off and the other began. It seemed, after a time, that I was floating head downward in a sea of light.

Then something righted me sharply. It was not sound nor was it thought. It appealed to subtler senses. It was as if the material body was endowed with a thinking machine and each pore contained a brain. It aroused some consciousness which the hypnotism of light had dulled. I knew then that I was standing, slim and white and frozen with terror, in the focus of the light.

I felt the cold diamonds shift their position upon my throat and breast and tremble as I breathed irregularly. I heard the sibilant slipping of the stiff satin as it fell into a changed position.

A powerful and dominant brain had touched my own. For one unconscious moment it had ruled it and set upon it the seal of its thought.

Such a passion of fear assailed me that it seemed as if I must choke. My fascinated eyes turned toward the end of the farthest room. From there the message came. There, I knew, was something compelling, something electric. Exactly in the center of that far room, and very erect, stood a man. He was coming toward me, too, slowly very slowly. Yet I heard not the slightest sound. Evidently he was shod with rubber. He moved as I have seen a malevolent spider move toward a prisoned fly, enjoying the pleasure of motion because he knows that there is no escape for his victim. Just as gracefully and easily did he move toward me. And as he came, I knew that he read my soul, measured my strength and my power of resistance, and at the same time admired the white erectness of my body.

Fear, as with a bitter acid, etched his picture on my brain. He was very tall, taller than I by a good inch and faultlessly attired; a patrician, but a degenerate patrician, the body alone having preserved its ancient dignity.

Ribboned decorations brightened his coat, and I saw a garter on his leg.

He was thinner than any one I ever saw and correspondingly supple. His movements had the fascination of a serpent. Thus might a serpent move, if its coiled length were poised erect.

His head would have been beautiful, had not the features been so delicately chiseled that strength and nobility had been refined away, and in their place had come effeminacy and a certain cold and delicate cruelty.

He was an old man, too, and his heavy hair was white. His brows, however, were black and youthful, and from beneath looked out blue eyes. The eyes were the color of light when it shines through thick ice. They were the color of the sharp edge of fine steel when it is bared too quickly to the sun. In the same hard way the light ran across them.

But the strangest part was that there seemed to be no limit to their depth. However far you looked within, you could not find a person. You could not surprise a consciousness. There was no soul there. In its stead there was merely a keen and destructive intelligence.

I realized that the man coming toward me did not live by means of the physical acts of life. He had learned to live by his brain. He was a cerebral!

I sensed his dominant personality and struggled against it. I sensed, too, the presence of a numbing mental fluid that crippled my will and dulled me as does that sweet-smelling death which surgeons call the ansesthetic.

He had stripped himself of human attributes. He knew nothing of fear, pity, love.

"I have the honor of meeting, I believe, the bride of the Leopardi." He bowed and spoke in an even, unemotional voice.

I bowed in return. "How is it possible for you to know that? I do not remember having met you."

"It is not necessary to have met me. No beautiful woman comes to Naples whom I do not know. I," bowing again, "am Count Ponteleone, painter of dead women. You have probably heard of me."

"Who has not!" I exclaimed, somewhat reassured and wondering that this could be the man whose name was resounding through two continents.

"This intrusion which I beg you to pardon is due to the coachman's mistake. I am expected at the Cinascalchi ball. My husband and cousin await me there. If you will send me on in your carriage, I shall be grateful."

"Oh, no, your coachman made no mistake," calmly ignoring my request. "I brought him here and you, too, as I have brought other women by this," tapping his forehead.

"You are graciously jesting to excuse my rudeness," I managed to stammer, summoning the ghost of a smile.

"Well, we may as well call it a jest if you wish. It is a jest which ought to flatter. I entertain only beautiful women here."

The glance that accompanied this enveloped me from head to foot. It was a glance of admiration, and yet in it there was none of the desire of would-be love. It was devoid of warmth and emotion. Nothing could be more impersonal. No mark of material beauty had escaped it. It was the trained glance of a connoisseur which measures accurately. I might have been a picture or a piece of furniture.

I felt that he knew my racial standing, my rank as a human animal, by the delicate roundness of my bones and the fine fiber of my flesh. I had been as glass to his intelligent gaze. Somehow, then, I felt that the body of me belonged to him because of this masterly penetration which substance could not resist.

"Since you are to be my guest, we might seek a more comfortable place to converse."

He led the way to the center of the great rooms where, touching an invisible spring, doors flew back, disclosing a drawing-room draped in red. As he bowed me to a seat, he remarked: "Here you look like a pearl dropped in a cup of blood."

I, too, thought that I had never seen so wicked a red nor one so suggestive of luxurious crime. The comparison jarred upon me and prickled me with fear.

As he sank back in an easy-chair opposite, I saw how the red walls touched with color the whiteness of his hair and sent occasional ruddy gleams into the depth of his eyes.

"You are an Englishwoman, too," he observed, with evident relish. "I knew it. Only the mists and rains of England can make color like yours. Did you notice how well we looked together as we walked along between the mirrors? Are we not as if made for each other, tall and regal both of us? What a picture we would make!"

It occurred to me then, with unpleasant appropriateness, that he was the painter of dead women.

"It is an English woman, too, that I lack for my collection," he mused meditatively.

"Collection! Have you a collection of women? That is certainly unique. I have heard of collections of bugs, birds, but women, never. Perhaps you would like me to join it!"

"Indeed I should! I never saw a woman I admired so tremendously."

I drew back in fear, silenced by the ardor of his words.

"Oh, you need not be afraid. I am not like other men. I do not love as they love. I love only with my brain. While you have been sitting here, I have caressed you a thousand times, and you have not even suspected it. I do not want the bestial common pleasures which my coachman can have, or my scullion can buy with a lira. Why should not I be as much superior to them in my loves as in my life? If I am not, then I am not their superior in any way. My pleasures are those of another plane of life, of a brain touched to a keener fire, of nerves that have reached the highest point of pleasurable vibration. Besides, when I love, I love only dead women. Life reaches its perfection only when death comes. *Life is never real until then*," he added.

"Perhaps you would like to kill me for your amusement tonight," I replied, still trying to keep up the jest. "I have always flattered myself, however, that I was better alive."

No sooner were the words out than I regretted them. His face grew thin and strained like a bird-dog's on the scent. His lips became expressive of a terrible desire, and his frail hands trembled with anticipation.

As I looked, his pupils disappeared, and his eyes became two pools of blue and blazing light. Unwittingly I had hit upon his object. I had surprised his purpose in a jest.

Who could have dreamed of this! At the worst, I thought, I might be detained for two or three days, forced to serve him for a model, and cause worry to my husband and gossiping comment.

But whose imagination could have reached this! Strangely enough, the decree of death that I read in his face dissipated my fear.

I became calm and collected. In an instant I was mistress of myself and ready to fight for life. The blood stopped pounding in my brain. I could think with normal clearness.

"The worst of it is," I reflected, "this man is not mad. If he were, I might be able to play upon some delusion for freedom. He has passed the point where madness begins. He has gone just so much too far the other way."

"Then you really think that you could love me if I were dead," I laughed, leaning toward him gayly. "Is it not rather a strange requisite for winning a woman's love? What would my reward be? Are you sure you could not endure me any other way?"

"Do not jest about sacred things! Death," he answered slowly and reprovingly, "is the thing most to be desired by beautiful women. It saves them from something worse—old age. An ugly woman can afford to live; a beautiful woman can not. The real object of life is to ripen the body to its limit of physical perfection, and then, just as you would a perfect fruit, pluck and preserve it. Death sets the definite seal upon its perfection, that is, if death can be controlled to prevent decay. And that is what I can do," he added proudly, getting up in his abstraction and pacing up and down the room. "And what difference does it make, what day it comes? All days march toward death."

I admired unreservedly the elegant, intellectualized figure, now that I had thrown fear to the winds.

"Come," he pleaded, "let me kill you! It is because I love you that I ask you. It is because I think that your physical self is worth being preserved. Your future will be assured. You will never be less happy than now, less lovely, less triumphant. You will always be an object of admiration."

"What a magician you are to picture death attractively! But tell me more about it first."

Joy leaped up and sang in my heart at the prospect of the struggle. I felt as the race horse feels when, knowing the strength and the suppleness of his limbs, he sees the long white track unfold before him.

"In ancient days my ancestors," he began, "were Roman Governors in Spain. At the court of one of them, Vitellius Ponteleone, lived a famous Jewish physician (in old Spanish days the Jews were the first of scientists), by name Ibn Ezra. He made a poison (poison is not the right word, I regret greatly its vulgar suggestiveness) from a mineral which has now vanished from the face of the earth. This poison causes a delicious, pleasureful death, and at the same time arrests physical decay. Now, if you will just let me inject one drop of it into that white arm of yours, you will be immortal superior to time and change, indestructibly young. You do not seem to realize the greatness of the offer. For this honor I have selected you from all the women in Naples."

"It is an honor, of course; but, like a proposal of marriage, it seems to me important and to require consideration."

"Oh, no, it is not important. We have to prepare for life, but for death we are always ready. Besides, I am offering you a chance to choose your own death. How many can do that!"

"Do not think that I am ungrateful, good Count, but—"

"One little drop of the liquid will run through your veins like flame, cutting off thought and all centers of painful sensation. Only a dim sweet memory of pleasant things will remain. Gradually, then, cells and arteries and flesh will harden. In time your body will attain the hardness of a diamond and the whiteness of fine marble. But it is months, years, before the brain dies. I am not really sure that it ever dies. In it, like the iridescent reflections upon a soap bubble, live the shadows of past pleasures. There is no other immortality that can equal this which I offer. Every day that you live now lessens your beauty. In a way every day is a vulgar death. It coarsens and over-colors your skin, dulls the gold of your hair, makes this bodily line, or this, a bit too full. That is why I brought you here to-night, at the height of your beauty, just as love and life have crowned you."

"It must be a remarkable liquid. Let me see it. Is it with you?"

"No, indeed! It is kept in a vault which it takes an hour to open. It is guarded as are the crown jewels of Italy," he responded proudly.

"There is no immediate danger," I thought. "There is time. Now the road lies long before me."

"I suppose there is an antidote for this liquid. I will not call it poison, since you dislike the word so greatly."

"None that is known now. You see it destroys instantly what only patient nature can rebuild."

"I am greatly interested in it. Show me the other women upon whom you have tried it. I am eager to see its effect."

"I knew you would be. Come this way."

We ascended a staircase, where again I felt the sting of light. Upon a landing, half way up, he paused and pointed to our reflected figures.

"Are we not as if made for each other you and I? When I sleep the white liquid sleep, I shall arrange that it be beside you."

My death evidently was firmly determined upon.

At the top he unlocked a door, and we entered a room where some fifty women were dancing a minuet. Above them great crystal chandeliers swung, giving to their jewels and their shimmering silks and satins reflected life. Each one was in an attitude of arrested motion. It was as if they had been frozen in the maddest moment of a dance. But what a horrible sight this dance of dead women, this mimic merriment of death!

"You know my picture of this scene, do you not?" said he, turning on more light. "They were perfect models, I can assure you. I can paint them for hours in any light.

"When I die I shall bequeath to Naples this art gallery. Will it not be a gift to be proud of? Nothing can surpass it in uniqueness. Then the bodies of these women will have attained the hardness and the whiteness of fine marble. They can in no way be distinguished from it except by their hair.

"Of course now, if the outside world knew of this, I should be punished as a murderer."

How firmly it is settled in his mind that the outside world is mine no more!

"But then I shall be revered as a scientist who preserved for posterity the most perfect human specimens of the age in which I lived. I shall be looked upon as a God. It is as great to preserve life as it is to make it."

The next room we entered was a luxurious boudoir. Before an exquisite French dressing-table sat a woman whose bronze hair swept the floor. On either side peacocks stood with outspread tails. Their backs served as a rest for a variety of jeweled hair pins, one of which she was in the act of picking up.

"That is the Contessa Fabriani. She is not dead yet. She hears every word we say, but she is unable to speak. I am painting her now. You can see the unfinished picture against the wall."

In an adjoining room a dark-skinned woman of the Orient, whose black and unbound hair showed purplish tints, was reclining upon the back of a Bengal tiger. Other Eastern women lay upon couches and divans.

"See, even in death, what enticing languor! See the arrested dreams in their dark eyes, deep as an Oriental night! These women I have loved very greatly. Sometimes I have a fancy that death cannot touch them. In them there is an electric energy, the stored-up indestructible ardor of the sun, which, I like to fancy, death cannot dissipate."

"Now here," said the Count, opening another door, "I will show you an effect I have tried for years to reproduce. This has been the desire of my life."

He flung back a row of folding windows, making the room on one side open to the sea.

"It is the effect of the blended radiance flung from the water here and the moon, upon dull silver, upon crystal, and the flesh of blond women."

He turned out the lights. The moon sent an eerie, shivering luster across the crystal and silver decorations, and touched three women in robes of white, who were standing in attitudes of dreaming indolence.

"This thin, ethereal, surface light, this *puissance de lumiere*, is what I have tried in vain to prison. I have always been greedy of the difficult and the unattainable. If I could do this, I should be the prince of painters! It is a fact, a real thing, and yet it possesses the magic of dreams, the enchantment of the fleeting and the illusory.

"I wish to be the wizard of light. I wish to be the only one to prison its bright, defiant insubstantiality. Can you not see how wonderful it is? It is the dust of light. Reflected upon silver and clear crystal it is what shadow is to sound. Sometimes it seems to me like a thin, clear acid; then like some blue, sweet-smelling volatile liquid, eager again to join the air. Have you noticed how it penetrates blond flesh? It reveals, yet transfigures it. I wish you could watch its effect often. Sometimes the wind churns the sea-light into transparent foam. Then I love its curd-like, piled-up whiteness. Sometimes when there is no moon, and only a wan, tremulous luster from the water, the light of a far star is focused on their satins, on their diamonds, struggles eeriely among their laces, or flickers mournfully from a pearl. The room then is filled with a regretful, metallic radiance. The stars caress them. They have become impersonal, you see, and the eternal things love them.

"When the autumn moons are high, the light that fills the room is resonant and yellow. It tingles like a crystal. It gives their cold white satins the yellow richness of the peach's heart, and to the women the enticing languor of life. On such nights the moonlight is musical and makes the crystal vibrate Now, to-night, the light is more like the vanishing ripple of the sea. Is it not wonderful? Look! It is the twin of silence, the ghost of light!"

In his excitement and exhilaration, his eyes shone like the moon-swept sea. I knew that in them, too, slept terrors inconceivable.

"This is the room I have in mind for you. You will queen it by a head over the other women. The color of your dress is right. Your gems, too, are white. Here, sometime, I promise to join you, and together we will be immortal.

"Excuse me just a moment. Wait here. Let me get the liquid and show it to you. You will be fascinated by it, just as other women have been. I never saw one who could resist it."

As he left, I heard the key turn in the lock. When we entered the other rooms, I remembered that he bolted the doors on the inside. This door, then, was the only one by which he could gain entrance. Swiftly I slipped the bolt. Now I was safe for a time, unless there was a secret entrance.

It was not far from the window to the water. I laughed with delight. I had dived that distance many a time for pleasure. I was one of the best swimmers in England, and I had always longed for a plunge in this sapphire sea. Now was my chance and life as the goal to gain. I took off my satin gown as gayly as I had put it on. Like the Count of Ponteleone, I, too, admired the play of light on its piled-up whiteness. How merrily the sea-wind came! How it counseled courage!

I took the plunge. Down, down, down I went, cleaving the clear water. The distance up seemed interminable. It was like being born again when at last I saw the white foam feather my arms and felt my lungs expand with air. I swam in the direction of Naples. I could not reach the city, but I could easily reach some fisher's hut and there gain shelter.

Oh, the delight of that warm, bright water under the moon! I felt that the strength of my arms and my legs was inexhaustible. I exulted in the water as a bird exults in its natural element, the air.

After I had covered what I thought to be a safe distance, I turned on my back and floated. Then I caught sight of the window from which I had leaped. It was brilliantly lighted. Count Ponteleone was leaning from it, his white hair shining like a malevolent flame. Despite the distance, I could feel the power of his wild blue eyes, which sparkled like the sea. Again I dived, lest they should reassert their power over me and draw me back.

I came up under the shadow of the shore, and made my way along until I reached a boat where Neapolitan fisherwomen were spreading their nets to dry.

They took me in, and for the doubled price of a good month's fishing brought me that night to Naples.

"Ah, Luigi," I sobbed, as he folded me in his arms, "little did I think, when you spoke of the dance this morning, that I should spend the night with the dead dancing women of Ponteleone."

"Nor I that you would solve Naples mystery of crime."

THE AUTOMATON EAR

Florence McLandburgh
(1850–1934)

The following is the earliest story in this book, dating from 1873. Its age perhaps betrays the comparatively impractical nature of the invention described, but who lets technicalities get in the way of an imaginative idea. The author wonders whether all sounds made throughout history can be captured and heard again, but she exercises caution over the idea by questioning the state of mind of the inventor.

Florence McLandburgh, who lived for much of her life in Chicago, though she was born and died in Ohio, was better known as a poet, often under the pseudonym McLandburgh Wilson. Her poetry was collected in The Little Flag on Main Street *(1917), which showed her support for the war effort. Her few short stories were collected as* The Automaton Ear and Other Stories *(1876), which includes several supernatural stories and shows her interest in music and the rhythm of words.*

THE DAY WAS hardly different from many another day, though I will likely recall it even when the mist of years has shrouded the past in an undefined hueless cloud. The sunshine came in at my open window. Out of doors it flooded all the land in its warm summer light—the spires of the town and the bare college campus; farther, the tall bearded barley and rustling oats; farther still, the wild grass and the forest, where the river ran and the blue haze dipped from the sky.

The temptation was greater than I could stand, and taking my book I shut up the "study," as the students called my small apartment, leaving it for one bounded by no walls or ceiling.

The woods rang with the hum and chirp of insects and birds. I threw myself down beneath a tall, broad-spreading tree. Against its moss-covered trunk I could hear the loud tap of the woodpecker secreted high up among its leaves, and off at the end of a tender young twig a robin trilled, swinging himself to and fro through the checkered sunlight. I never grew weary listening to the changeful voice of the forest and the river, and was hardly conscious of reading until I came upon this paragraph:

> As a particle of the atmosphere is never lost, so sound is never lost. A strain of music or a simple tone will vibrate in the air forever and ever, decreasing according to a fixed ratio. The diffusion of the agitation extends in all directions, like the waves in a pool, but the ear is unable to detect it beyond a certain point. It is well known that some individuals can distinguish sounds which to others under precisely similar circumstances are wholly lost. Thus the fault is not in the sound itself, but in our organ of hearing, and a tone once in existence is always in existence.

This was nothing new to me. I had read it before, though I had never thought of it, particularly; but while I listened to the robin, it seemed singular to know that all the sounds ever uttered, ever born, were floating in the air *now*—all music, every tone, every bird-song—and we, alas! could not hear them.

Suddenly a strange idea shot through my brain—Why not? Ay, *why not hear*? Men had constructed instruments which could magnify to the eye and—was it possible?—Why not?

I looked up and down the river, but saw neither it, nor the sky, nor the moss that I touched. Did the woodpecker still tap secreted among the leaves, and the robin sing, and the hum of insects run along the bank as before? I cannot recollect, I cannot recollect anything, only Mother Flinse, the deaf and dumb old crone that occasionally came to beg, and sell nuts to the students, was standing in the gateway. I nodded to her as she passed, and walked up her long, slim shadow that lay on the path. It was a strange idea that had come so suddenly into my head and startled me. I hardly dared to think of it, but I could think of nothing else. It could not be possible, and yet—why not?

Over and over in the restless hours of the night, I asked myself, I said aloud, Why not? Then I laughed at my folly, and wondered what I was thinking of and tried to sleep—but if it *could* be done?

The idea clung to me. It forced itself up in class hours and made confusion in the lessons. Some said the professor was ill those two or three days before the vacation; perhaps I was. I scarcely slept; only the one thought grew stronger—Men had done more wonderful things, it certainly was possible, and I would accomplish this grand invention. I would construct the king of all instruments—I would construct an instrument which could catch these faint tones vibrating in the air and make them audible. Yes, and I would labor quietly until it was perfected, or the world might laugh.

The session closed, and the college was deserted, save by the few musty students whom, even in imagination, one could hardly separate or distinguish from the old books on the library shelves. I could wish for no better opportunity to begin my great work. The first thing would be to prepare for it by a careful study of acoustics, and I buried myself among volumes on the philosophy of sound.

I went down to London and purchased a common ear-trumpet. My own ear was exceedingly acute, and to my great delight I found that, with the aid of the trumpet just as it was, I could distinguish sounds at a much greater distance, and those nearer were magnified in power. I had only to improve upon this instrument; careful study, careful work, careful experiment, and my hopes would undoubtedly be realized.

Back to my old room in the college I went with a complete set of tools. So days and weeks I shut myself in, and every day and every week brought nothing but disappointment. The instrument seemed only to diminish sound rather than increase it, yet still I worked on and vowed I would not grow discouraged.

Hour after hour I sat, looking out of my narrow window. The fields of barley and waving oats had been reaped, the wheat too had ripened and gone, but I did not notice. I sprang up with a joyful exclamation—Strange never to have thought of it before! Perhaps I had not spent my time in vain, after all. How could I expect to test my instrument in this close room with only that little window? It should be removed from immediate noises, high up in the open air, where there would be no obstructions. I would never succeed here—but where should I go? It must be some place in which I would never be liable to interruption, for my first object was to be shielded and work in secret.

I scoured the neighborhood for an appropriate spot without success, when it occurred to me that I had heard some say the old grey church was shut up. The church was situated just beyond the suburbs of the town. It was built of rough stone, mottled and stained by unknown years. The high, square tower, covered by thick vines that clung and crept round its base, was the most venerable monument among all the slabs and tombs where it stood sentinel. Only graves deserted and uncared for by the living kept it company. People said the place was too damp for use, and talked of rebuilding, but it had never been done. Now if I could gain access to the tower, that was the very place for my purpose.

I found the door securely fastened, and walked round and round without discovering any way of entrance; but I made up my mind, if it were possible to get inside of that church I would do it, and without the help of keys. The high windows were not to be thought of; but in the rear of the building, lower down, where the fuel had probably been kept, there was a narrow opening which was boarded across. With very little difficulty I knocked out the planks and crept through. It was a cellar, and, as I had anticipated, the coal receptacle. After feeling about, I found a few rough steps which led to a door that was unlocked and communicated with the passage back of the vestry-room.

The tower I wished to explore was situated in the remote corner of the building. I passed on to the church. Its walls were discolored by green mould, and blackened where the water had dripped through. The sun, low down in the sky, lit the tall, arched windows on the west, and made yellow strips across the long aisles, over the faded pews with their stiff, straight backs, over the chancel rail, over the altar with its somber wood-work; but there was no warmth; only the cheerless glare seemed to penetrate the cold, dead atmosphere,—only the cheerless glare, without sparkle, without life, came into that voiceless sanctuary where the organ slept. At the right of the vestibule, a staircase led to the tower; it ascended to a platform laid on a level with the four windows and a little above the point of the church roof. These four windows were situated one on each side of the tower, running high up, and the lower casement folding inward.

Here was my place. Above the tree-tops, in the free open air, with no obstacle to obstruct the wind, I could work unmolested by people or noise. The fresh breeze that fanned my face was cool and pleasant. An hour ago I had been tired, disappointed, and depressed; but now, buoyant with hope, I was ready to begin work again—work that I was determined to accomplish.

The sun had gone. I did not see the broken slabs and urns in the shadow down below; I did not see the sunken graves and the rank grass and the briers. I looked over them and saw the gorgeous fringes along the horizon, scarlet and gold and pearl; saw them quiver and brighten to flame, and the white wings of pigeons whirl and circle in the deepening glow.

I closed the windows, and when I had crawled out of the narrow hole, carefully reset the boards just as I had found them. In another day all the tools and books that I considered necessary were safely deposited in the tower. I only intended to make this my workshop, still, of course, occupying my old room in the college.

Here I matured plan after plan. I studied, read, worked, knowing, *feeling* that at last I must succeed; but failure followed failure, and I sank into despondency only to begin again with a kind of desperation. When I went down to London and wandered about, hunting up different metals and hard woods, I never encountered a concert-room or an opera-house. Was there not music in store for me, such as no mortal ear had ever heard? *All* the music, every strain that had sounded in the past ages? Ah, I could wait; I would work patiently and wait.

I was laboring now upon a theory that I had not tried heretofore. It was my last resource; if this failed, then—but it would not fail! I resolved not to make any test, not to put it near my ear until it was completed. I discarded all woods and used only the metals which best transmitted sound. Finally it was finished, even to the ivory ear-piece. I held the instrument all ready—I held it and looked eastward and westward and back again. Suddenly all control over the muscles of my hand was gone, it felt like stone; then the strange sensation passed away. I stood up and lifted the trumpet to my ear—What! Silence? No, no—I was faint, my brain was confused, whirling. I would not believe it; I would wait a moment until this dizziness was gone, and then—then I would be able to hear. I was deaf now. I still held the instrument; in my agitation the ivory tip shook off and rolled down rattling on the floor. I gazed at it mechanically, as if it had been a pebble; I never thought of replacing it, and, mechanically, I raised the trumpet a second time to my ear. A crash of discordant sounds, a confused jarring noise broke upon me and I drew back, trembling, dismayed.

Fool! O fool of fools never to have thought of this, which a child, a dunce, would not have over-looked! My great invention was nothing, was worse than nothing, was worse than a failure. I might have known that my instrument would magnify present sounds in the air to such a degree as to make them utterly drown all others, and, clashing together, produce this noise like the heavy rumble of thunder.

The college reopened, and I took up my old line of duties, or at least attempted them, for the school had grown distasteful to me. I was restless, moody, and discontented. I tried to forget my disappointment, but the effort was in vain.

The spires of the town and the college campus glittered white, the fields of barley and oats were fields of snow, the forest leaves had withered and fallen, and the river slumbered, wrapped in a sheeting of ice. Still I brooded over my failure, and when again the wild grass turned green, I no longer cared. I was not the same man that had looked out at the waving grain and the blue haze only a year before. A gloomy despondency had settled upon me, and I grew to hate the students, to hate the college, to hate society. In the first shock of discovered failure I had given up all hope, and the Winter passed I know not how. I never wondered if the trouble could be remedied. Now it suddenly occurred to me, perhaps it was no failure after all. The instrument might be made adjustable, so as to be sensible to faint or severe vibrations at pleasure of the operator, and thus separate the sounds. I remembered how but for the accidental removal of the ivory my instrument perhaps would not have reflected any sound. I would work again and persevere.

I would have resigned my professorship, only it might create suspicion. I knew not that already they viewed me with curious eyes and sober faces. When the session finally closed, they tried to persuade me to leave the college during vacation and travel on the continent. I would feel much fresher, they told me, in the Autumn. In the Autumn? Ay, perhaps I might, perhaps I might, and I would not go abroad.

Once more the reapers came unnoticed. My work progressed slowly. Day by day I toiled up in the old church tower, and night by night I dreamed. In my sleep it often seemed that the instrument was suddenly completed, but before I could raise it to my ear I would always waken with a nervous start, So the feverish time went by, and at last I held it steady for a second trial. Now the instrument was adjustable, and I had also improved it so far as to be able to set it very accurately for any particular period, thus rendering it sensible only to sounds of that time, all heavier and fainter vibrations being excluded.

I drew it out almost to its limits.

All the maddening doubts that had haunted me like grinning specters died. I felt no tremor, my hand was steady, my pulse-beat regular.

The soft breeze had fallen away. No leaf stirred in the quiet that
seemed to await my triumph. Again the crimson splendor of sunset
illumined the western sky and made a glory overhead—and the
dusk was thickening down below among the mouldering slabs.
But that mattered not.

I raised the trumpet to my ear.

Hark!—The hum of mighty hosts! It rose and fell, fainter and
more faint; then the murmur of water was heard and lost again, as
it swelled and gathered and burst in one grand volume of sound
like a hallelujah from myriad lips. Out of the resounding echo, out
of the dying cadence a single female voice arose. Clear, pure, rich,
it soared above the tumult of the host that hushed itself, a living
thing. Higher, sweeter, it seemed to break the fetters of mortality
and tremble in sublime adoration before the Infinite. My breath
stilled with awe. Was it a spirit-voice one of the glittering host in
the jasper city "that had no need of the sun, neither of the moon
to shine in it?" And the water, was it the river flowing clear as
crystal from the great white throne? But no! The tone now floated
out soft, sad, human. There was no sorrowful strain in that night-
less land where the leaves of the trees were for the healing of the
nations. The beautiful voice was of the earth and sin-stricken.
From the sobbing that mingled with the faint ripple of water it
went up once more, ringing gladly, joyfully; it went up inspired
with praise to the sky, and—hark! the Hebrew tongue:

"The horse and his rider hath he thrown into the sea."

Then the noise of the multitude swelled again, and a crash of
music broke forth from innumerable timbrels. I raised my head
quickly—it was the song of Miriam after the passage of the Red Sea.

I knew not whether I lived.

I bent my ear eagerly to the instrument again and heard—the
soft rustle, the breathing as of a sleeping forest. A plaintive note
stole gently out, more solemn and quiet than the chant of the
leaves. The mournful lay, forlorn, frightened, trembled on the air
like the piteous wail of some wounded creature. Then it grew
stronger. Clear, brilliant, it burst in a shower of silver sounds like
a whole choir of birds in the glitter of the tropical sunlight. But the
mournful wail crept back, and the lonely heart-broken strain was
lost, while the leaves still whispered to one another in the
midnight.

Like the light of a distant star came to me this song of some
nightingale, thousands of years after the bird had mouldered to

nothing. At last my labor had been rewarded, As sound travels in waves, and these waves are continually advancing as they go round and round the world, therefore I would never hear the same sound over again at the same time, but it passed beyond and another came in its stead.

All night I listened with my ear pressed to the instrument. I heard the polished, well-studied compliments, the rustle of silks, and the quick music of the dance at some banquet. I could almost see the brilliant robes and glittering jewels of the waltzers, and the sheen of light, and the mirrors. But hush! a cry, a stifled moan. Was that at the—No, the music and the rustle of silk were gone.

"Mother, put your hand here—I am tired, and my head feels hot and strange. Is it night, already, that it has grown so dark? I am resting now, for my book is almost done, and then, mother, we can go back to the dear old home where the sun shines so bright and the honeysuckles are heavy with perfume. And, mother, we will never be poor any more. I know you are weary, for your cheeks are pale and your fingers are thin; but they shall not touch a needle then, and you will grow better, mother, and we will forget these long, bitter years. I will not write in the evenings then, but sit with you and watch the twilight fade as we used to do and listen to the murmur of the frogs. I described the little stream, our little stream, mother, in my book.—Hark! I hear the splash of its waves now. Hold me by the hand tight, mother. I am tired, but we are almost there. See! the house glimmers white through the trees, and the red bird has built its nest again in the cedar. Put your arm around me, mother, mother—"

Then single, echoless, the mother's piercing cry went up—"O my God!"

Great Heaven! It would not always be music that I should hear. Into this ear, where all the world poured its tales, sorrow and suffering and death would come in turn with mirth and gladness.

I listened again. The long-drawn ahoy!—ahoy!—of the sailor rang out in slumbrous musical monotone, now free, now muffled—gone. The gleeful laugh of children at play, then the drunken boisterous shout of the midnight reveler—What was that? A chime of bells, strange, sublime, swimming in the air they made a cold, solemn harmony. But even over them dashed the storm-blast of passion that sweeps continually up and down the earth, and the harmony that bound them in peace broke up in a wild, angry clamor, that set loose shrill screams which were swallowed up in a savage tumult of discord, like a mad carnical of yelling demons. Then, as if terrified by their own fiendish rage, they retreated shivering, remorseful, and hushed themselves in hoarse whispers about the gray belfry. It was the Carillonneur, Matthias Vander Gheyn, playing at Louvain on the first of July, 1745.

Yes, my invention had proved a grand success. I had worked and worked in order to give this instrument to the world; but now when it was finished, strange to say, all my ambition, all my desire for fame left me, and I was anxious only to guard it from discovery, to keep it secret, to keep it more jealously than a miser hoards his gold. An undefinable delight filled my soul that I alone out of all humanity possessed this treasure, this great Ear of the World, for which kings might have given up their thrones. Ah! they dreamed not of the wonders I could relate. It was a keen, intense pleasure to see the public for which I had toiled live on, deaf forever save to the few transient sounds of the moment, while I, their slave, reveled in another world, above, beyond theirs. But they should never have this instrument; no, not for kingdoms would I give it up, not for life itself.

It exerted a strange fascination over me, and in my eager desire to preserve my secret a tormenting fear suddenly took possession of me that someone might track me to the tower and discover all. It seemed as if the people looked after me with curious faces as I passed. I went no longer on the main road that led to the church, but, when I left my room, took an opposite direction until out of sight, and then made a circuit across the fields. I lived in a continual fear of betraying myself, so that at night I closed my window and door lest I might talk aloud in my sleep. I could never again bear the irksome duties of my office, and when the college re-opened I gave up my situation and took lodgings in town. Still the dread of detection haunted me. Every day I varied my route to the church, and every day the people seemed to stare at me with a more curious gaze. Occasionally some of my old pupils came to visit me, but they appeared constrained in my presence and were soon gone. However, no one seemed to suspect my secret; perhaps all this was merely the work of my imagination, for I had grown watchful and reticent.

I hardly ate or slept. I lived perpetually in the past listening to the echoing song of the Alpine shepherd; the rich, uncultivated soprano of the Southern slave making strange, wild melody. I heard grand organ fugues rolling, sweeping over multitudes that kneeled in awe, while a choir of voices broke into a gloria that seemed to sway the great cathedral. The thrilling artistic voices of the far past rang again, making my listening soul tremble in their magnificent harmony. It was music of which we could not dream.

Then suddenly I determined to try the opera once more; perhaps I was prejudiced: I had not been inside of a concert-room for more than a year.

I went down to London. It was just at the beginning of the season. I could hardly wait that evening until the curtain rose; the orchestra was harsh and discordant, the house hot and disagreeable, the gas painfully bright. My restlessness had acquired a feverish pitch before the prima donna made her appearance. Surely that voice was not the one before which the world bowed! Malibran's song stood out in my memory clearly defined and complete, like a magnificent cathedral of pure marble, with faultless arches and skilfully chiseled carvings, where the minarets rose from wreaths of lilies and vine leaves cut in bas-relief, and the slender spire shot high, glittering yellow in the upper sunlight, its golden arrow, burning like flame, pointing towards the East. But this prima donna built only a flat, clumsy structure of wood ornamented by gaudily painted lattice. I left the opera amid the deafening applause of the audience with a smile of scorn upon my face. Poor deluded creatures! they knew nothing of music, they knew not what they were doing.

I went to St. Paul's on the Sabbath. There was no worship in the operatic voluntary sung by hired voices; it did not stir my soul and their cold hymns did not warm with praise to the Divine Creator, or sway the vast pulseless congregation that came and went without one quickened breath.

All this time I felt a singular, inexpressible pleasure in the consciousness of my great secret, and I hurried back with eager haste. In London I had accidentally met two or three of my old acquaintances. I was not over glad to see them myself: as I have said, I had grown utterly indifferent to society; but I almost felt ashamed when they offered me every attention within their power, for I had not anticipated it, nor was it deserved on my part. Now, when I returned, everybody in the street stopped to shake hands with me and inquire for my health. At first, although I was surprised at the interest they manifested, I took it merely as the common civility on meeting, but when the question was repeated so particularly by each one, I thought it appeared strange, and asked if they had ever heard to the contrary; no, oh no, they said, but still I was astonished at the unusual care with which they all made the same inquiry.

I went up to my room and walked directly to the glass. It was the first time I had consciously looked into a mirror for many weeks. Good Heavens! The mystery was explained now. *I could hardly recognise myself.* At first the shock was so great that I stood gazing, almost petrified. The demon of typhus fever could not have wrought a more terrific change in my face if he had held it in his clutches for months. My hair hung in long straggling locks around my neck. I was thin and fearfully haggard. My eyes sunken far back in my head, looked out from dark, deep hollows; my heavy black eyebrows were knit together by wrinkles that made seams over my forehead: my fleshless cheeks clung tight to the bone, and a bright red spot on either one was half covered by thick beard. I had thought so little about my personal appearance lately that I had utterly neglected my hair, and I wondered that it had given me no annoyance. I smiled while I still looked at myself. This was the effect of the severe study and loss of sleep, and the excitement under which I had labored for months, yes, for more than a year. I had not been conscious of fatigue, but my work was done now and I would soon regain my usual weight. I submitted myself immediately to the hands of a barber, dressed with considerable care, and took another look in the glass. My face appeared pinched and small since it had been freed from beard. The caverns around my eyes seemed even larger, and the bright color in my cheeks contrasted strangely with the extremely sallow tint of my complexion. I turned away with an uncomfortable feeling, and started on a circuitous route to the church, for I never trusted my instrument in any other place.

It was a sober autumn day. Everything looked dreary with that cold, gray, sunless sky stretched overhead. The half-naked trees shivered a little in their scared garments of ragged leaves. Occasionally a cat walked along the fence-top, or stood trembling on three legs. Sometimes a depressed bird tried to cheer its drooping spirits and uttered a few sharp, discontented chirps. Just in front of me two boys were playing ball on the road-side. As I passed I accidentally caught this sentence:

"They say the professor ain't just right in his head."'

For a moment I stood rooted to the ground; then wheeled round and cried out fiercely,

"What did you say?"

"Sir?"

"What was that you said just now?" I repeated still more fiercely.

The terrified boys looked at me an instant, then without answering turned and ran as fast as fright could carry them.

So the mystery now was really explained! It was not sick the people thought me, but crazy. I walked on with a queer feeling and began vaguely to wonder why I had been so savage to those boys. The fact which I had learned so suddenly certainly gave me a shock, but it was nothing to me. What did I care, even if the people did think me crazy? Ah! perhaps if I told my secret they would consider it a desperate case of insanity. But the child's words kept ringing in my ears until an idea flashed upon me even more terrifying than death itself. How did I know that I was *not* insane? How did I know that my great invention might be only a hallucination of my brain?

Instantly a whole army of thoughts crowded up like ghostly witnesses to affright me. I had studied myself to a shadow; my pallid face, with the red spots on the cheeks and the blue hollows around the eyes, came before my mental vision afresh. The fever in my veins told me I was unnaturally excited. I had not slept a sound, dreamless sleep for weeks. Perhaps in the long, long days and nights my brain, like my body, had been over-wrought; perhaps in my eager desire to succeed, in my desperate determination, the power of my will had disordered my mind, and it was all deception: the sounds, the music I had heard, merely the creation of my diseased fancy, and the instrument I had handled useless metal. The very idea was inexpressible torture to me. I could not bear that a single doubt of its reality should exist; but after once entering my head, how would I ever be able to free myself from distrust? I could not do it; I would be obliged to live always in uncertainty. It was maddening: now I felt as if I might have struck the child in my rage if I could have found him. Then suddenly it occurred to me, for the first time, that my invention could easily be tested by some other person. Almost instantly I rejected the thought, for it would compel me to betray my secret, and in my strange infatuation I would rather have destroyed the instrument. But the doubts of my sanity on this subject returned upon me with tenfold strength, and again I thought in despair of the only method left me by which they could ever be settled.

In the first shock, when the unlucky sentence fell upon my ear, I had turned after the boys, and then walked on mechanically

towards the town. Now, when I looked up I found myself almost
at the college gate. No one was to be seen, only Mother Flinse
with her basket on her arm was just raising the latch. Half bewildered I turned hastily round and bent my steps in the direction of
my lodgings, while I absently wondered whether that old woman
had stood there ever since, since—when? I did not recollect, but
her shadow was long and slim—no, there were no shadows this
afternoon; it was sunless.

As I reached the stairs leading to my room, my trouble, which
I had forgotten for the moment, broke upon me anew. I dragged
myself up and sat down utterly overwhelmed. As I have said, I
would sooner destroy the instrument than give it to a thankless
world; but to endure the torturing doubt of its reality was impossible. Suddenly it occurred to me that Mother Flinse was mute. I
might get her to test my invention without fear of betrayal, for she
could neither speak nor write, and her signs on this subject, if she
attempted to explain, would be altogether unintelligible to others.
I sprang up in wild delight, then immediately fell back in my chair
with a hoarse laugh—Mother Flinse was *deaf* as well as dumb. I had
not remembered that. I sat quietly a moment trying to calm myself
and think. Why need this make any difference? The instrument
ought to, at least it was possible that it might, remedy loss of hearing. I too was deaf to these sounds in the air that it made audible.
They would have to be magnified to a greater degree for her. I
might set it for the present and use the full power of the instrument: there certainly would be no harm in trying, at any rate, and
if it failed it would prove nothing, if it did not fail it would prove
everything. Then a new difficulty presented itself. How could I
entice the old woman into the church?

I went back towards the college expecting to find her, but she
was nowhere to be seen, and I smiled that only a few moments ago
I had wondered if she did not always stand in the gateway. Once,
I could not exactly recall the time, I had passed her hut. I remembered distinctly that there was a line full of old ragged clothes
stretched across from the fence to a decayed tree, and a bright red
flannel petticoat blew and flapped among the blackened branches.
It was a miserable frame cabin, set back from the Spring road,
about half a mile out of town. There I went in search of her.

The blasted tree stood out in bold relief against the drab sky.
There appeared no living thing about the dirty, besmoked hovel
except one lean rat, that squatted with quivering nose and stared a

moment, then retreated under the loose plank before the door, leaving its smellers visible until I stepped upon the board. I knocked loudly without receiving any reply; then, smiling at the useless ceremony I had performed, pushed it open. The old woman, dressed in her red petticoat and a torn calico frock, with a faded shawl drawn over her head, was standing with her back towards me, picking over a pile of rags. She did not move. I hesitated an instant, then walked in. The moment I put my foot upon the floor she sprang quickly round. At first she appeared motionless, with her small, piercing gray eyes fixed upon me, holding a piece of orange-and-black spotted muslin; evidently she recognized me, for, suddenly dropping it, she began a series of wild gestures, grinning until all the wrinkles of her skinny face converged in the region of her mouth, where a few scattered teeth, long and sharp, gleamed strangely white. A rim of grizzled hair stood out round the edge of the turbaned shawl and set off the withered and watchful countenance of the speechless old crone. The yellow, shriveled skin hung loosely about her slim neck like leather, and her knotted hands were brown and dry as the claws of an eagle.

I went through the motion of sweeping and pointed over my shoulder, making her understand that I wished her to do some cleaning. She drew the seams of her face together into a new grimace by way of assent, and, putting the piece of orange-and-black spotted muslin around her shoulders in lieu of a cloak, preceded me out of the door. She started immediately in the direction of the college, and I was obliged to take hold of her before I could attract her attention; then, when I shook my head, she regarded me in surprise, and fell once more into a series of frantic gesticulations. With considerable trouble I made her comprehend that she was merely to follow me. The old woman was by no means dull, and her small, steel-gray eyes had a singular sharpness about them that is only found in the deaf-mute, where they perform the part of the ear and tongue. As soon as we came in sight of the church she was perfectly satisfied. I walked up to the main entrance, turned the knob and shook it, then suddenly felt in all my pockets, shook the door over, and felt through all my pockets again. This hypocritical pantomime had the desired effect. The old beldam slapped her hands together and poked her lean finger at the hole of the lock, apparently amused that I had forgotten the key. Then of her own accord she went round and tried the other doors, but without success. As we passed the narrow window in the rear I made a violent effort in knocking out the loose boards. The old woman seemed greatly delighted, and when I crawled through willingly followed. I gave her a brush, which fortunately one day I had discovered lying in the vestibule, and left her in the church to dust, while I went up in the tower to prepare and remove from sight all the tools which were scattered about. I put them in a recess and screened it from view by a map of the Holy Land. Then I took my instrument and carefully adjusted it, putting on its utmost power.

In about an hour I went down and motioned to Mother Flinse that I wanted her up stairs. She came directly after me without hesitation, and I felt greatly relieved, for I saw that I would likely have no trouble with the old woman. When we got into the tower she pointed down to the trees and then upward, meaning, I presume, that it was high. I nodded, and taking the instrument placed my ear to it for a moment. A loud blast of music, like a dozen bands playing in concert, almost stunned me. She watched me very attentively, but when I made signs for her to come and try, she drew back. I held up the instrument and went through all manner of motions indicating that it would not hurt her, but she only shook her head. I persevered in my endeavor to coax her until she seemed to gain courage and walked up within a few feet of me, then suddenly stopped and stretched out her hands for the instrument. As she did not seem afraid, provided she had it herself, I saw that she took firm hold.

In my impatience to know the result of this experiment, I was obliged to repeat my signs again and again before I could prevail upon her to raise it to her ear. Then breathlessly I watched her face, a face I thought which looked as if it might belong to some mummy that had been withering for a thousand years. Suddenly it was convulsed as if by a galvanic shock, then the shriveled features seemed to dilate, and a great light flashed through them, transforming them almost into the radiance of youth; a strange light as of some seraph had taken possession of the wrinkled old frame and looked out at the gray eyes, making them shine with unnatural beauty. No wonder the dumb countenance reflected a brightness inexpressible, for the Spirit of Sound had just alighted with silvery wings upon a silence of seventy years.

A heavy weight fell unconsciously from my breast while I stood almost awed before this face, which was transfigured, as if it might have caught a glimmer of that mystical morn when, in a moment, in the twinkling of an eye, we shall all be changed.

My instrument had stood the test; it was proved forever. I could no longer cherish any doubts of its reality, and an indescribable peace came into my soul, like a sudden awakening from some frightful dream. I had not noticed the flight of time. A pale shadow hung already over the trees—yes, and under them on the slime-covered stones. Ay! and a heavier shadow than the coming night was even then gathering its rayless folds. The drab sky had blanched and broken, and the sinking sun poured a fading light through its ragged fissures.

The old woman, as if wrapped in an enchantment, had hardly moved. I tried vainly to catch her attention; she did not even appear conscious of my presence. I walked up and shook her gently by the shoulder, and, pointing to the setting sun, held out my hand for the instrument. She looked at me a moment with the singular unearthly beauty shining through every feature; then suddenly clutching the trumpet tight between her skinny claws, sprang backward towards the stairs, uttering a sound that was neither human nor animal, that was not a wail or a scream, but it fell upon my ears like some palpable horror. Merciful Heaven! Was that thing yonder a woman? The shriveled, fleshless lips gaped apart, and a small pointed tongue lurked behind five glittering, fang-like teeth. The wild beast had suddenly been developed in the hag. Like a hungry tigress defending its prey, she stood hugging the trumpet to her, glaring at me with stretched neck and green eyes.

A savage fierceness roused within me when I found she would not give up the instrument, and I rushed at her with hands ready to snatch back the prize I valued more than my life—*or hers*; but, quicker than a hunted animal, she turned and fled with it down the stairs, making the tower ring with the hideous cries of her wordless voice. Swiftly—it seemed as if the danger of losing the trumpet gave me wings to fly in pursuit—I crossed the vestibule. She was not there. Everything was silent, and I darted with fleet steps down the dusky aisle of the church, when suddenly the jarring idiotic sounds broke loose again, echoing up in the organ-pipes and rattling along the galleries. The fiend sprang from behind the altar, faced about an instant with flashing eyes and gleaming teeth, then fled through the vestry-room into the passage. The sight of her was fresh fuel to my rage, and it flamed into a frenzy that seemed to burn the human element out of my soul. When I gained the steps leading into the coal-room, she was already in the window, but I cleared the distance at a single bound and caught hold of her clothes as she leaped down. I crawled through, but she clutched the instrument tighter. I could not prize it out of her grasp; and in her ineffectual efforts to free herself from my hold she made loud, grating cries, that seemed to me to ring and reverberate all through the forest; but presently they grew smothered, gurgled, then ceased. Her clasp relaxed in a convulsive struggle, and the trumpet was in my possession. It was easily done, for her neck was small and lean, and my hands made a circle strong as a steel band.

The tremor died out of her frame and left it perfectly still. Through the silence I could hear the hiss of a snake in the nettle-weeds, and the flapping wings of some night bird fanned my face as it rushed swiftly through the air in its low flight. The gray twilight had deepened to gloom and the graves seemed to have given up their tenants. The pale monuments stood out like shrouded specters. But all the dead in that church-yard were not under the ground, for on the wet grass at my feet there was something stark and stiff, more frightful than any phantom of imagination—something that the daylight would not rob of its ghastly features. It must be put out of my sight, yes, it must be hid, to save my invention from discovery. The old hag might be missed, and if she was found here it would ruin me and expose my secret. I placed the trumpet on the window-ledge, and, carrying the grim burden in my arms, plunged into the damp tangle of weeds and grass.

In a lonesome corner far back from the church, in the dense shade of thorn-trees, among the wild brambles where poisonous vines grew, slippery with the mould of forgotten years, unsought, uncared for by any human hand, was a tomb. Its sides were half buried in the tall under-brush, and the long slab had been broken once, for a black fissure ran zigzag across the middle. In my muscles that night there was the strength of two men. I lifted off one-half of the stone and heard the lizards dart startled from their haunt, and felt the spiders crawl. When the stone was replaced it covered more than the lizards or the spiders in the dark space between the narrow walls.

As I have said, the instrument possessed a singular fascination over me. I had grown to love it, not alone as a piece of mechanism for the transmission of sound, but like a living thing, and I replaced it in the tower with the same pleasure one feels who has rescued a friend from death. My listening ear never grew weary, but now I drew quickly away. It was not music I heard, or the ripple of water, or the prattle of merry tongues, but the harsh grating cries that had echoed in the church, that had rattled and died out in the forest—that voice which was not a voice. I shivered while I readjusted the instrument; perhaps it was the night wind which chilled me, but the rasping sounds were louder than before. *I could not exclude them.* There was no element of superstition in my nature, and I tried it over again: still I heard them—sometimes sharp, sometimes only a faint rumbling. Had the soul of the deaf-mute come in retribution to haunt me and cry eternally in my instrument? Perhaps on the morrow it would not disturb me, but there was no difference. I could hear only it, though I drew out the trumpet for vibrations hundreds of years old. I had rid myself of the withered hag who would have stolen my treasure, but now I could not rid myself of her invisible ghost. She had conquered, even through death, and come from the spirit world to gain possession of the prize for which she had given up her life. The instrument was no longer of any value to me, though cherishing a vague hope I compelled myself to listen, even with chattering teeth; for it was a terrible thing to hear those hoarse, haunting cries of the dumb soul—of the soul I had strangled from its body, a soul which I would have killed itself if it were possible. But my hope was vain, and the trumpet had become not only worthless to me, but an absolute horror.

Suddenly I determined to destroy it. I turned it over ready to dash it in pieces, but it cost me a struggle to destroy this work of my life, and while I stood irresolute a small green-and-gold beetle crawled out of it and dropped like a stone to the floor. The insect was an electric flash to me, that dispelled the black gloom through which I had been battling. It had likely fallen into the instrument down in the church-yard, or when I laid it upon the window-sill, and the rasping of its wings, magnified, had produced the sounds which resembled the strange grating noise uttered by the deaf-mute.

Instantly I put the trumpet to my ear. Once more the music of the past surged in. Voices, leaves, water, all murmured to me their changeful melody; every zephyr wafting by was filled with broken but melodious whispers.

Relieved from doubts, relieved from fears and threatening dangers, I slept peacefully, dreamlessly as a child. With a feeling of rest to which I had long been unused, I walked out in the soft, clear morning. Everything seemed to have put on new life, for the sky was not gray or sober, and the leaves, if they were brown, trimmed their edges in scarlet, and if many had fallen, the squirrels played among them on the ground. But suddenly the sky and the leaves and the squirrels might have been blotted from existence. I did not see them, but I saw—*I saw Mother Flinse come through the college gateway and walk slowly down the road!*

The large faded shawl pinned across her shoulders nearly covered the red flannel petticoat and the orange-and-black spotted muslin was wrapped in a turban on her head. Without breathing, almost without feeling, I watched the figure until at the corner it turned out of sight, and a long dark outline on the grass behind it ran into the fence. The shadow? Then it was not a ghost. Had the grave given up its dead? I would see.

At the churchyard the briars tore my face and clothes, but I plunged deeper where the shade thickened under the thorn-trees. There in the corner I stooped to lift the broken slab of a tomb, but all my strength would not avail to move it. As I leaned over, bruising my hands in a vain endeavor to raise it, my eyes fell for an instant on the stone, and with a start I turned quickly and ran to the church; then I stopped—the narrow fissure that cut zigzag across the slab on the tomb was filled with green moss, and this window was nailed up, and hung full of heavy cobwebs.

And my instrument?

Suddenly, while I stood there, some substance in my brain seemed to break up—it was the fetters of monomania which had bound me since that evening long ago, when, by the river in the oak-forest, I had heard the robin trill.

No murder stained my soul: and there, beside the black waves of insanity through which I had passed unharmed, I gave praise to the great Creator—praise silent, but intense as Miriam's song by the sea.

ELY'S AUTOMATIC HOUSEMAID

Elizabeth W. Bellamy
(1837–1900)

After the darkness of the previous stories it is time to have something a little more light-hearted. The end of the nineteenth century saw a rapid growth in the number of new inventions, thanks in part to the industry of Thomas Edison, who is credited with over a thousand patents alone. Inevitably, as with all new technology, things do not always work as they should. So the same period saw a rise in humorous stories looking at madcap inventions that go awry. Automatons and clockwork toys had long been a fascination, but the idea of mechanical beings created to undertake housework was relatively new in fiction. In effect the housemaids in the following story are robots, though that word did not pass into the language until 1921 with the premiere of Karel Capek's play R. U. R. (Rossum's Universal Robots).

The humor of this story is a far cry from the life of its author. Elizabeth Croom came from a prosperous merchant family. She was born in Florida but the family settled in Georgia, partly so that she and her brother could benefit from a better education. She married her cousin, Charles Bellamy, in 1858 and they had two children. However tragedy struck during the Civil War. Both her children died within months of each other in 1862 and her husband died of typhoid the following summer. Her parents' cotton plantation in Alabama was ruined during the War and her father was declared bankrupt in 1868. The now widowed Elizabeth turned to teaching to help support them. Thankfully her brother had good work as a lawyer and he encouraged her to write. Although she had little financial success she did achieve a certain national reputation, notably with the idiosyncratic Four Oaks (1867), written under the alias Kamba Thorpe. After her father's death, Elizabeth settled with her brother and his family and continued to write, though her main income came from teaching. After his death in 1884 from bronchitis, aged only 45, Elizabeth stayed with his widow Mary and ran a school from their home.

Somehow she found the time to produce a steady stream of fiction. The following story was one of her last, written when her health had deteriorated and she was suffering from kidney failure. She died just four months after it was published in The Black Cat. *She was four days away from her sixty-third birthday.*

IN ORDER FOR a man to have faith in such an invention, he would have to know Harrison Ely. For Harrison Ely was a genius. I had known him in college, a man amazingly dull in Latin and Greek and even in English, but with ideas of his own that could not be expressed in language. His bent was purely mechanical, and found expression in innumerable ingenious contrivances to facilitate the study to which he had no inclination. His self-acting lexicon-holder was a matter of admiring wonder to his classmates, but it did not serve to increase the tenacity of his mental grasp upon the contents of the volume, and so did little to recommend him to the faculty. And his self-feeding safety student-lamp admirably illuminated everything for him save the true and only path to an honorable degree.

It had been years since I had seen him or thought of him, but the memory is tenacious of small things, and the big yellow envelope which I found one morning awaiting me upon my breakfast-table brought his eccentric personality back to me with a rush. It was addressed to me in the Archimedean script always so characteristic of him, combining, as it seemed to do, the principles of the screw and of the inclined plane, and in its superscription Harrison Ely stood unmistakably revealed.

It was the first morning of a new cook, the latest potentate of a dynasty of ten who had briefly ruled in turn over our kitchen and ourselves during the preceding three months, and successively abdicated in favor of one another under the compelling influences of popular clamor, and in the face of such a political crisis my classmate's letter failed to receive immediate attention. Unfortunately but not unexpectedly the latest occupant of our culinary throne began her reign with no conspicuous reforms, and we received in gloomy silence her preliminary enactments in the way of greasy omelette and turbid and flavorless coffee, the yellow screed of Harrison Ely looking on the while with bilious sympathy as it leaned unopened against the water-bottle beside me.

As I drained the last medicinal drop of coffee my eye fell upon it, and needing a vicarious outlet for my feelings toward the cook, I seized it and tore it viciously open. It contained a letter from my classmate and half a dozen printed circulars. I spread open the former, and my eye fastened at once upon this sympathetic exordium:

"Doubtless, my dear friend, you have known what discomfort it is to be at the mercy of incompetent domestics—"

But my attention was distracted at this point by one of the circulars, which displayed an array of startling, cheering, alluring words, followed by plentiful exclamation points, that, like a bunch of keys, opened to my enraptured vision the gates of a terrestrial Paradise, where Bridgets should be no more, and where ill-cooked meals should become a mechanical impossibility. The boon we had been sighing for now presented itself for my acceptance, an accomplished fact. Harrison Ely had invented "An Automatic Household Beneficent Genius.—A Practical Realization of the Fabled Familiar of the Middle Ages." So the circular set forth.

Returning to the letter, I read that Harrison Ely, having exhausted his means in working out his invention, was unable to manufacture his "machine" in quantity as yet; but that he had just two on hand which he would sell in order to raise some ready money. He hoped that I would buy one of his automatons, and aid him to sell the other.

Never did a request come at a more propitious moment. I had always entertained a kindness for Harrison Ely, and now such was my disgust at the incompetence of Bridget and Juliana and their predecessors that I was eager to stake the price of a "Household Beneficent Genius" on the success of my friend's invention.

So, having grasped the purport of the circulars and letter, I broke forth to my wife:

"My dear, you've heard me speak of Harrison Ely—"

"That man who is always so near doing something great, and never *has* done anything?" said she.

"He has done it at last!" I declared. "Harrison Ely is one of the greatest geniuses the world has ever seen. He has invented an 'Automatic-Electric Machine-Servant.'"

My wife said, "Oh!"

There was not an atom of enthusiasm in that "Oh!" but I was not to be daunted.

"I am ready," I resumed, "to invest my bottom dollar in *two* of Harrison Ely's machine-servants."

Her eyes were fixed upon me as if they would read my very soul. "What do they cost?" she mildly asked.

"In comparison with the benefits to be derived, little enough. Listen!" I seized a circular at random, and began to read:

"The Automatic Household Genius, a veritable Domestic Fairy, swift, silent, sure; a Permanent, Inalienable, First-class Servant, warranted to give Satisfaction."

"Ah!" said my wife; and the enthusiasm that was lacking in the "Oh!" made itself eloquent in that "Ah!" "What is the price?" she asked again.

"The price is all right, and we are going to try the experiment."

"Are we though?" said she, between doubt and desire.

"Most assuredly; it will be a saving in the end. I shall write to Harrison Ely this very night."

The return mail brought me a reply stating that two Electric-Automatic Household Beneficent Geniuses had been shipped me by express. The letter enclosed a pamphlet that gave a more particular account of the E. A. H. B. G. than the circulars contained. My friend's invention was shaped in the likeness of the human figure, with body, head, arms, legs, hands and feet. It was clad in waterproof cloth, with a hood of the same to protect the head, and was shod with felt. The trunk contained the wheels and springs, and in the head was fixed the electric battery. The face, of bisque, was described as possessing "a very natural and pleasing expression."

Just at dusk an oblong box arrived by express and was duly delivered in our hall, but at my wife's urgent entreaty I consented not to unpack the machines until next day.

"If we should not get the knack of managing them, they might give us trouble," said this wise wife of mine.

I agreed to this, and having sent away Bridget with a week's wages, to the satisfaction of all parties, we went to bed in high hopes.

Early next morning we were astir.

"My dear," I said, "do not give yourself the least concern about breakfast; I am determined that Harrison's invention shall have fair play."

"Very well," my wife assented; but she prudently administered bread and butter to her offspring.

I opened the oblong box, where lay the automatons side by side, their hands placidly folded upon their waterproof breasts, and their eyes looking placidly expectant from under their waterproof hoods.

I confess the sight gave me a shock. Anna Maria turned pale; the children hid their faces in her skirts.

"Once out of the box," I said to myself, "and the horror will be over."

The machines stood on their feet admirably, but the horror was not materially lessened by this change of position. However, I assumed a bold front, and said, jocosely:

"Now, which is Bridget, and which is Juliana—which the cook, and which the housemaid?"

This distinction was made clear by dial-plates and indicators, set conspicuously between the shoulders, an opening being cut in the waterproof for that purpose. The housemaid's dial-plate was stamped around the circumference with the words: Bed, Broom, Duster, Door-bell, Dining-room Service, Parlor Service, etc. In like manner, the cook's dial-plate bore the words that pertained to her department. I gave myself first to "setting" the housemaid, as being the simpler of the two.

"Now, my dear," said I, confidently, "we shall see how *this* Juliana can make the beds."

I proceeded, according to the pamphlet's directions, to point the indicator to the word "Bed." Next, as there were three beds to be made, I pushed in three of the five little red points surrounding the word. Then I set the "clock" connected with the indicator, for a thirty minutes' job, thinking it might take about ten minutes to a bed. I did not consult my wife, for women do not understand machinery, and any suggestion of hesitancy on my part would have demoralized her.

The last thing to be done was to connect the indicator with the battery, a simple enough performance in itself, but the pamphlet of directions gave a repeated and red-lettered "CAUTION," never to interfere with the machine while it was at work! I therefore issued the command, "Non-combatants to the rear!" and was promptly obeyed.

What happened next I do not pretend to account for. By what subtle and mysterious action of electricity, by what unerring affinity, working through a marvellous mechanism, that Electric-Automatic Household Beneficent Genius, whom—or which, for short—we called Juliana, sought its appropriate task, is the inventor's secret. I don't undertake to explain, I merely narrate. With a "click" the connection was made, and the new Juliana *went up-stairs* at a brisk and business-like pace.

We followed in breathless amazement. In less than five minutes, bed number one was made, and in a twinkling the second was taken in hand, and number three also was fairly accomplished, long before the allotted thirty minutes had expired. By this time, familiarity had somewhat dulled that awe and wonder with which we had gaped upon the first performance, and I beheld a smile of hopeful satisfaction on my wife's anxious countenance.

Our youngest, a boy aged three, was quick to feel the genial influence of this smile, and encouraged thereby, he bounced into the middle of the first bed. Hardly had he alighted there, when our automaton, having finished making the third bed, returned to her first job, and, before we could imagine mischief, the mattresses were jerked about, and the child was tumbled, headforemost on the floor!

Had the flesh-and-blood Juliana been guilty of such an act, she should have been dismissed on the spot; but, as it was, no one of us ventured so much as a remonstrance. My wife lifted the screaming child, and the imperturbable machine went on to readjust the bed with mechanical exactitude.

At this point a wild shout of mingled exultation, amazement and terror arose from below, and we hastened down-stairs to find our son John hugging his elbows and capering frantically in front of the kitchen-door, where the electric cook was stirring empty nothing in a pan, with a zeal worthy a dozen eggs.

My eldest hopeful, impelled by that spirit of enterprise and audacity characteristic of nine-year-old boys, had ventured to experiment with the kitchen automaton, and by sheer accident had effected a working connection between the battery and the indicator, and the machine, in "going off," had given the boy a blow that made him feel, as he expressed it, "like a funny-bone all over."

"And served you right!" cried I. The thing was set for an hour and a half of work, according to the showing of the dial-plate, and no chance to stop it before I must leave for my office. Had the materials been supplied, we might have had breakfast; but, remembering the red-lettered "CAUTION," we dared not supply materials while that indefatigable spoon was gyrating in the empty pan. For my distraction, Kitty, my daughter of seven years, now called to me from up-stairs:

"Papa, you *better* come, quick! *It's* a-tearin' up these beds!"

"My dear," I sighed, "there's no way to stop it. We'll have to wait for the works to run down. I must call Harrison's attention to this defect. He ought to provide some sort of brake."

We went up-stairs again. The B. G. Juliana stood beside the bed which she had just torn up for the sixth or seventh time, when suddenly she became, so to speak, paralyzed; her arms, in the act of spreading the sheets, dropped by her sides, her back stiffened, and she stood absolutely motionless, leaving her job unfinished— the B. G. would move no more until duly "set" again.

I now discovered that I was hungry. "If that Fiend in the kitchen were only at work about something substantial, instead of whipping the air into imaginary omelettes!" I groaned.

"Never mind," said my wife; "I've a pot of coffee on the kerosene stove."

Bless her! She was worth a thousand Beneficent Geniuses, and so I told her.

I did not return until late, but I was in good spirits, and I greeted my wife gayly:

"Well, how do they work?"

"*Like fiends!*" my usually placid helpmeet replied, so vehemently that I was alarmed. "They flagged at first," she proceeded, excitedly, "and I oiled them, which *I* am not going to do, ever again. According to the directions, I poured the oil down their throats. It was horrible! They seemed to me to *drink it greedily*."

"Nonsense! That's your imagination."

"Very well," said Anna Maria. "You can do the oiling in future. They took a good deal this morning; it wasn't easy to stop pouring it down. And they worked—*obstreperously*. That Fiend in the kitchen has cooked all the provisions I am going to supply *this* day, but still she goes on, and it's no use to say a word."

"Don't be absurd," I remonstrated. "The thing is only a machine."

"I'm not so sure about that!" she retorted. "As for the other one—I set it sweeping, and it is sweeping still!"

We ate the dinner prepared by the kitchen Fiend, and really, I was tempted to compliment the cook in a set speech, but recollected myself in time to spare Anna Maria the triumph of saying, "I told you so!"

Now, that John of mine, still in pursuit of knowledge, had spent the day studying Harrison Ely's pamphlet, and he learned that the machines could be set, like an alarm-clock, for any given hour. Therefore, as soon as the Juliana had collapsed over a pile of dust in the middle of the hall, John, unknown to us, set her indicator to the broom-handle for seven o'clock the following morning. When the Fiend in the kitchen ran down, leaving everything in confusion, my much-tried wife persuaded me to give my exclusive attention to that machine, and the Juliana was put safely in a corner. Thus it happened that John's interference escaped detection. I set Bridget's indicator for kitchen-cleaning at seven-thirty the next morning.

"When we understand them better," I said to my wife, "we will set their morning tasks for an earlier hour, but we won't put it too early now, since we must first learn their ways."

"That's the trouble with all new servants," said Anna Maria.

The next morning at seven-thirty, precisely, we were awakened by a commotion in the kitchen.

"By George Washington!" I exclaimed. "The Thing's on time!"

I needed no urging to make me forsake my pillow, but Anna Maria was ahead of me.

"Now, my dear, don't get excited," I exhorted, but in vain.

"Don't you hear?" she whispered, in terror. "*The other one*—swe—eep—ing!" And she darted from the room.

I paused to listen, and heard the patter of three pairs of little bare feet across the hall up-stairs. The children were following their mother. The next sound I heard was like the dragging of a rug along the floor. I recognized this peculiar sound as the footsteps of the B. G. Then came a dull thud, mingled with a shout from Johnnie, a scream from my wife, and the terrified cries of the two younger children. I rushed out just in time to see John, in his night-clothes, with his hair on end, tear down-stairs like a streak of lightning. My little Kitty and the three-year-old baby stood clasped in each other's arms at the head of the stairs, sobbing in terror, and, half-way down, was my wife, leaning over the railing, with ashen face and rigid body, her fascinated gaze fixed upon a dark and struggling mass in the hall below.

John, when he reached the bottom of the stairs, began capering like a goat gone mad, digging the floor with his bare heels, clapping his hands with an awful glee, and shouting:

"Bet your bottom dollar on the one that whips!"

The Juliana and the Bridget were fighting for the broom!

I comprehended the situation intuitively. The kitchen-cleaning, for which the Fiend had been "set," had reached a point that demanded the broom, and that subtle, attractive affinity, which my friend's genius had known how to produce, but had not learned to regulate, impelled the unerring automaton towards the only broom in the house, which was now in the hands of its fellow-automaton, and a struggle was inevitable. What I could not understand—Johnnie having kept his own counsel—was this uncontrollable sweeping impulse that possessed the Juliana.

However, this was no time for investigating the exact cause of the terrific row now going on in our front hall. The Beneficent Geniuses had each a firm grip of the broom-handle, and they might have performed the sweeping very amicably together, could they but have agreed as to the field of labor, but their conflicting tendencies on this point brought about a rotary motion that sent them spinning around the hall, and kept them alternately cracking each other's head with a violehce that ought to have drawn blood. Considering their life-likeness, we should hardly have thought it strange if blood *had* flowed, and it would have been a relief had the combatants but called each other names, so much did their dumbness intensify the horror of a struggle, in the midst of which the waterproof hoods fell off, revealing their startlingly human countenances, not distorted by angry passions, but resolute, inexorable, calm, as though each was sustained in the contest by a lofty sense of duty.

"They're alive! Kill 'em! Kill 'em quick!" shrieked my wife, as the gyrating couple moved towards the stair-case.

"Let 'em alone," said Johnnie—his sporting blood, which he inherits from his father, thoroughly roused—dancing about the automatic pugilists in delight, and alternately encouraging the one or the other to increased efforts.

Thus the fight went on with appalling energy and reckless courage on both sides, my wife wringing her hands upon the staircase, our infants wailing in terror upon the landing above, and I wavering between an honest desire to see fair play and an apprehensive dread of consequences which was not unjustified.

In one of their frantic gyrations the figures struck the hat-rack and promptly converted it into a mass of splinters. In a minute more they became involved with a rubber plant—the pride of my wife's heart—and distributed it impartially all over the premises. From this they caromed against the front door, wrecking both its stained-glass panes, and then down the length of the hall they sped again, fighting fiercely and dealing one another's imperturbable countenances ringing blows with the disputed broom.

We became aware through Johnnie's excited comments, that Juliana had lost an ear in the fray, and presently it was discernible that a fractured nose had somewhat modified the set geniality of expression that had distinguished Bridget's face in its prime.

How this fierce and equal combat would have culminated if further prolonged no one but Harrison Ely can conjecture, but it came to an abrupt termination as the parlor clock chimed eight, the hour when the two automatons should have completed their appointed tasks.

Though quite late at my office that morning, I wired Ely before attending to business. Long-haired, gaunt and haggard, but cheerful as ever, he arrived next day, on fire with enthusiasm. He could hardly be persuaded to refresh himself with a cup of coffee before he took his two recalcitrant Geniuses in hand. It was curious to see him examine each machine, much as a physician would examine a patient. Finally his brow cleared, he gave a little puff of satisfaction, and exclaimed:

"Why, man alive, there's nothing the matter—not a thing! What you consider a defect is really a merit—merely a surplus of mental energy. They've had too big a dose of oil. Few housekeepers have any idea about proper lubrication," and he emitted another little snort, at which my wife colored guiltily.

"I see just what's wanted," he resumed. "The will-power generated and not immediately expended becomes cumulative and gets beyond control. I'll introduce a little compensator, to take up the excess and regulate the flow. Then a child can operate them."

It was now Johnnie's turn to blush.

"Ship 'em right back to the factory, and we'll have 'em all right in a few days. I see where the mechanism can be greatly improved, and when you get 'em again I know you'll never consent to part with 'em!"

That was four months ago. The "Domestic Fairies" have not yet been returned from Harrison's laboratory, but I am confidently looking for the familiar oblong packing case, and expect any day to see in the papers the prospectus of the syndicate which Ely informs me is being "promoted" to manufacture his automatic housemaid.

THE RAY OF DISPLACEMENT

Harriet Prescott Spofford
(1835–1921)

Unlike the previous writers in this volume, Harriet Elizabeth Prescott, who became Harriet Spofford after her marriage in 1865, delighted in the weird and unusual. She made her mark with her first novel, the gothic Sir Rohan's Ghost *(1860) and several macabre stories which were collected as* The Amber Gods *(1863). Though born in Maine, she lived all her teenage and adult life in Massachusetts. However, she was unlike many of the other New England regional writers, being a true romantic rather than a realist. Her stories have a dark uncertainty, her characters haunted by a spiritual or psychological threat that is never fully understood. As a result, a few of her stories qualify as borderline science fiction, such as* "The Moonstone Mass" *(1868), about the discovery of something unusual in the Arctic wastes of northern Canada or her last ghost story,* "The Mad Lady" *(1916), which includes a motor-car which may have a mind of its own.*

"The Ray of Displacement" is her most overt science fiction story and dates from late in her career. It takes on board some of the thinking about atomic theory and looks at how matter may be dissipated so that an individual can pass through walls. It's a theme uncommon in early science fiction, and this story is certainly amongst the first of its kind.

> *"We should have to reach the Infinite*
> *to arrive at the Impossible."*

IT WOULD INTEREST none but students should I recite the circumstances of the discovery. Prosecuting my usual researches, I seemed rather to have stumbled on this tremendous thing than to have evolved it from formulæ.

Of course, you already know that all molecules, all atoms, are separated from each other by spaces perhaps as great, when

53

compared relatively, as those which separate the members of the
stellar universe. And when by my Y-ray I could so far increase
these spaces that I could pass one solid body through another,
owing to the differing situation of their atoms, I felt no disembod-
ied spirit had wider, freer range than I. Until my discovery was
made public my power over the material universe was practically
unlimited.

Le Sage's theory concerning ultra-mundane corpuscles was
rejected because corpuscles could not pass through solids. But here
were corpuscles passing through solids. As I proceeded, I found
that at the displacement of one one-billionth of a centimeter the
object capable of passing through another was still visible, owing
to the refraction of the air, and had the power of communicating
its polarization; and that at two one-billionths the object became
invisible, but that at either displacement the subject, if a person,
could see into the present plane; and all movement and direction
were voluntary. I further found my Y-ray could so polarize a substance that its touch in turn temporarily polarized anything with
which it came in contact, a negative current moving atoms to the
left, and a positive to the right of the present plane.

My first experience with this new principle would have made a
less determined man drop the affair. Brant had been by way of
dropping into my office and laboratory when in town. As I afterwards recalled, he showed a signal interest in certain toxicological
experiments. "Man alive!" I had said to him once, "let those crys-
tals alone! A single one of them will send you where you never see
the sun!" I was uncertain if he brushed one off the slab. He did not
return for some months. His wife, as I heard afterwards, had a long
and baffling illness in the meantime, divorcing him on her recov-
ery; and he had remained out of sight, at last leaving his native
place for the great city. He had come in now, plausibly to ask my
opinion of a stone—a diamond of unusual size and water.

I put the stone on a glass shelf in the next room while looking
for the slide. You can imagine my sensation when that diamond,
with something like a flash of shadow, so intense and swift it was,
burst into a hundred rays of blackness and subsided—a pile of carbon! I had forgotten that the shelf happened to be negatively
polarized, consequently everything it touched sharing its polarization, and that in pursuing my experiment I had polarized myself
also, but with the opposite current; thus the atoms of my fingers
passing through the spaces of the atoms of the stone already

polarized, separated them negatively so far that they suffered disintegration and returned to the normal. "Good heavens! What has happened!" I cried before I thought. In a moment he was in the rear room and bending with me over the carbon. "Well," he said, straightening himself directly, "you gave me a pretty fright. I thought for a moment that was my diamond."

"But it is!" I whispered.

"Pshaw!" he exclaimed roughly. "What do you take me for? Come, come, I'm not here for tricks. That's enough damned legerdemain. Where's my diamond?"

With less dismay and more presence of mind I should have edged along to my batteries, depolarized myself, placed in vacuum the tiny shelf of glass and applied my Y-ray; and with, I knew not what, of convulsion and flame the atoms might have slipped into place. But, instead, I stood gasping. He turned and surveyed me; the low order of his intelligence could receive but one impression.

"Look here," he said, "you will give me back my stone! Now! Or I will have an officer here!"

My mind was flying like the current through my coils. How could I restore the carbon to its original, as I must, if at all, without touching it, and how could I gain time without betraying my secret? "You are very short," I said. "What would you do with your officer?"

"Give you up! Give you up, appear against you, and let you have a sentence of twenty years behind bars."

"Hard words, Mr. Brant. You could say I had your property. I could deny it. Would your word outweigh mine? But return to the office in five minutes—if it is a possible thing you shall ——"

"And leave you to make off with my jewel! Not by a long shot! I'm a bad man to deal with, and I'll have my stone or ——"

"Go for your officer," said I.

His eye, sharp as a dagger's point, fell an instant. How could he trust me? I might escape with my booty. Throwing open the window to call, I might pinion him from behind, powerful as he was. But before he could gainsay, I had taken half a dozen steps backward, reaching my batteries.

"Give your alarm," I said. I put out my hand, lifting my lever, turned the current into my coils, and blazed up my Y-ray for half a heart-beat, succeeding in that brief time in reversing and in receiving the current that so far changed matters that the thing I touched would remain normal, although I was left still so far subjected to the ray of the less displacement that I ought, when the thrill had subsided, to be able to step through the wall as easily as if no wall were there. "Do you see what I have here?" I most unwisely exclaimed. "In one second I could annihilate you ——" I had no time for more, or even to make sure I was correct, before, keeping one eye on me, he had called the officer.

"Look here," he said again, turning on me. "I know enough to see you have something new there, some of your damned inventions. Come, give me my diamond, and if it is worth while I'll find the capital, go halves, and drop this matter."

"Not to save your life!" I cried.

"You know me, officer," he said, as the blue coat came running in. "I give this man into custody for theft."

"It is a mistake, officer," I said. "But you will do your duty."

"Take him to the central station," said Mr. Brant, "and have him searched. He has a jewel of mine on his person."

"Yer annar's sure it's not on the primmises?" asked the officer.

"He has had no time ——"

"Sure, if it's quick he do be he's as like to toss it in a corner ——"

I stretched out my hand to a knob that silenced the humming among my wires, and at the same time sent up a thread of white fire whose instant rush and subsidence hinted of terrible power behind. The last divisible particle of radium—their eyeballs throbbed for a week.

"Search," I said. "But be careful about shocks. I don't want murder here, too."

Apparently they also were of that mind. For, recovering their sight, they threw my coat over my shoulders and marched me between them to the station, where I was searched, and, as it was already late, locked into a cell for the night.

I could not waste strength on the matter. I was waiting for the dead middle of the night. Then I should put things to proof.

I confess it was a time of intense breathlessness while waiting for silence and slumber to seal the world. Then I called upon my soul, and I stepped boldly forward and walked through that stone wall as if it had been air.

Of course, at my present displacement I was perfectly visible, and I slipped behind this and that projection, and into that alley, till sure of safety. There I made haste to my quarters, took the shelf holding the carbon, and at once subjected it to the necessary treatment. I was unprepared for the result. One instant the room seemed full of a blinding white flame, an intolerable heat, which shut my eyes and singed my hair and blistered my face.

"It is the atmosphere of a fire-dissolving planet," I thought. And then there was darkness and a strange odor.

I fumbled and stumbled about till I could let in the fresh air; and presently I saw the dim light of the street lamp. Then I turned on my own lights—and there was the quartz slab with a curious fusing of its edges, and in the center, flashing, palpitating, lay the diamond, all fire and whiteness. I wondered if it were not considerably larger; but it was hot as if just fallen from Syra Vega; it contracted slightly after subjection to dephlogistic gases.

It was near morning when, having found Brant's address, I passed into his house and his room, and took my bearings. I found his waistcoat, left the diamond in one of its pockets, and returned. It would not do to remain away, visible or invisible. I must be vindicated, cleared of the charge, set right before the world by Brant's appearing and confessing his mistake on finding the diamond in his pocket.

Judge Brant did nothing of the kind. Having visited me in my cell and in vain renewed his request to share in the invention which the habit of his mind convinced him must be of importance, he appeared against me. And the upshot of the business was that I went to prison for the term of years he had threatened.

I asked for another interview with him; but was refused, unless on the terms already declined. My lawyer, with the prison chaplain, went to him, but to no purpose. At last I went myself, as I had gone before, begging him not to ruin the work of my life. He regarded me as a bad dream, and I could not undeceive him without betraying my secret. I returned to my cell and again waited. For to escape was only to prevent possible vindication. If Mary had lived—but I was alone in the world.

The chaplain arranged with my landlord to take a sum of money I had, and to keep my rooms and apparatus intact till the expiration of my sentence. And then I put on the shameful and degrading prison garb and submitted to my fate.

It was a black fate. On the edge of the greatest triumph over matter that had ever been achieved, on the verge of announcing the actuality of the Fourth Dimension of Space, and of defining and declaring its laws, I was a convict laborer at a prison bench.

One day Judge Brant, visiting a client under sentence of death, in relation to his fee, made pretext to look me up, and stopped at my bench. "And how do you like it as far as you've gone?" he said.

"So that I go no farther," I replied. "And unless you become accessory to my taking off, you will acknowledge you found the stone in your pocket ———"

"Not yet, not yet," he said, with an unctuous laugh. "It was a keen jest you played. Regard this as a jest in return. But when you are ready, I am ready."

The thing was hopeless. That night I bade good-bye to the life that had plunged me from the pinnacle of light to the depths of hell.

When again conscious I lay on a cot in the prison hospital. My attempt had been unsuccessful. St. Angel sat beside me. It was here, practically, he came into my life. Alas, that I came into his.

In the long nights of darkness and failing faintness, when horror had me by the throat, he was beside me, and his warm, human touch was all that held me while I hung over the abyss. When I swooned off again his hand, his voice, his bending face recalled me. "Why not let me go, and then an end?" I sighed.

"To save you from a great sin," he replied. And I clung to his hand with the animal instinct of living.

I was well, and in my cell, when he said. "You claim to be an honest man ———"

"And yet?"

"You were about taking that which did not belong to you."

"I hardly understand—"

"Can you restore life once taken?"

"Oh, life! That worthless thing!"

"Lent for a purpose."

"For torture!"

"If by yourself you could breathe breath into any pinch of feathers and toss it off your hand a creature—but, as it is, life is a trust. And you, a man of parts, of power, hold it only to return with usury."

"And stripped of the power of gathering usury! Robbed of the work about to revolutionize the world!"

"The world moves on wide waves. Another man will presently have reached your discovery."

As if that were a thing to be glad of! I learned afterwards that St. Angel had given up the sweetness of life for the sake of his enemy. He had gone to prison, and himself worn the stripes, rather than the woman he loved should know her husband was the criminal. Perhaps he did not reconcile this with his love of inviolate truth. But St. Angel had never felt so much regard for his own soul as for the service of others. Self-forgetfulness was the dominant of all his nature.

"Tell me," he said, sitting with me, "about your work."

A whim of trustfulness seized me. I drew an outline, but paused at the look of pity on his face. He felt there was but one conclusion to draw—that I was a madman.

"Very well," I said, "you shall see." And I walked through the wall before his amazed eyes, and walked back again.

For a moment speechless, "You have hypnotic power," then he said. "You made me think I saw it."

"You did see it. I can go free any day I choose."

"And you do not?"

"I must be vindicated." And I told exactly what had taken place with Brant and his diamond. "Perhaps that vindication will never come," I said at last. "The offended *amour propre*, and the hope of gain, hindered in the beginning. Now he will find it impossible."

"That is too monstrous to believe!" said St. Angel. "But since you can, why not spend an hour or two at night with your work?"

"In these clothes! How long before I should be brought back? The first wayfarer—oh, you see!"

St. Angel thought a while. "You are my size," he said then. "We will exchange clothes. I will remain here. In three hours return, that you may get your sleep. It is fortunate the prison should be in the same town."

Night after night then, I was in my old rooms, the shutters up, lost in my dreams and my researches, arriving at great ends. Night after night I reappeared on the moment, and St. Angel went his way.

I had now found that molecular displacement can be had in various directions. Going further, I saw that gravity acts on bodies whose molecules are on the same plane, and one of the possible results of the application of the Y-ray was the suspension of the laws of gravity. This possibly accounted for an almost inappreciable buoyancy and the power of directing one's course. My last studies showed that a substance thus treated has the degenerative power of attracting the molecules of any norm into its new orbit—a disastrous possibility. A chair might disappear into a table previously treated by a Y-ray. In fact, the outlook was to infinity. The change so slight the result so astonishing! The subject might go into molecular interstices as far removed, to all essential purpose, as if billions of miles away in interstellar space. Nothing was changed, nothing disrupted; but the thing had stepped aside to let the world go by. The secrets of the world were mine. The criminal was at my mercy. The lover had no reserves from me. And as for my enemy, the Lord had delivered him into my hand. I could leave him only a puzzle for the dissectors. I could make him, although yet alive, a conscious ghost to stand or wander in his altered shape through years of nightmare alone and lost. What wonders of energy would follow this ray of displacement. What withdrawal of malignant growth and deteriorating tissue was to come. "To what heights of succor for humanity the surgeon can rise with it!" said St. Angel, as, full of my enthusiasm, I dilated on the marvel.

"He can work miracles!" I exclaimed. "He can heal the sick, walk on the deep, perhaps—who knows—raise the dead!"

I was at the height of my endeavor when St. Angel brought me my pardon. He had so stated my case to the Governor, so spoken of my interrupted career, and of my prison conduct, that the pardon had been given. I refused to accept it. "I accept," I said, "nothing but vindication, if I stay here till the day of judgment!"

"But there is no provision for you now," he urged. "Officially you no longer exist."

"Here I am," I said, "and here I stay."

"At any rate," he continued, "come out with me now and see the Governor, and see the world and the daylight outdoors, and be a man among men a while!"

With the stipulation that I should return, I put on a man's clothes again and went out the gates.

It was with a thrill of exultation that, exhibiting the affairs in my room to St. Angel, finally I felt the vibrating impulse that told me I had received the ray of the larger displacement. In a moment I should be viewless as the air.

"Where are you?" said St. Angel, turning this way and that. "What has become of you?"

"Seeing is believing," I said. "Sometimes not seeing is the naked truth."

"Oh, but this is uncanny!" he exclaimed. "A voice out of empty air."

"Not so empty! But place your hand under the second coil. Have no fear. You hear me now," I said. "I am in perhaps the

Fourth Dimension. I am invisible to any one not there—to all the world, except, presently, yourself. For now you, you also, pass into the unseen. Tell me what you feel."

"Nothing," he said. "A vibration—a suspicion of one. No, a blow, a sense of coming collapse, so instant it has passed."

"Now," I said, "there is no one on earth with eyes to see you but myself!"

"That seems impossible."

"Did you see me? But now you do. We are on the same plane. Look in that glass. There is the reflection of the room, of the window, the chair. Do you see me? Yourself?"

"Powers of the earth and air, but this is ghastly!" said St. Angel.

"It is the working of natural law. Now we will see the world, ourselves unseen."

"An unfair advantage."

"Perhaps. But there are things to accomplish to-day." What things I never dreamed; or I had stayed on the threshold.

I wanted St. Angel to know the manner of man this Brant was. We went out, and arrested our steps only inside Brant's office.

"This door is always blowing open!" said the clerk, and he returned to a woman standing in a suppliant attitude. "The Judge has gone to the races," he said, "and he's left word that Tuesday morning your goods'll be put out of the house if you don't pay up!" The woman went her way weeping.

Leaving, we mounted a car; we would go to the races ourselves. I doubt if St. Angel had ever seen anything of the sort. I observed him quietly slip a dime into the conductor's pocket—he felt that even the invisible, like John Gilpin, carried a right. "This opens a way for the right hand undreamed of the left," he said to me later.

It was not long before we found Judge Brant, evidently in an anxious frame, his expanse of countenance white with excitement. He had been plunging heavily, as I learned, and had big money staked, not upon the favorite but upon *Hannan*, the black mare. "That man would hardly put up so much on less than a certainty," I thought. Winding our way unseen among the grooms and horses, I found what I suspected—a plan to pocket the favorite. "But I know a game worth two of that," I said. I took a couple of small smooth pebbles, previously prepared, from the chamois bag into which I had put them with some others and an aluminum wafer treated for the larger displacement, and slipped one securely under the favorite's saddle-girth. When he warmed to his work he should be, for perhaps half an hour, at the one-billionth point, before the virtue expired, and capable of passing through every obstacle as he was directed.

"Hark you, Danny," then I whispered in the jockey's ear.

"Who are you? What—I—I—don't ——" looking about with terror.

"It's no ghost," I whispered hurriedly. "Keep your nerve. I am flesh and blood—alive as you. But I have the property which for half an hour I give you—a new discovery. And knowing Bub and Whittler's game, it's up to you to knock 'em out. Now, remember, when they try the pocket ride straight through them!"

Other things kept my attention; and when the crucial moment came I had some excited heart-beats. And so had Judge Brant. It was in the instant when Danny, having held the favorite well in hand for the first stretch, *Hannan* and *Darter* in the lead and the field following, was about calling on her speed, that suddenly Bub and Whittler drew their horses' heads a trifle more closely together, in such wise that it was impossible to pass on either side, and a horse could no more shoot ahead than if a stone wall stood there. "Remember, Danny!" I shouted, making a trumpet of my hands. "Ride straight through!"

And Danny did. He pulled himself together, and set his teeth as if it were a compact with powers of evil, and rode straight through without turning a hair, or disturbing either horse or rider. Once more the Y-ray was triumphant.

But about Judge Brant the air was blue. It would take a very round sum of money to recoup the losses of those few moments. I disliked to have St. Angel hear him; but it was all in the day's work.

The day had not been to Judge Brant's mind, as at last he bent his steps to the club. As he went it occurred to me to try upon him the larger ray of displacement, and I slipped down the back of his collar the wafer I had ready. He would not at once feel its action, but in the warmth either of walking or dining, its properties should be lively for nearly an hour. I had curiosity to see if the current worked not only through all substances, but through all sorts and conditions.

"I should prefer a better pursuit," said St. Angel, as we reached the street. "Is there not something ignoble in it?"

"In another case. Here it is necessary to hound the criminal, to see the man entirely. A game not to be played too often, for there is work to be done before establishing the counteracting currents that may ensure reserves and privacies to people. To-night let us go to the club with Judge Brant, and then I will back to my cell."

As you may suppose, Brant was a man neither of imagination nor humor. As you have seen, he was hard and cruel, priding himself on being a good hater, which in his contention meant indulgence of a preternaturally vindictive temper when prudence allowed. With more cunning than ability, he had achieved some success in his profession, and he secured admission to a good club, recently crowning his efforts, when most of the influential members were absent, by getting himself made one of its governors.

It would be impossible to find a greater contrast to this wretch than in St. Angel—a man of delicate imagination and pure fancy, tender to the child on the street, the fly on the wall; all his atmosphere that of kindness. Gently born, but too finely bred, his physical resistance was so slight that his immunity lay in not being attacked. His clean, fair skin, his brilliant eyes, spoke of health, but the fragility of frame did not speak of strength. Yet St. Angel's life was the active principle of good; his neighborhood was purification.

I was revolving these things while we followed Judge Brant, when I saw him pause in an agitated manner, like one startled out of sleep. A quick shiver ran over his strong frame; he turned red and pale, then with a shrug went on. The displacement had occurred. He was now on the plane of invisibility, and we must have a care ourselves.

Wholly unconscious of any change, the man pursued his way. The street was as usual. There was the boy who always waited for him with the extra but to-night was oblivious; and failing to get his attention the Judge walked on. A shower that had been threatening began to fall, the sprinkle becoming a downpour, with umbrellas spread and people hurrying. The Judge hailed a car; but the motorman was as blind as the newsboy. The shower stopped as suddenly as it had begun, but he went on some paces before perceiving that he was perfectly dry, for as he shut and shook his umbrella not a drop fell, and as he took off his hat and looked at it, not an atom of moisture was to be found there. Evidently bewildered, and looking about shamefacedly, I fancied I could hear him saying, with his usual oaths, "I must be deucedly overwrought, or this is some blue devilment."

As the Judge took his accustomed seat in the warm and brilliantly lighted room, and picking up the evening paper, looked over the columns, the familiar every-day affair quieting his nerves so that he could have persuaded himself he had been half asleep as he walked, he was startled by the voice, not four feet away, of one of the old officers who made the Kings County their resort. Something had ruffled the doughty hero. "By the Lord Harry, sir," he was saying in unmodulated tones, "I should like to know what this club is coming to when you can spring on it the election of such a man as this Brant! Judge? What's he Judge of? Beat his wife, too, didn't he? The governors used to be gentlemen!"

"But you know, General," said his *vis-à-vis*, "I think no more of him than you do; but when a man lives at the Club ——"

"Lives here!" burst in the other angrily. "He hasn't anywhere else to live! Is there a decent house in town open to him? Well, thank goodness, I've somewhere else to go before he comes in! The sight of him gives me a fit of the gout!" And the General stumped out stormily.

"Old boy seems upset!" said someone not far away. "But he's right. It was sheer impudence in the fellow to put up his name."

I could see Brant grow white and gray with anger, as surprised and outraged, wondering what it meant—if the General intended insult—if Scarsdale—but no, apparently they had not seen him. The contemptuous words rankled; the sweat stood on his forehead.

Had not the moment been serious, there were a thousand tricks to play. But the potency of the polarization was subsiding and in a short time the normal molecular plane would be re-established. It was there that I made my mistake. I should not have allowed him to depolarize so soon. I should have kept him bewildered and foodless till famished and weak. Instead, as ion by ion the effect of the ray decreased, his shape grew vague and misty, and then one and another man there rubbed his eyes, for Judge Brant was sitting in his chair and a waiter was hastening towards him.

It had all happened in a few minutes. Plainly the Judge understood nothing of the circumstances. He was dazed, but he must put the best face on it; and he ordered his dinner and a pony of brandy, eating like a hungry animal.

He rose, after a time, refreshed, invigorated, and all himself. Choosing a cigar, he went into another room, seeking a choice lounging place, where for a while he could enjoy his ease and wonder if anything worse than a bad dream had befallen. As for the General's explosion, it did not signify; he was conscious of such opinion; he was overliving it; he would be expelling the old cock yet for conduct unbecoming a gentleman.

Meanwhile, St. Angel, tiring of the affair, and weary, had gone into this room, and in an arm-chair by the hearth was awaiting me—the intrusive quality of my observations not at all to his mind. He had eaten nothing all day, and was somewhat faint. He had closed his eyes, and perhaps fallen into a light doze when he must have been waked by the impact of Brant's powerful frame, as the latter took what seemed to him the empty seat. I expected to see Brant at once flung across the rug by St. Angel's natural effort in rising. Instead, Brant sank into the chair as into down pillows.

I rushed, as quickly as I could, to seize and throw him off, "Through him! Pass through him! Come out! Come to me!" I cried. And people to-day remember that voice out of the air, in the Kings County Club.

It seemed to me that I heard a sound, a sob, a whisper, as if one cried with a struggling sigh, "Impossible!" And with that a strange trembling convulsed Judge Brant's great frame, he lifted his hands, he thrust out his feet, his head fell forward, he groaned gurglingly, shudder after shudder shook him as if every muscle quivered with agony or effort, the big veins started out as if every pulse were a red-hot iron. He was wrestling with something, he knew not what, something as antipathetic to him as white is to black; every nerve was concentrated in rebellion, every fiber struggled to break the spell.

The whole affair was that of a dozen heart-beats—the attempt of the opposing molecules each to draw the other into its own orbit. The stronger physical force, the greater aggregation of atoms was prevailing. Thrust upward for an instant, Brant fell back into his chair exhausted, the purple color fading till his face shone fair as a girl's, sweet and smiling as a child's, white as the face of a risen spirit—Brant's!

Astounded, I seized his shoulder and whirled him about. There was no one else in the chair. I looked in every direction. There was no St. Angel to be seen. There was but one conclusion to draw—the molecules of Brant's stronger material frame had drawn into their own plane the molecules of St. Angel's.

I rushed from the place, careless if seen or unseen, howling in rage and misery. I sought my laboratory, and in a fiend's fury

depolarized myself, and I demolished every instrument, every for
mula, every vestige of my work. I was singed and scorched and
burned, but I welcomed any pain. And I went back to prison,
admitted by the officials who hardly knew what else to do. I would
stay there, I thought, all my days. God grant they should be few!
It would be seen that a life of imprisonment and torture were too
little punishment for the ruin I had wrought.

It was after a sleepless night, of which every moment seemed
madness, that, the door of my cell opening, I saw St. Angel. St.
Angel? God have mercy on me, no, it was Judge Brant I saw!

He came forward, with both hands extended, a grave, imploring
look on his face. "I have come," he said, a singular sweet overtone
in his voice that I had never heard before, yet which echoed like
music in my memory, "to make you all the reparation in my
power. I will go with you at once before the Governor, and
acknowledge that I have found the diamond. I can never hope to
atone for what you have suffered. But as long as I live, all that I
have, all that I am, is yours!"

There was a look of absolute sweetness on his face that for a
dizzy moment made me half distraught. "We will go together," he
said. "I have to stop on the way and tell a woman whose mortgage
comes due to-day that I have made a different disposition; and, do
you know," he added brightly, after an instant's hesitation, "I
think I shall help her pay it!" and he laughed gayly at the jest
involved.

"Will you say that you have known my innocence all these
years?" I said sternly.

"Is not that," he replied, with a touching and persuasive quality
of tone, "a trifle too much? Do you think this determination has
been reached without a struggle? If you are set right before the
world, is not something due to—Brant?"

"If I did not know who and what you are," I said, "I should
think the soul of St. Angel had possession of you!"

The man looked at me dreamily. "Strange!" he murmured. "I
seem to have heard something like that before. However," as if he
shook off a perplexing train of thought, "all that is of no consequence. It is not who you are, but what you do. Come, my friend,
don't deny me, don't let the good minute slip. Surely the undoing
of the evil of a lifetime, the turning of that force to righteousness,
is work outweighing all a prison chaplain's ——"

My God, what had the intrusion of my incapable hands upon forbidden mysteries done!

"Come," he said. "We will go together. We will carry light into dark places—there are many waiting ——"

"St. Angel!" I cried, with a loud voice, "are you here?"

And again the smile of infinite sweetness illuminated the face even as the sun shines up from the depths of a stagnant pool.

THOSE FATAL FILAMENTS

Mabel Ernestine Abbott

I can find very little about Mabel Ernestine Abbott. She was a fairly regular contributor to the popular magazines and pulps from at least 1902 to 1940. Her output included detective stories and mysteries and the following unusual story dating from 1903. Supposing we could build a device that could read thoughts. Would it be beneficial or not?

I AM AN electrician.

I suppose I may say that I am an electrician of note; at least, my name is on most of the electrical appliances which make life worth living nowadays, and the income from these, together with my published lectures, etc., supports my rather expensive family in sufficient comfort.

Two or three months ago an idea which had long lain in embryo in my brain suddenly developed form, and I hastened to put it in practical shape.

An instrument which should respond to unspoken thought had long seemed to me not an impossibility, but to make it of practical value, I deemed it necessary that it should transmit the thought in words. The solution flashed upon me, as these things usually do, when I had given over the effort to solve the problem.

It was so simple as to seem almost trivial, but the more I pondered over its possibilities, the more enthusiastic I became.

I said nothing to anyone of my discovery, but occupied myself for several days in constructing the little apparatus which I hoped was to make my name a household word for all time. I wonder what I would have said had anyone told me that in two months the thing would have become so hateful to me that neither gold nor glory could tempt me to touch it.

I experimented with it myself until I was convinced that it was successful.

It transmitted spoken words much more clearly than the telephone, reproducing the exact quality and volume of tone of the speaker.

Unexpressed thoughts were given in a thin, sibilant whisper which was very impressive. It made my own flesh fairly creep the first time I heard my inmost thoughts hissed into my ear while my lips remained closed.

The operator needed only to place his bare hand in contact, no matter how slightly, with an infinitely fine filament of a substance which I may be pardoned for not specifying here, as no patent has been issued.

This filament connected with ordinary telephone wires by means of a device in which was embodied the new principle I had discovered, and these wires led to a very delicately adjusted telephone, with a phonograph attachment, which transmitted to the listener both the words and thoughts of the operator.

There was always a whispering, rustling undercurrent of thought speech running through the spoken words, sometimes coinciding exactly with them, sometimes differing.

This was not ordinarily distinct enough to be confusing, but if the operator's wandering thoughts gained sufficient clearness to be distinctly audible over the thinkophone, the natural consequence was that his words either ceased or became of subordinate importance.

The final test as to the perfection of the instrument, of course, must be to cause it to transmit to my ears the thoughts of others; otherwise, there was always the possibility of self deception; and, to make the result absolutely convincing, I thought best that the subject of the first experiment should be ignorant of what was being done.

The thing had been in working order for a week, and yet I had had no opportunity to test it.

I had located it upstairs in my dressing room, instead of in the workshop, but I feared that Little, my assistant, suspected something.

I thought a great deal of Little, who had been with me for over a year and gave promise of becoming in time a real coadjutor. I even had dreams of sometimes handing my work on to him, as I would have done to my son, had I had one.

I had said nothing to him of my discovery, and pleased myself with the notion of his surprise and delight; but the surprise was in danger of being forestalled unless I made the test soon.

I resolved to connect a chair in the library and experiment with the first person who chanced to occupy it.

With this idea, I conducted a slender bundle of the filaments down the stairs and across the hall. While I was at work, Julie passed through the hall.

"What are you doing, papa?" she inquired, patting my incipient bald spot as I crouched.

I mumbled something in my beard, but she was already answering herself:

"Oh, yes, fixing the bells."

She did not move on, however, as promptly as I could have wished.

"There is something in my overcoat pocket, in the back hall," I suggested, "that a certain young lady might make use of."

"What is it?" she demanded, instead of going to see.

"Well, tomorrow is that young lady's birthday, and it is conceivable that she might like to give a party, and my overcoat pocket is pretty big, and it might be—"

"*Not* a box at the theater?" she shrieked, flying at me.

I had already braced myself in expectation of the onslaught. In a minute she let me go, but instead of taking herself away, what should the incomprehensible child do but actually bury her face in her hands.

"Oh, you are too good to me, papa—far too good!" she cried.

A man with two daughters learns not to be much surprised at anything, as I accepted this new phenomenon philosophically.

"Well, I'll try to balance matters some other time," I observed. "Just now I'm busy. And by the way, pet, you'd better get the order out of my pocket right away. I might forget it, you know. In the back hall."

Even then she had to stop for another hug and a kiss before she went.

I looked after her. She was tall and there were rounded lines about her slim figure which half pleased, half pained me. Julie was growing up, and I should miss my baby.

I ran the filaments into the library, behind a bookcase and along the floor to a big Morris chair, and distributed them liberally over the arms, where anyone occupying the chair could hardly fail to touch one or more.

As I turned to go, my wife entered the room.

"Aha!" thought I. "Excellent! Couldn't be better!"

She traced her pretty morning gown slowly across the floor, hesitated before a bookcase, turned to the desk, rustled over the daily paper, and finally took up a magazine and sank softly into the Morris chair.

I fairly rubbed my hands with satisfaction.

My beautiful young wife is only two years older than my eldest daughter, and very dear to me.

I suppose people think me an elderly idiot, for I often find my eyes following her when they should be decorously employed elsewhere; but the wonder of it is as fresh to me now as when I married her five years ago—how she should have chosen me— *me*—from among the many younger and more attractive men who sought her.

Through the quiet happiness of marriage, the old, first thrill still makes itself felt at the turn of her head, the tone of her voice, the glance of her eye.

She smiled up at me from her magazine now, as I still stood in the doorway, looking at her.

"What is it?" she asked.

"Nothing, my dear," I answered; "nothing but the old, old story."

She still smiled at me, without replying; I thought she seemed a little pale.

"Aren't you well?" I asked.

"My head aches a little; it is the heat, I think. Are you going to work now?"

"Yes," I answered. I had actually forgotten the experiment for a moment. I paused again to say, "Oh, Margaret, I shall keep Herman Little to lunch today. We shall be working at some matters which I don't want to drop longer than necessary."

"Very well, dear," she replied. The arrangement was not an unusual one.

"You are as flushed now as you were pale a moment ago," I went on. "You must take something for your headache."

"I will if it does not leave me soon," she assented, and then I went upstairs two steps at a time in my eagerness to see if the machine was working.

Little was safe in the workshop in the backyard. With fingers that trembled with excitement, I pushed over the switch.

Blank silence! A second passed—a minute—a minute and a half. I was sick with disappointment.

Suddenly a soft, sighing sound was audible, then inarticulate whispers, tantalizingly like speech, but wholly unintelligible.

I waited, straining ears and nerves to make out something definite. Slowly the lisping and whispering crystallized into disconnected words, into phrases, but the more distinctly I heard, the more incomprehensible did the stuff become.

He has never suspected—never dreamed for an instant. And he is so kind—so good—how can I—how can I tell him that there is another dearer—how will he take it? What will he say?

I stood bewildered. If the machine was going to mistranslate, it was worse than useless.

I fumbled impatiently with the adjustments, but the thought-speech rolled on as incoherently as before.

Thoroughly disgusted, I reached for the switch to disconnect it. I did not care to invent a machine to grind out cheap melodrama; we have plenty of two-legged ones already.

Just then a familiar name in the midst of the rubbish arrested my hand.

Herman, Herman—my darling—my darling! What does it matter— what does anything matter—if you love me—as I love you—forever and ever! But he does not know—he does not realize—how can I hurt him— he is so kind, so good—how can I tell him—

On it went, over and over, always coming back to the same thing, but—God help me—incomprehensible no longer.

I jerked the switch violently, cutting a word in the middle. I was trembling and felt cold and numb, and the chair seemed a long way off.

In a moment I was able to think again. It seemed as if I had always known it. Even the ache in my heart seemed old.

I bent my head on my hands, nerving myself to action.

This could not go on. How far it had already gone, God only knew, but now I would put a stop to it, one way or the other.

But which way? That was the question and whirled around in my aching head.

One point was clear; for the sake of the love I had borne her—ah me, that I still bore her—she should be happy if possible.

I followed this determination to its logical outcome. Clearly, pitilessly, the conclusion confronted me.

I must set her free. Youth was for youth, and I felt very old and feeble just then.

I rose weakly to go to her. A step sounded outside on the cement. Through the window, I saw Little coming from the workshop. He entered the side door; he, too, was going to her!

Perhaps she was waiting for him; she had paled and flushed when I spoke his name! Perhaps they would speak to me—angrily?—pityingly?

Things flew around me in a black and red whirl. I sprang to the door, upsetting as I did so the table on which sat the devilish little machine, but before the crash came, I was already at the head of the stair.

Little was just passing the foot of the staircase, and without a word I hurled myself down and at him like a thunderbolt. His horrified face gleamed before me for the fraction of a second as he sprang backward, and then, as I struck the polished floor, Julie's scream came from the library and my wife's great cry from the opposite side of the hall.

Even in that instant, I half grasped the significance of the location of the two cries, and as my wife reached me, I gasped: "Margaret—for God's sake, where are you?"

"My darling! Are you—"

"*Where were you?*"

"In the dining room, getting some headache drops. Quick, darling, tell me, where are you hurt?"

"Then who was in the library? Answer me."

"Julie, I think. What is the matter? Help, Julie! Herman! He is badly hurt."

"Thank God! Thank God!" I breathed, and tried to draw her agonized face down to mine, but my right arm was broken.

I told them that I had missed my footing at the head of the stairs and had taken them in two or three leaps in order to save myself.

I don't think they tried to account for my irrelevant inquiries. Herman did say something about my face having frightened him as I came down, but I suppose they thought that natural under the circumstances.

The wrecked thinkophone is in the ash barrel. My arm is still in its sling, and even if it were not, I should not feel inclined to reproduce the infernal little machine that so nearly caused a tragedy. Someday I will explain the principle to my son-in-law, Herman Little, and he may have the pleasure of introducing it to the public; it would be none to me.

THE THIRD DRUG

Edith Nesbit
(1858–1924)

Edith Nesbit will always be remembered as the author of that timeless children's book The Railway Children *(1904). She wrote so many books for children, such as* The Story of the Treasure Seekers *(1899) and* Five Children and It *(1902) that it's easy to overlook that she also wrote for adults, and often very dark tales. The titles of her first two story collections suggest as much,* Grim Tales *(1893) and* Something Wrong *(1893). It's also easy to forget that she was a strong and resilient woman, an early socialist, being one of the founders of the Fabian Society, and someone sufficiently prepared to put up with the philandering of her husband, Hubert Bland, and to adopt his illegitimate child as her own.*

Amongst her stories are several classifiable as science fiction. 'The Five Senses' (1909) considers what might happen if all of your senses are enhanced at once. 'The Haunted House' (1913) is about immortality through blood transfusion. The following, dating from 1908, explores the possibility of using drugs to become super-human.

I

ROGER WROXHAM LOOKED round his studio before he blew out the candle, and wondered whether, perhaps, he looked for the last time. It was large and empty, yet his trouble had filled it, and, pressing against him in the prison of those four walls, forced him out into the world, where lights and voices and the presence of other men should give him room to draw back, to set a space between it and him, to decide whether he would ever face it again—he and it alone together. The nature of his trouble is not germane to this story. There was a woman in it, of course, and money, and a friend, and regrets and embarrassments—and all of

these reached out tendrils that wove and interwove till they made
a puzzle-problem of which heart and brain were now weary. It
was as though his life depended on his deciphering the straggling
characters traced by some spider who, having fallen into the ink-
well, had dragged clogged legs in a black zig-zag across his map of
the world.

He blew out the candle and went quietly downstairs. It was nine
at night, a soft night of May in Paris. Where should he go? He
thought of the Seine, and took—an omnibus. The chestnut trees of
the Boulevards brushed against the sides of the one that he boarded
blindly in the first light street. He did not know where the omnibus
was going. It did not matter. When at last it stopped he got off, and
so strange was the place to him that for an instant it almost seemed
as though the trouble itself had been left behind. He did not feel it
in the length of three or four streets that he traversed slowly. But in
the open space, very light and lively, where he recognised the
Taverne de Paris and knew himself in Montmartre, the trouble set
its teeth in his heart again, and he broke away from the lamps and
the talk to struggle with it in the dark quiet streets beyond.

A man braced for such a fight has little thought to spare for the
details of his surroundings. The next thing that Wroxham knew of
the outside world was the fact that he had known for some time
that he was not alone in the street. There was someone on the
other side of the road keeping pace with him—yes, certainly keeping pace, for, as he slackened his own, the feet on the other pavement also went more slowly. And now they were four feet, not
two. Where had the other man sprung from? He had not been
there a moment ago. And now, from an archway a little ahead of
him, a third man came.

Wroxham stopped. Then three men converged upon him, and,
like a sudden magic-lantern picture on a sheet prepared, there
came to him all that he had heard and read of Montmartre—dark
archways, knives, Apaches, and men who went away from homes
where they were beloved and never again returned. He, too—
well, if he never returned again, it would be quicker than the
Seine, and, in the event of ultramundane possibilities, safer.

He stood still and laughed in the face of the man who first
reached him.

"Well, my friend?" said he, and at that the other two drew close.

"Monsieur walks late," said the first, a little confused, as it
seemed, by that laugh.

"And will walk still later, if it pleases him," said Roger. "Good-night, my friends."

"Ah!" said the second, "friends do not say adieu so quickly. Monsieur will tell us the hour."

"I have not a watch," said Roger, quite truthfully.

"I will assist you to search for it," said the third man, and laid a hand on his arm.

Roger threw it off. That was instinctive. One may be resigned to a man's knife between one's ribs, but not to his hands pawing one's shoulders. The man with the hand staggered back.

"The knife searches more surely," said the second.

"No, no," said the third quickly, "he is too heavy. I for one will not carry him afterwards."

They closed round him, hustling him between them. Their pale, degenerate faces spun and swung round him in the struggle. For there was a struggle. He had not meant that there should be a struggle. Someone would hear—someone would come.

But if any heard, none came. The street retained its empty silence, the houses, masked in close shutters, kept their reserve. The four were wrestling, all pressed close together in a writhing bunch, drawing breath hardly through set teeth, their feet slipping, and not slipping, on the rounded cobble-stones.

The contact with these creatures, the smell of them, the warm, greasy texture of their flesh as, in the conflict, his face or neck met neck or face of theirs—Roger felt a cold rage possess him. He wrung two clammy hands apart and threw something off—something that staggered back clattering, fell in the gutter, and lay there.

It was then that Roger felt the knife. Its point glanced off the cigarette-case in his breast pocket and bit sharply at his inner arm. And at the sting of it Roger knew that he did not desire to die. He feigned a reeling weakness, relaxed his grip, swayed sideways, and then suddenly caught the other two in a new grip, crushed their faces together, flung them off, and ran. It was but for an instant that his feet were the only ones that echoed in the street. Then he knew that the others too were running.

It was like one of those nightmares wherein one runs for ever, leaden-footed, through a city of the dead. Roger turned sharply to the right. The sound of the other footsteps told that the pursuers also had turned that corner. Here was another street—a steep ascent. He ran more swiftly—he was running now for his life—the life that he held so cheap three minutes before. And all the streets

were empty—empty like dream-streets, with all their windows
dark and unhelpful, their doors fast closed against his need.

Far away down the street and across steep roofs lay Paris, poured
out like a pool of light in the mist of the valley. But Roger was
running with his head down—he saw nothing but the round heads
of the cobble stones. Only now and again he glanced to the right
or left, if perchance some window might show light to justify a cry
for help, some door advance the welcome of an open inch.

There was at last such a door. He did not see it till it was almost
behind him. Then there was the drag of the sudden stop—the
eternal instant of indecision. Was there time? There must be. He
dashed his fingers through the inch-crack, grazing the backs of
them, leapt within, drew the door after him, felt madly for a lock
or bolt, found a key, and, hanging his whole weight on it, strove
to get the door home. The key turned. His left hand, by which he
braced himself against the door-jamb, found a hook and pulled on
it. Door and door-post met—the latch clicked—with a spring as it
seemed. He turned the key, leaning against the door, which shook
to the deep sobbing breaths that shook him, and to the panting
bodies that pressed a moment without. Then someone cursed
breathlessly outside; there was the sound of feet that went away.

Roger was alone in the strange darkness of an arched carriage-
way, through the far end of which showed the fainter darkness of
a courtyard, with black shapes of little formal tubbed orange trees.
There was no sound at all there but the sound of his own desperate
breathing; and, as he stood, the slow, warm blood crept down his
wrist, to make a little pool in the hollow of his hanging, half-
clenched hand. Suddenly he felt sick.

This house, of which he knew nothing, held for him no terrors.
To him at that moment there were but three murderers in all the
world, and where they were not, there safety was. But the spacious
silence that soothed at first, presently clawed at the set, vibrating
nerves already overstrained. He found himself listening, listening,
and there was nothing to hear but the silence, and once, before he
thought to twist his handkerchief round it, the drip of blood from
his hand.

By and by, he knew that he was not alone in this house, for from
far away there came the faint sound of a footstep, and, quite near,
the faint answering echo of it. And at a window, high up on the
other side of the courtyard, a light showed. Light and sound and
echo intensified, and light passing window after window, till at last

it moved across the courtyard, and the little trees threw back shifting shadows as it came towards him—a lamp in the hand of a man.

It was a short, bald man, with pointed beard and bright, friendly eyes. He held the lamp high as he came, and when he saw Roger, he drew his breath in an inspiration that spoke of surprise, sympathy, and pity.

"Hold! hold!" he said, in a singularly pleasant voice, "there has been a misfortune? You are wounded, monsieur?"

"Apaches," said Roger, and was surprised at the weakness of his own voice.

"Your hand?"

"My arm," said Roger.

"Fortunately," said the other, "I am a surgeon. Allow me."

He set the lamp on the step of a closed door, took off Roger's coat, and quickly tied his own handkerchief round the wounded arm.

"Now," he said, "courage! I am alone in the house. No one comes here but me. If you can walk up to my rooms, you will save us both much trouble. If you cannot, sit here and I will fetch you a cordial. But I advise you to try and walk. That *porte cochère* is, unfortunately, not very strong, and the lock is a common spring lock, and your friends may return with *their* friends; whereas the door across the courtyard is heavy and the bolts are new."

Roger moved towards the heavy door whose bolts were new. The stairs seemed to go on for ever. The doctor lent his arm, but the carved bannisters and their lively shadows whirled before Roger's eyes. Also, he seemed to be shod with lead, and to have in his legs bones that were red-hot. Then the stairs ceased, and there was light, and a cessation of the dragging of those leaden feet. He was on a couch, and his eyes might close. There was no need to move any more, nor to look, nor to listen.

When next he saw and heard, he was lying at ease, the close intimacy of a bandage clasping his arm, and in his mouth the vivid taste of some cordial.

The doctor was sitting in an armchair near a table, looking benevolent through gold-rimmed pince-nez.

"Better?" he said. "No, lie still, you'll be a new man soon."

"I am desolated," said Roger, "to have occasioned you all this trouble."

"Not at all," said the doctor. "We live to heal, and it is a nasty cut, that in your arm. If you are wise, you will rest at present. I shall be honoured if you will be my guest for the night."

Roger again murmured something about trouble.

"In a big house like this," said the doctor, as it seemed a little sadly, "there are many empty rooms, and some rooms which are not empty. There is a bed altogether at your service, monsieur, and I counsel you not to delay in seeking it. You can walk?"

Wroxham stood up. "Why, yes," he said, stretching himself. "I feel, as you say, a new man."

A narrow bed and rush-bottomed chair showed like doll's-house furniture in the large, high, gaunt room to which the doctor led him.

"You are too tired to undress yourself," said the doctor, "rest— only rest," and covered him with a rug, roundly tucked him up, and left him.

"I leave the door open," he said, "in case you have any fever. Good night. Do not torment yourself. All goes well."

Then he took away the lamp, and Wroxham lay on his back and saw the shadows of the window-frames cast on the wall by the moon now risen. His eyes, growing accustomed to the darkness, perceived the carving of the white panelled walls and mantelpiece. There was a door in the room, another door from the one which the doctor had left open. Roger did not like open doors. The other door, how-ever, was closed. He wondered where it led, and whether it were locked. Presently he got up to see. It was locked. He lay down again.

His arm gave him no pain, and the night's adventure did not seem to have overset his nerves. He felt, on the contrary, calm, confident, extraordinarily at east, and master of himself. The trou-ble—how could that ever have seemed important? This calmness— it felt like the calmness that precedes sleep. Yet sleep was far from him. What was it that kept sleep away? The bed was comfortable— the pillows soft. What was it? It came to him presently that it was the scent which distracted him, worrying him with a memory that he could not define. A faint scent of—what was it? Perfumery? Yes—and camphor—and something else—something vaguely dis-quieting. He had not noticed it before he had risen and tried the handle of that other door. But now—— He covered his face with the sheet, but through the sheet he smelt it still. He rose and threw back one of the long French windows. It opened with a click and a jar, and he looked across the dark well of the courtyard. He leaned out, breathing the chill, pure air of the May night, but when he withdrew his head, the scent was there again. Camphor— perfume—and something else. What was it that it reminded him of? He had his knee on the bed-edge when the answer came to that question. It was the scent that had struck at him from a darkened room when, a child, clutching at a grown-up hand, he had been led to the bed where, amid flowers, something white lay under a sheet—his mother they had told him. It was the scent of death, disguised with drugs and perfumes.

He stood up and went, with carefully controlled swiftness, towards the open door. He wanted light and a human voice. The doctor was in the room upstairs; he——

The doctor was face to face with him on the landing, not a yard away, moving towards him quietly in shoeless feet.

"I can't sleep," said Wroxham, a little wildly, "it's too dark——"

"Come upstairs," said the doctor, and Wroxham went.

There was comfort in the large, lighted room, with its shelves and shelves full of well-bound books, its tables heaped with papers and pamphlets—its air of natural everyday work. There was a warmth of red curtain at the windows. On the window ledge a plant in a pot, its leaves like red misshapen hearts. A green-shaded lamp stood on the table. A peaceful, pleasant interior.

"What's behind that door," said Wroxham, abruptly—"that door downstairs?"

"Specimens," the doctor answered "preserved specimens. My line is physiological research. You understand?"

So that was it.

"I feel quite well, you know," said Wroxham, laboriously explaining—"fit as any man—only I can't sleep."

"I see," said the doctor.

"It's the scent from your specimens, I think," Wroxham went on; "there's something about that scent——"

"Yes," said the doctor.

"It's very odd." Wroxham was leaning his elbow on his knee and his chin on his hand. "I feel so frightfully well—and yet—there's a strange feeling——"

"Yes," said the doctor. "Yes, tell me exactly what you feel."

"I feel," said Wroxham, slowly, "like a man on the crest of a wave."

The doctor stood up.

"You feel well, happy, full of life and energy—as though you could walk to the world's end, and yet——"

"And yet," said Roger, "as though my next step might be my last—as though I might step into my grave."

He shuddered.

"Do you," asked the doctor, anxiously—"do you feel thrills of pleasure—something like the first waves of chloroform—thrills running from your hair to your feet?"

"I felt all that," said Roger, slowly, "downstairs before I opened the window."

The doctor looked at his watch, frowned and got up quickly. "There is very little time," he said.

Suddenly Roger felt an unexplained opposition stiffen his mind.

The doctor went to a long laboratory bench with bottle-filled shelves above it, and on it crucibles and retorts, test tubes, beakers—all a chemist's apparatus—reached a bottle from a shelf, and measured out certain drops into a graduated glass, added water, and stirred it with a glass rod.

"Drink that," he said.

"No," said Roger, and as he spoke a thrill like the first thrill of the first chloroform wave swept through him, and it was a thrill, not of pleasure, but of pain. "No," he said, and "Ah!" for the pain was sharp.

"If you don't drink," said the doctor, carefully, "you are a dead man."

"You may be giving me poison," Roger gasped, his hands at his heart.

"I may," said the doctor. "What do you suppose poison makes you feel like? What do you feel like now?"

"I feel," said Roger, "like death."

Every nerve, every muscle thrilled to a pain not too intense to be underlined by a shuddering nausea.

"Then drink," cried the doctor, in tones of such cordial entreaty, such evident anxiety, that Wroxham half held his hand out for the glass. "Drink! Believe me, it is your only chance."

Again the pain swept through him like an electric current. The beads of sweat sprang out on his forehead.

"That wound," the doctor pleaded, standing over him with the glass held out. "For God's sake, drink! Don't you understand, man? You *are* poisoned. Your wound——"

"The knife?" Wroxham murmured, and as he spoke, his eyes seemed to swell in his head, and his head itself to grow enormous. "Do you know the poison—and its antidote?"

"I know all." The doctor soothed him. "Drink, then, my friend."

As the pain caught him again in a clasp more close than any lover's he clutched at the glass and drank. The drug met the pain and mastered it. Roger, in the ecstasy of pain's cessation, saw the world fade and go out in a haze of vivid violet.

II

Faint films of lassitude, shot with contentment, wrapped him round. He lay passive, as a man lies in the convalescence that follows a long fight with Death. Fold on fold of white peace lay all about him.

"I'm better now," he said, in a voice that was a whisper—tried to raise his hand from where it lay helpless in his sight, failed, and lay looking at it in confident repose—"much better."

"Yes," said the doctor, and his pleasant, soft voice had grown softer, pleasanter. "You are now in the second stage. An interval is necessary before you can pass to the third. I will enliven the interval by conversation. Is there anything you would like to know?"

"Nothing," said Roger; "I am quite contented."

"This is very interesting," said the doctor. "Tell me exactly how you feel."

Roger faintly and slowly told him.

"Ah!" the doctor said, "I have not before heard this. You are the only one of them all who ever passed the first stage. The others—"

"The others? said Roger, but he did not care much about the others.

"The others," said the doctor frowning, "were unsound. Decadent students, degenerates, Apaches. You are highly trained—in fine physical condition. And your brain! God be good to the Apaches, who so delicately excited it to just the degree of activity needed for my purpose."

"The others?" Wroxham insisted.

"The others? They are in the room whose door was locked. Look—you should be able to see them. The second drug should lay your consciousness before me, like a sheet of white paper on which I can write what I choose. If I choose that you should see my specimens—*Allons donc.* I have no secrets from you now. Look—look—strain your eyes. In theory, I know all that you can do and feel and see in this second stage. But practically—enlighten me—look—shut your eyes and look!"

Roger closed his eyes and looked. He saw the gaunt, uncarpeted staircase, the open doors of the big rooms, passed to the locked door, and it opened at his touch. The room inside was like the others, spacious and panelled. A lighted lamp with a blue shade hung from the ceiling, and below it an effect of spread whiteness. Roger looked. There *were* things to be seen.

With a shudder he opened his eyes on the doctor's delightful room, the doctor's intent face.

"What did you see?" the doctor asked. "Tell me!"

"Did you kill them all?" Roger asked back.

"They died—of their own inherent weakness," the doctor said. "And you saw them?"

"I saw," said Roger, "the quiet people lying all along the floor in their death clothes—the people who have come in at that door of yours that is a trap—for robbery, or curiosity, or shelter, and never gone out any more."

"Right," said the doctor. "Right. My theory is proved at every point. You can see what I choose you to see. Yes, decadents all. It was in embalming that I was a specialist before I began these other investigations."

"What," Roger whispered—"what is it all for?"

"To make the superman," said the doctor. "I will tell you."

He told. It was a long story—the story of a man's life, a man's work, a man's dreams, hopes, ambitions.

"The secret of life," the doctor ended. "This is what all the alchemists sought. They sought it where Fate pleased. I sought it where I have found it—in death."

Roger thought of the room behind the locked door.

"And the secret is?" he asked.

"I have told you," said the doctor impatiently; "it is in the third drug that life—splendid, superhuman life—is found. I have tried it on animals. Always they became perfect, all that an animal should be. And more, too—much more. They were too perfect, too near humanity. They looked at me with human eyes. I could not let them live. Such animals it is not necessary to embalm. I had a laboratory in those days—and assistants. They called me the Prince of Vivisectors."

The man on the sofa shuddered.

"I am naturally," the doctor went on, "a tender-hearted man. You see it in my face; my voice proclaims it. Think what I have suffered in the sufferings of these poor beasts who never injured me. My God! Bear witness that I have not buried my talent. I have been faithful. I have laid down all—love, and joy, and pity, and the little beautiful things of life—all, all, on the altar of science, and seen them consume away. I deserve my heaven, if ever man did. And now by all the saints in heaven I am near it!"

"What is the third drug?" Roger asked, lying limp and flat on his couch.

"It is the Elixir of Life," said the doctor. "I am not its discoverer; the old alchemists knew it well, but they failed because they sought to apply the elixir to a normal—that is, a diseased and faulty—body. I knew better. One must have first a body abnormally healthy, abnormally strong. Then, not the elixir, but the two drugs that prepare. The first excites prematurely the natural conflict between the principles of life and death, and then, just at the point where Death is about to win his victory, the second drug intensifies life so that it conquers—intensifies, and yet chastens. Then the whole life of the subject, risen to an ecstasy, falls prone in an almost voluntary submission to the coming super-life. Submission—submission! The garrison must surrender before the splendid conqueror can enter and make the citadel his own. Do you understand? Do you submit?"

"I submit," said Roger, for, indeed, he did. "But—soon—quite soon—I will not submit."

He was too weak to be wise, or those words had remained unspoken.

The doctor sprang to his feet.

"It works too quickly!" he cried. "Everything works too quickly with you. Your condition is too perfect. So now I bind you."

From a drawer beneath the bench where the bottles gleamed, the doctor drew rolls of bandages—violet, like the haze that had drowned, at the urgence of the second drug, the consciousness of Roger. He moved, faintly resistant, on his couch. The doctor's hands, most gently, most irresistibly, controlled his movement.

"Lie still," said the gentle, charming voice. "Lie still; all is well." The clever, soft hands were unrolling the bandages—passing them round arms and throat—under and over the soft narrow couch. "I cannot risk your life, my poor boy. The least movement of yours might ruin everything. The third drug, like the first, must be offered directly to the blood which absorbs it. I bound the first drug as an unguent upon your knife-wound."

The swift hands, the soft bandages, passed back and forth, over and under—flashes of violet passed to and fro in the air, like the shuttle of a weaver through his warp. As the bandages clasped his knees, Roger moved.

"For God's sake, no!" the doctor cried; "the time is so near. If you cease to submit it is death."

With an incredible, accelerated swiftness he swept the bandages round and round knees and ankles, drew a deep breath—stood upright.

"I must make an incision," he said—"in the head this time. It will not hurt. See! I spray it with the Constantia Nepenthe; that also I discovered. My boy, in a moment you know all things—you are as God. For God's sake, be patient. Preserve your submission."

And Roger, with life and will resurgent hammering at his heart, preserved it.

He did not feel the knife that made the cross-cut on his temple, but he felt the hot spurt of blood that followed the cut; he felt the cool flap of a plaster, spread with some sweet, clean-smelling unguent that met the blood and stanched it. There was a moment—or was it hours?—of nothingness. Then from that cut on his forehead there seemed to radiate threads of infinite length, and of a strength that one could trust to—threads that linked one to all knowledge past and present. He felt that he controlled all wisdom, as a driver controls his four-in-hand. Knowledge, he perceived, belonged to him, as the air belongs to the eagle. He swam in it, as a great fish in a limitless ocean.

He opened his eyes and met those of the doctor, who sighed as one to whom breath has grown difficult.

"Ah, all goes well. Oh, my boy, was it not worth it? What do you feel?"

"I. Know. Everything," said Roger, with full stops between the words.

"Everything? The future?"

"No. I know all that man has ever known."

"Look back—into the past. See someone. See Pharaoh. You see him—on his throne?"

"Not on his throne. He is whispering in a corner of his great gardens to a girl, who is the daughter of a water-carrier."

"Bah! Any poet of my dozen decadents, who lie so still could have told me that. Tell me secrets—the *Masque de Fer*."

The other told a tale, wild and incredible, but it satisfied the teller.

"That too—it might be imagination. Tell me the name of the woman I loved and——"

The echo of the name of the anæsthetic came to Roger; "Constantia," said he, in an even voice.

"Ah," the doctor cried, "now I see you know all things. It was not murder. I hoped to dower her with all the splendours of the superlife."

"Her bones lie under the lilacs, where you used to kiss her in the spring," said Roger, quite without knowing what it was that he was going to say.

"It is enough," the doctor cried. He sprang up, ranged certain bottles and glasses on a table convenient to his chair. "You know all things. It is not a dream, this, the dream of my life. It is true. It is a fact accomplished. Now I, too, will know all things. I will be as the gods."

He sought among leather cases on a far table, and came back swiftly into the circle of light that lay below the green-shaded lamp.

Roger, floating contentedly on the new sea of knowledge that seemed to support him, turned eyes on the trouble that had driven him out of that large, empty studio so long ago, so far away. His new-found wisdom laughed at that problem, laughed and solved it. "To end that trouble I must do so-and-so, say such-and-such," Roger told himself again and again.

And now the doctor, standing by the table, laid on it his pale, plump hand outspread. He drew a knife from a case—a long, shiny knife—and scored his hand across and across its back, as a cook scores pork for cooking. The slow blood followed the cuts in beads and lines.

Into the cuts he dropped a green liquid from a little bottle, replaced its stopper, bound up his hand and sat down.

"The beginning of the first stage," he said; "almost at once I shall begin to be a new man. It will work quickly. My body, like yours, is sane and healthy."

There was a long silence.

"Oh, but this is good," the doctor broke it to say. "I feel the hand of Life sweeping my nerves like harp-strings."

Roger had been thinking, the old common sense that guides an ordinary man breaking through this consciousness of illimitable wisdom. "You had better," he said, "unbind me; when the hand of Death sweeps your nerves you may need help."

"No," the doctor said, "and no, and no, and no many times. I am afraid of you. You know all things, and even in your body you

are stronger than I. When I, too, am a god, and filled with the
wine of knowledge, I will loose you, and together we will drink
of the fourth drug—the mordant that shall fix the others and set us
eternally on a level with the immortals."

"Just as you like, of course," said Roger, with a conscious effort
after commonplace. Then suddenly, not commonplace any more—
"Loose me!" he cried; "loose me, I tell you! I am wiser than you."

"You are also stronger," said the doctor, and then suddenly and
irresistibly the pain caught him. Roger saw his face contorted with
agony, his hands clench on the arm of his chair; and it seemed that,
either this man was less able to bear pain than he, or that the pain
was much more violent than had been his own. Between the grip-
pings of the anguish the doctor dragged on his watch-chain; the
watch leapt from his pocket, and rattled as his trembling hand laid
it on the table.

"Not yet," he said, when he had looked at its face, "not yet, not
yet, not yet." It seemed to Roger, lying there bound, that the other
man repeated those words for long days and weeks. And the
plump, pale hand, writhing and distorted by anguish, again and
again drew near to take the glass that stood ready on the table, and
with convulsive self-restraint again and again drew back without it.

The short May night was waning—the shiver of dawn rustled
the leaves of the plant whose leaves were like red misshaped hearts.

"Now!" The doctor screamed the word, grasped the glass,
drained it and sank back in his chair. His hand struck the table
beside him. Looking at his limp body and head thrown back, one
could almost see the cessation of pain, the coming of kind
oblivion.

III

The dawn had grown to daylight, a poor, gray, rain-stained daylight, not strong enough to pierce the curtains and persiennes, and
yet not so weak but that it could mock the lamp, now burnt low
and smelling vilely.

Roger lay very still on his couch, a man wounded, anxious, and
extravagantly tired. In those hours of long, slow dawning, face to
face with the unconscious figure in the chair, he had felt, slowly
and little by little, the recession of that sea of knowledge on which
he had felt himself float in such content. The sea had withdrawn
itself, leaving him high and dry on the shore of the normal. The

only relic that he had clung to and that he still grasped was the answer to the problem of the trouble—the only wisdom that he had put into words. These words remained to him, and he knew that they held wisdom—very simple wisdom, too.

"To end the trouble, I must do so-and-so and say such-and-such."

But of all that had seemed to set him on a pinnacle, had evened him with the immortals, nothing else was left. He was just Roger Wroxham—wounded, and bound, in a locked house, one of whose rooms was full of very quiet people, and in another room himself and a dead man. For now it was so long since the doctor had moved that it seemed he must be dead. He had got to know every line of that room, every fold of drapery, every flower on the wall-paper, the number of the books, the shapes and sizes of things. Now he could no longer look at these. He looked at the other man.

Slowly a dampness spread itself over Wroxham's forehead and tingled among the roots of his hair. He writhed in his bonds. They held fast. He could not move hand or foot. Only his head could turn a little, so that he could at will see the doctor or not see him. A shaft of desolate light pierced the persienne at its hinge and rested on the table, where an overturned glass lay.

Wroxham thrilled from head to foot. The body in the chair stirred—hardly stirred—shivered rather—and a very faint, faraway voice said:—

"Now the third—give me the third."

"What?" said Roger, stupidly; and he had to clear his throat twice before he could say even that.

"The moment is now," said the doctor. "I remember all. I made you a god. Give me the third drug."

"Where is it?" Roger asked.

"It is at my elbow," the doctor murmured. "I submit—I submit. Give me the third drug, and let me be as you are."

"As *I* am?" said Roger. "You forget. *I* am bound."

"Break your bonds," the doctor urged, in a quick, small voice. "I trust you now. You are stronger than all men, as you are wiser. Stretch your muscles, and the bandages will fall asunder like snow-wreaths."

"It is too late," Wroxham said, and laughed; "all that is over. I am not wise any more, and I have only the strength of a man. I am tired and wounded. I cannot break your bonds—I cannot help you!"

"But if you cannot help me—it is death," said the doctor.

"It is death," said Roger. "Do you feel it coming on you?"

"I feel life returning," said the doctor; "it is now the moment—the one possible moment. And I cannot reach it. Oh, give it me—give it me!"

Then Roger cried out suddenly, in a loud voice: "Now, by God in heaven, you damned decadent, I am _glad_ that I cannot give it. Yes, if it costs me my life, it's worth it, you madman, so that your life ends too. Now be silent, and die like a man, if you have it in you."

Only one word seemed to reach the man in the chair.

"A decadent!" he repeated. "I? But no, I am like you—I see what I will. I close my eyes, and I see—no—not that—ah!—not that!" He writhed faintly in his chair, and to Roger it seemed that for that writhing figure there would be no return of power and life and will.

"Not that," he moaned. "Not that," and writhed in a gasping anguish that bore no more words.

Roger lay and watched him, and presently he writhed from the chair to the floor, tearing feebly at it with his fingers, moaned, shuddered, and lay very still.

Of all that befell Roger in that house, the worst was now. For now he knew that he was alone with the dead, and between him and death stretched certain hours and days. For the _porte cochère_ was locked; the doors of the house itself were locked—heavy doors and the locks new.

"I am alone in the house," the doctor had said. "No one comes here but me."

No one would come. He would die there—he, Roger Wroxham—"poor old Roger Wroxham, who was no one's enemy but his own." Tears pricked his eyes. He shook his head impatiently and they fell from his lashes.

"You fool," he said, "can't _you_ die like a man either?"

Then he set his teeth and made himself lie still. It seemed to him that now Despair laid her hand on his heart. But, to speak truth, it was Hope whose hand lay there. This was so much more than a man should be called on to bear—it could not be true. It was an evil dream. He would wake presently. Or if it were, indeed, real—then someone would come, someone must come. God could not let nobody come to save him.

And late at night, when heart and brain had been stretched to the point where both break and let in the sea of madness, someone came.

The interminable day had worn itself out. Roger had screamed, yelled, shouted till his throat was dried up, his lips baked and cracked. No one heard. How should they? The twilight had thickened and thickened, till at last it made a shroud for the dead man on the floor by the chair. And there were other dead men in that house; and as Roger ceased to see the one he saw the others—the quiet, awful faces, the lean hands, the straight, stiff limbs laid out one beyond another in the room of death. They at least were not bound. If they should rise in their white wrappings and, crossing that empty sleeping chamber very softly, come slowly up the stairs—

A stair creaked.

His ears, strained with hours of listening, thought themselves befooled. But his cowering heart knew better.

Again a stair creaked. There was a hand on the door.

"Then it is all over," said Roger in the darkness, "and I *am* mad."

The door opened very slowly, very cautiously. There was no light. Only the sound of soft feet and draperies that rustled.

Then suddenly a match spurted—light struck at his eyes; a flicker of lit candle-wick steadying to flame. And the things that had come were not those quiet people creeping up to match their death with his death in life, but human creatures, alive, breathing, with eyes that moved and glittered, lips that breathed and spoke.

"He must be here," one said. "Lisette watched all day; he never came out. He must be here—there is nowhere else."

Then they set up the candle-end on the table, and he saw their faces. They were the Apaches who had set on him in that lonely street, and who had sought him here—to set on him again.

He sucked his dry tongue, licked his dry lips, and cried aloud:—

"Here I am! Oh, kill me! For the love of God, brothers, kill me *now!*"

And even before they spoke, they had seen him, and seen what lay on the floor.

"He died this morning. I am bound. Kill me, brothers; I cannot die slowly here alone. Oh, kill me, for Christ's sake!"

But already the three were pressing on each other at the doorway suddenly grown too narrow. They could kill a living man, but they could not face death, quiet, enthroned.

"For the love of Christ," Roger screamed, "have pity! Kill me outright! Come back—come back!"

And then, since even Apaches are human, one of them did come back. It was the one he had flung into the gutter. The feet of the others sounded on the stairs as he caught up the candle and bent over Roger, knife in hand.

"Make sure," said Roger, through set teeth.

"*Nom d'un nom,*" said the Apache, with worse words, and cut the bandages here, and here, and here again, and there, and lower, to the very feet.

Then this good Samaritan helped Roger to rise, and when he could not stand, the Samaritan half pulled, half carried him down those many steps, till they came upon the others putting on their boots at the stair-foot.

Then between them the three men who could walk carried the other out and slammed the outer door, and presently set him against a gate-post in another street, and went their wicked ways.

And after a time, a girl with furtive eyes brought brandy and hoarse, muttered kindnesses, and slid away in the shadows.

Against that gate-post the police came upon him. They took him to the address they found on him. When they came to question him he said, "Apaches," and his late variations on that theme were deemed sufficient, though not one of them touched truth or spoke of the third drug.

There has never been anything in the papers about that house. I think it is still closed, and inside it still lie in the locked room the very quiet people; and above, there is the room with the narrow couch and the scattered, cut, violet bandages, and the thing on the floor by the chair, under the lamp that burned itself out in that May dawning.

A DIVIDED REPUBLIC
—AN ALLEGORY OF THE FUTURE

Lillie Devereux Blake
(1833–1913)

This story, and the one after, both look at the idea of feminist societies. Lillie Devereux Blake was a renowned suffragist and reformer of her day. Born in North Carolina, she was raised and educated in Connecticut and developed strong views on the treatment of women in society. Her first husband, whom she married in 1855, died (perhaps a suicide) in 1859 leaving her with two small children to raise and she turned to writing for financial support. She had several successful early novels but achieved fame chiefly as a reporter during the Civil War. After the War she married a New York merchant, Grinfill Blake, and his wealth allowed her to pursue her mission to bring attention to the plight of women. Her best known novel on the subject was Fettered for Life *(1872). Blake also drummed up support for women's rights through her lectures, and she published them as* Woman's Place To-Day *(1883). She was President of the New York State Woman's Suffrage Association from 1879 to 1890.*

The following story, first published in 1887, considers the plight of men if women declared their independence, left them behind, and set up their own society.

THE FORTY-NINTH CONGRESS adjourned without enfranchising the women of the Republic, and many state legislatures, where pleas were made for justice, refused to listen to the suppliants. The women of the nation grow more and more indignant over the denial of equality. Great conventions were held and monster mass meetings took place all over the land. But although men had been declaring that so soon as women wanted to vote they would be allowed to, they still continued to assert in the face of all those efforts that only a few agitators were making the demand. An

93

enormous petition was sent to the fiftieth Congress containing the signatures of twenty millions of women praying for suffrage, and still Senator Edmunds and Senator Vest insisted that the best women would not vote if they could.

Matters began actually to grow worse for women. The more honors they carried off at college the less were they allowed to hold places of public trust or given equal pay for equal work. Taxes of oppressive magnitude were imposed on women, for a new idea had seized the masculine brains of the country. They wanted to fortify our sea-coast. The women protested in vain; they said they did not want war, that they never would permit war, and that all difficulties with foreign nations, if any arose, should be settled by arbitration.

The men paid no attention whatever to their protests, but went right on levying heavy taxes and imposing a high tariff on foreign goods, and spending the money in monstrous forts and bristling cannon that looked out over the wide waters of the Atlantic in useless menace.

Drunkenness, too, increased in the land. It is true that sometimes women were able to procure the passage of some law to restrain the sale of liquors, but the enactments were always dead letters; the men would not enforce the laws they themselves had made, and mothers saw their sons led away and their families broken up, and still no man heeded their protests.

The murmurs of discontent among women grew louder and deeper, and a grand national council was called.

Now the great leader among women in this time was Volumnia, a matron of noble appearance, whose guidance the women gladly followed. When the great council met at Washington every state was represented by the foremost women of the day, and all were eager for some radical action that should force the men of the nation to give them a voice in the laws.

All were assembled, and the great hall filled to its utmost limit by eager delegates, when Volumnia arose to speak. "Women of America," she said, "we have borne enough! We have appealed to the men to set us free. They have refused. We have protested against the imposition of taxes. They have increased them. We have implored them to protect our homes from the curse of intemperance. They have passed prohibition laws on one day, and permitted saloons to be opened the next. We are tired of argument, entreaty and persuasion. Patience is no longer becoming in the women of America. The time for action has come."

And this vast assemblage of women stirred to the utmost shouted "ACTION!"

"I have a proposal to make to you," she continued, "the result of long study and consultation with the profoundest female minds of the country. It is this: Within the limits of this so-called Republic there is one spot where the Women are free. I mean in Washington Territory, that great state that has been refused admission to the Union, solely because women there are voters. I have communicated with the leading women of that region; some of them are here to speak for themselves, and others are here from the sister Territory of Wyoming. With their approval and aid I propose that all the women of the United States leave the East where ancient customs oppress us and where old fogyism prevails, and emigrate in a body to the free West, the lofty heights of the mountains and the broad slopes on the coast of the majestic Pacific."

Wild and tumultuous applause followed this proposal, which was at once enthusiastically adopted by the assembled multitude, who after a few days of discussion as to the means to carry out these designs dispersed to their homes to make preparations for the greatest exodus of modern times.

In the early spring all arrangements were complete, and then was seen a wonderful sight: women leaving their homes all over the land, and marching by night and by day in great armies, westward. All the means of conveyance were crowded. The railroads were loaded with women, the boats on the great lakes were thronged with them; the Northern and Central Pacific roads ran immense extra trains to convey the women to their new homes.

It must not be supposed that their departure took place without protest on the part of the men. Some of them were greatly dismayed when they heard that wife and daughters were going away, and essayed remonstrance, but the women had borne so much so long that they were inexorable—not always without a pang, however.

Volumnia had long been a widow, and therefore owed allegiance to no man; but she had a young daughter named Rose, who was as pretty as she was accomplished, and who cherished a fondness for a young man who admired her.

When he learned of the proposed exodus, this youth, whose name was Flavius, hurried to the railway station, reaching there a few moments before the departure of the train. The waiting-room was crowded with a great throng of women, but Rose was lingering near the door, Flavius seized her hand and he drew her aside and with eyes full of love and longing, said: "You surely will not go, Rose; stay and let us be married at once."

Rose blushed, and for a moment trembled under his ardent gaze. "Oh, Flavius, if it only could be," she whispered.

There was a stir in the crowd as someone announced that the train was ready. Rose started as if to go.

"Stay, love, stay," entreated Flavius.

She hesitated and raised her eyes; they were swimming with tears; "I cannot," she said, "honor before love,"—then she drew a little nearer—"but you can help to bring us back—obtain justice!"

She broke off abruptly as she heard her mother calling her name and hurried away.

Volunmia's great co-worker was a certain lady called Cecilia, and to her also there was a trial in parting. Her father was elderly and infirm, and although possessed of ample means, he depended much on the companionship of his daughter. For a brief moment she hesitated to leave him; then she said sternly: "The Roman father sacrificed his child; Jeptha gave up his daughter at the call of his country; then so will I leave my father for the demands of my sex and of humanity."

Then despite all entreaties and expostulations and even threats, which the men at some points vainly tried, the women every one departed, and after a few days in all the great Atlantic seaboard, from the pine forests of Maine to the wave-washed Florida Keys there was not a woman to be seen.

At first, most of the men pretended that they were glad.

"We can go to the club whenever we like," said a certain married man.

"And no one will find fault with us if we drop into a saloon," added another.

"Or say that tobacco is nasty stuff," suggested a third.

Other individuals, too, were outspoken in regard to the relief they felt. Dr. Hammond declared that the neurological conditions which afflicted women had always rendered them unfit for the companionship of intelligent men. Carl Schurz said that the whole thing was a matter of indifference to him. No one took any interest in the woman question anyway. John Boyle O'Reilly was relieved that no Irish women would hereafter ask him hard questions as to what freedom really meant.

There was much rejoicing among the writers also. Mr. Howells remarked that now he could describe New England girls just as he pleased and no one would find fault with him; and Mr. Henry James was certain that the men would all buy the "Bostonians," which proved so conclusively that no matter how much of a stick a man might be, it was far better for a woman to marry him than to follow even the most brilliant career.

On some points the rejoicing was open. The men in Massachusetts declared that they were well-rid of the Women; there were too many of them anyhow. The members of the New York Legislature held a caucus, irrespective of party, and passed resolutions of congratulation that they would not be plagued with a woman's suffrage bill.

Meantime Volumnia and her hosts had swept across the Rocky Mountains and taken possession of the Pacific slope. Not Wyoming and Washington alone, but Idaho and Montana, and all the region between the two enfranchised territories.

By an arrangement previously made with the women who dwelt in these lands the few men were sent eastward, and in all that wide expanse of territory there were only women to be seen.

Under these circumstances they made such laws as suited them. The Territorial Legislature, consisting wholly of women, speedily passed bills giving women the right to vote. There was no need to pass prohibition measures, as the saloon-keepers had gone East. Peace and tranquillity prevailed through all the borders of the feminine Republic.

There were no policemen, for there was no disorder, but thrift, sobriety and decorum ruled, and the days passed in calm monotony.

Very different was the condition of affairs on the Eastern coast. The men for a while after the departure of the women went bravely about their vocations, many of them, as we have seen, pretending that they were glad that the women were gone. But presently signs of a change appeared. While the saloons did a roaring business the barber shops were deserted—men began to say there was no use in shaving as there were no women to see how they looked; the tailors also suffered, for the men grew careless in their dress; what was the use of fresh linen and gorgeous cravats with never a pretty girl to smile at them? White shirts rapidly gave place to red and gray flannel ones; old hats were worn with calm indifference, even on Fifth Avenue, and after a time men went up and down to business unshaven, and slouchy.

Within the houses there was also a marked change. One of the first sources of rejoicing among men had been that now they would be rid of the slavery of dusters and brooms, and after the women were gone the houses were allowed to fall into confusion. As no one objected that the curtains would be ruined, the men smoked in drawing-room and parlor as well as study, and knocked the ashes from cigar or pipe on the carpet without fearing a remonstrance.

At the end of some months affairs grew worse. The amount of liquor consumed was enormous, the police force was doubled, and then was inefficient because it was impossible to find policemen who would not drink. Brawling was incessant; the men had become cross and sulky, and murderous rows were of constant occurrence. Burglaries and other violent crimes increased and the jails were over-crowded with inmates.

From the first the churches had been nearly empty, as there were no women to attend them, and after awhile they were all closed until the next Legislature ordered that they be turned over to the State; after which some of them were used for sparring exhibitions, and others were turned into gambling saloons, for draw poker had become the fashionable game, and men having no longer any homes gathered every night at some place of amusement. The theatres were obliged to change their attractions and instead of comedies or operas, feats of strength were exhibited. The laws against prize-fighting were repealed, and slugging matches took place nightly; dog-fights and cocking-mains also were popular and the Madison Square Garden, once the scene of a moral "Wild-West" was even turned into an arena for bull-fights.

It was about this time that Henry Bergh, who had vainly protested against some of these things, was defeated for Congress by a man who had won distinction by catching five hundred live rats and putting them into a barrel in fifty minutes. Matters went rapidly from bad to worse after this. John Sullivan was elected President. The men were about to declare war against all the world, so as to have a chance to use their new fortifications when Flavius, who had never ceased to long for Rose, called a secret council at the house of Cecilia's father and proposed that a deputation should be sent with a flag of truce to the women. To his astonishment and delight the idea was received with wild enthusiasm, and he and the host were appointed a committee to lay the question before Congress.

On their appearance at the Capitol, the Senate and House of Representatives were hastily assembled in joint session to receive them, and as they entered the hall the air rang with cries and cheers. It was with great difficulty that General Blair, who had been chosen to preside, could put the motion, which was carried with a wild hurrah of applause, and for many moments thereafter the noise and cheering continued; men hugged each other with delight; some tore off their coats to wave them in the air; many wept tears of joy—in short the scene of enthusiasm exceeded that which is sometimes witnessed at a Presidential nominating convention when a favorite candidate has been selected.

In the fervor of delight which followed all those who had ever opposed the women's wishes fell into the deepest disfavor. It was proposed to expel from the Senate-House Edmunds and Tucker and every other man who had voted against a woman suffrage bill. One member alone suggested that they be banished to the Dry Tortugas with the Rev. M. D. as attendant chaplain.

Calmer counsels ultimately prevailed, as it was discovered that the worst offenders were now thoroughly penitent, and discussion followed as to what terms should be offered to the Women to induce them to return. Everything was conceded, everything accepted, and a deputation of the foremost men was appointed to convey their propositions to the feminine Republic.

But when these reverend seigneurs started they found that a vast array of volunteers was ready to accompany them, a throng that constantly increased as the news spread, and the train moved Westward, for men left their farms, their counting houses and their stores, at the joyful words, "We are going to bring back the women."

Reforms in dress took place as if by magic: no man not properly attired was permitted to join the train. The barbers who had all disappeared, most of them having become butchers, were rediscovered, and although rather out of practice, succeeded in putting heads and beards in presentable trim. Tobacco was positively forbidden; any man detected with even an odor of smoke in his garments was instantly sent to the'rear. Alcoholic stimulants of all sorts were also strictly prohibited, and draw poker went suddenly out of fashion.

Meantime, in the feminine Republic matters moved on serenely but it must be confessed a little slowly. The most absolute order prevailed; the homes were scrupulousy tidy; the streets of the city were always clean. The public money, which was no longer needed for the support of police officers and jails, was spent in the construction of schoolhouses, and other beautiful public buildings. Artificers of all sorts had been found among the women whose natural talents had heretofore been suppressed. Female architects designed houses with innumerable closets. Female contractors built them without developing a female Buddensick, and female plumbers repaired pipes and presented only moderate bills.

But despite the calm and peaceful serenity that prevailed, it was not to be denied that life was rather dull. Women who would not admit it publicly, whispered to themselves that existence would be a little gayer if there were some men to talk to occasionally. Mothers longed in secret for news from their sons; wives dreamed of their husbands, and young girls sighed as they thought of lovers left at home.

Certain great advantages had undoubtedly flowed from the new order of things. Women thrown wholly on their own resources had grown self-reliant, their imposed out-door lives had developed them physically. A complete revolution in dress had taken place; compressed waists had totally disappeared, and loose garments were invariably worn. For out-door labours blouse waists, short skirts and long boots were in fashion; for home life graceful and flowing ones of Grecian design were worn. Common-sense shoes were universal. The schools under the care of feminine Boards of Education were brought to great perfection; the buildings, large and well ventilated, offered ample accommodation, as over-crowding was not permitted. Individual character was carefully studied and each child was trained to develop a special gift. Ethical instruction was daily given and children were rewarded for good conduct even more than for proficiency in study.

Music was carefully taught, and, undismayed by men, women wrote operas and oratorios. Free lectures were given on all branches of knowledge by scientific women who were supported by the State, and debating societies met nightly for the discussion of questions of public policy.

Still, despite all this the women, as we have seen, sent many a thought across the rocky barrier that separated them from the East, and under the leadership of Rose some of the younger ones had formed a league having for its object the opening of communication with husbands and brothers in the masculine Republic.

Thus matters stood when, on a soft June morning, word came to the Capital from the sentinels on the watch-towers of the mountains, that a great horde of men was advancing up the South Pass. Now across this road, the most convenient to the other world, there had been built a wall in the center of which was a massive gate of silver, and at this point the masculine army had halted. The news of the arrival of the men occasioned great commotion, and a joyful host of women started forth to meet them, so that when Volumnia and the other dignitaries of the State reached the Pass, the heights above were filled with a great throng of women who, recognizing in the crowd below sons and brothers, husbands and fathers, were waving joyous greetings, which were answered by the men with every demonstration of delight.

By the order of Volumnia the great silver gate was opened, and the envoys were admitted. They were received in a tent of purple satin which had been quickly erected and their leader made haste to lay before the assembled women the terms they proposed. If the women would only return to their homes the men promised that all wage-workers should have equal pay for equal work; that women should be equally eligible with men to all official positions; that the fortifications should be turned into schoolhouses; that the control of the sale of liquors should be in the hands of women; and that universal suffrage, without regard to sex, should be everywhere established.

When the women heard these words they raised a chorus that was caught up and re-echoed by the crowd outside. At this moment, Cecilia, who saw her father just behind the envoys, went forward to embrace him, and Flavius, taking advantage of the movement advanced to where Rose stood beside her mother. Clasping the blushing girl by the hand he whispered, "At last, love, at last."

Wives rushed into their husband's arms, mothers kissed their sons; the men hurried up from the Pass, the women came down from the mountain; there were broken whispers and fervent prayers, sobs mingled with smiles, and bright eyes shone through tears, as loved ones separated by the stern call of duty were reunited.

After this, there followed a mighty movement, in prairie and forest, by lakeside and river. Over all the land, homes were rebuilt, and society reconstructed. The divided States, now reunited, formed a Republic where all the people were in reality free.

VIA THE HEWITT RAY

M. F. Rupert

I have deliberately paired this story with the previous one because, although written over forty years later, it also portrays a female society and its relationship with men—or, at least, the few that survive. The story is quite shocking in parts, not least in the description of the merciless genocide of another race, making it all the more surprising that the story was by a young woman.

M. F. Rupert, though, is a real mystery. All that we know about her comes from a small sketch that accompanied the original publication of the story in the Spring 1930 issue of Science Wonder Quarterly, *and a letter of comment that was published in the July 1930* Wonder Stories. *The first shows a woman of perhaps mid-30s or early 40s, and the second, which still only uses her initials preceded by 'Miss,' reveals that she lived in Chicago. But a search of census and other records for the time reveals no individual that fits those criteria. It has been suggested her first name was Margaret and, if so, she may be the Margaret Rupert who became a doctor and was practising in Cleveland, Ohio, in the 1940s.*

Whoever she was, this is her only known story and it has never been reprinted outside of the old pulp magazines until now.

Chapter I

LETTER TO LUCILE HEWITT from her father, John J. Hewitt:

My Dear Daughter:

It is now eleven o'clock and I have one hour in which to give you my farewell message. Do not be alarmed, Lucile. I am not contemplating suicide, but as a climax to my life-long studies, I am now going to put to the final test my latest discoveries. Should I be successful in this experiment, you will not see me for a long time. When you find that I am missing, do not fear for me but rejoice that I have succeeded in the great undertaking.

You have now finished college and are engrossed in your own work so, although I shall miss you and do not doubt you will miss me, I feel free to make this experiment. Financially, you do not need me as you are now a self-supporting young woman and I have left provision wherein you will receive this house and all that I own after a year. The greatest hardship is severing, for the time being, our dear comradeship, but I know you will join with me in making this sacrifice.

Do you remember, dear, that about a year ago I told you of the experiments I was making in light waves? It is about those experiments and what they led up to that I wish to write. I will try not to be too technical.

In the laboratory you will find my equipment, electrical apparatus, and light-wave machine, and also the Hewitt Ray machine. In the top right-hand drawer of my desk is a manuscript explaining fully the new discoveries I have made. Please do not allow anything to be disturbed in the laboratory while I am gone. If I do not return within a year, you may publish the manuscript. I hope to be back before the year is up and attend to those things myself, but if I do not return then you, my beloved daughter, may present to the world my life's work.

No doubt, you remember when I erected the light-wave machine. I told you then that it was similar to a radio receiving set, but instead of receiving radio waves, it was intended to receive light waves. Just as sound is transmitted from a source through the air by a series of waves, so light is transmitted through space by a series of ether waves. This machine receives the light waves just as radio receives the radio waves. Of course the real explanation is much more complicated and only a physicist could really understand and appreciate the beauty and immensity of the idea, but as I am writing simply for your benefit, the explanation I gave you a year ago is sufficient.

Messages from Beyond

When I built the machine I had no idea of the astounding revelations I was to receive. But one day, while twirling the dial, I noticed a peculiar arrangement of spectral lines showing on the screen.

Do you remember enough of your physics to understand what this means? The spectrum is the colored band which is produced by placing a prism in the path of a beam of light. When the spectrum is studied minutely with a spectroscope it is found not to be a continuous band of colors, but to be crossed by many dark lines called Fraunhofer lines, which are familiar to all who study light waves. It is also well known that the difference in color in the spectrum corresponds to the difference of wavelength. Keep this explanation in mind as you read what follows.

As soon as I noticed these peculiar lines showing through the spectrum I immediately ceased twirling the dials and studied the spectral lines, the characteristics of which were totally unfamiliar. I made a careful note of the arrangement of the lines; I also noted at what numbers the dials were set, and the time, which was five o'clock in the evening. For fifteen minutes this peculiar spectrum appeared on the screen and was then displaced by the usual Fraunhofer lines. Not touching the dials, I waited carefully for a reappearance of the dark lines, but not until five o'clock the next evening did they come. I compared them line for line with my drawing of the day before and they were exactly the same! For many nights at five o'clock these unusual lines appeared on the screen. Finally I dared to change the dials, to see whether, if I restored those numbers, the phenomenon would occur.

It did, but only at five o'clock. With the help of Professor Hendricks, who died last month, I built a light-wave sending set and after a vast amount of research and labor we found the combination of prisms and lenses that produced the correct spectrum. By manipulating the wavelengths we produced the dark line spectrum which had at first amazed me when beholding it on my own screen.

Do not be impatient with me for this long, dry discourse on light waves and spectra. I am apt to forget that you are not as intensely interested in the details as I. I know that by now you are impatiently asking yourself, "But what's it all about?"

I will try to tell you. You know that Professor Hendricks and myself have always believed in the reality of the fourth and even the fifth and sixth dimensions. Remember how you laughed at us and told us that theoretically we were correct, but you declared actual and tangible proof was impossible? Now do not laugh, dear, when I say that Professor Hendricks and myself believed that these unusual lines were being sent by intelligent beings but *not of our dimension!* The elements of these lines are not known to us.

Do I make myself clear? If these strange spectral lines showed on my receiving screen, they were being sent by someone. The fact that they showed night after night at the same time and only when

the dials were set in a certain manner proved that it was no accidental short-circuiting of the wavelength but that they were being
sent deliberately. The precise and undeviating arrangement of lines
argued that a message of some kind was being sent. What the message meant and who was sending it we did not know but we
intended to find out if possible.

One evening immediately after receiving what we had by now
come to call 'our message', we switched on our sending set and
repeated the message line for line. After a few moments, there
flashed back on our receiving screen the identical lines! For the
first time the message had come through again! We were highly
elated, you may be sure, and figured that whoever was sending that
message had received our repetition of their code and was indicating that.

What to do now? We could, of course, repeat the message every
night after we received it and in this way keep in touch with the
beings who were communicating with us. But as we had no means
of finding out what the lines meant, we could not get very far by
that method.

Determined to Go

Then came the illness and death of Professor Hendricks and I was
left to carry on alone. I almost despaired of making any progress
when there flashed into my mind another possible way of communicating with these strangers.

Several years ago I was working on a series of experiments in
short wavelengths, especially cathode and X-rays. As you may
remember, cathode rays are streams of electrons shot off from a
surface at very high velocity. Just as the X-ray was discovered by
experimenting with the cathode rays, so one day, experimenting
with the X-ray, I discovered an entirely new ray which I called the
Hewitt Ray. No doubt you remember the excitement that the
publication of its discovery caused.

Like the X-ray, the Hewitt Ray will penetrate any substance
opaque to ordinary light, but the great difference is that it does not,
like the X-ray, stop at forming a shadow picture, for by diminish-
ing the gas pressure within the tube and by increasing the voltage
across the electrodes, the penetrating power of the resulting rays is
increased to such an extent that the object on which the ray is
focused is disintegrated. And what is stranger still, not the picture

of the object appears at the focal point, but the actual object itself is reassembled and reappears, none the worse for its experience.

You were just a young girl then, but you must remember all the talk and conjecture aroused by the discovery of this new ray. It was thought for a time that it would revolutionize transportation. In fact, it was proved practical for swift traveling. Huge Hewitt Ray machines were built with a focus of many miles and a few intrepid souls were found to lend themselves to the experiment; but although they arrived safely at their destination and were loud in their praise of this method of traveling, the general public would have none of it. Humanity has not yet evolved to the point where it is willing to travel 186,000 miles per second. So my Hewitt Ray, conceded to be a marvelous thing, was put on the shelf like many other revolutionary inventions. No doubt, a few thousand years from now, it will be used universally.

So, as I thought of this ray, I wondered if, by experimenting a little further, I could possibly change the ray so that it would not merely reassemble the object which it disintegrated but allow the object to travel on. Into what, you may ask? Space? The fourth dimension, or wherever it is that a light wave goes when it has passed beyond our eye?

I will not weary you, Lucile, with the details but I have succeeded in changing the rays as I wanted to and have discovered that the light waves do not die out but by an energy transformation they pass off into another plane of energy.

You ask how I know? I know because with my improved Hewitt Ray I have disintegrated objects such as books, vases, flowers, and live animals and sent them traveling as part of the wave of light into the unknown world from which I have been receiving messages.

With the dials of my light-wave machine set to receive an answer from the beings with whom I have been in communication, I sent through the medium of the Hewitt Ray these objects and animals; and every time I sent something through, no matter at what time of the day or night, I received a message which I interpreted to mean that the objects were received.

Now, Lucile, all this preliminary explanation over, we come to the vital part of my letter. I have determined to go to this new world. It will be a simple accomplishment. I have built a large Hewitt Ray projector which will be automatically shut off after I have passed through. What sort of world I will find or what kind of people or beings I will meet I do not know. I believe they are friendly and will welcome me, but anyway I will soon find out.

Now, dear daughter, I will leave you. Enclosed you will find the keys to the laboratory and detailed instructions for working the light-wave receiving and sending set. Every evening at five o'clock I will endeavor to send you a message, according to the light-wave code I have worked out. It will make me very happy if you will answer.

Goodbye, dear. That you may keep well and happy is the wish of

Your loving father,
JOHN J. HEWITT.

CHAPTER II

Lucile Hewitt's Story

To say that I was astonished and alarmed to receive this letter is describing my feeling feebly. Darling old Dad, to travel along a light wave, into a new world filled, no doubt, with unknown dangers! Why, he was forever cautioning me to be careful! Even as late as 1945 he thought airplanes were dangerous! I have often begged him to let me take him for a ride in my fly-about but he declared he did not have the necessary courage. Yet he risked his life daily in his beloved laboratory.

It is really too bad that I am not scientifically inclined. What a help I might have been to Dad! But I honestly tried to fit myself for a scientific career and it was not my fault that I failed miserably.

When Dad got out his Hewitt Ray and there was talk of utilizing it for travel, then my interest in science awoke. To travel with the speed of light! Imagine the thrill! Unknown to Dad, for I knew he would forbid me, I slipped away from school and volunteered for a demonstration trip along the Hewitt Ray. I was one of the 'intrepid souls' Dad speaks of. It was glorious! To place yourself before the ray and in a flash be hundreds of miles away! That is traveling!

When the use of the Hewitt Ray was discontinued my interest in science dropped. But my one great interest in life had been revealed to me. Travel—and travel with limitless speed! The next speediest thing I could find was the airplane and you may be sure I got one.

At the time I learned to operate my first plane I was sixteen years old, a wild, harum-scarum girl. As public interest in aviation grew, I grew right with it, until now, at twenty-six, I have been piloting a huge commercial airliner between New York and Honolulu for five years.

At first the public was sceptical about trusting its life to a woman's hands but now the New York-Honolulu Air Line uses only women pilots, as statistics show that a plane is ten percent safer with a woman pilot than with a man.

The morning I had received Dad's letter I had just come off duty. I had been on a six-day shift and now I had before me three days of rest. That was the regular schedule.

After reading the letter I went immediately to the laboratory. There the large Hewitt Ray machine attracted my attention. After examining it closely, I found the controls and with a little trepidation turned them on. A soft, almost invisible amber ray shone from the funnel-shaped aperture. Emboldened a little I took off my glove and placed it experimentally on the platform immediately in the glow of the ray. At first nothing happened, but then the glove began to glow with the same soft radiance of the ray and almost imperceptibly it disappeared, becoming a part of the surrounding light.

I next turned my attention to the light-wave receiver, tuning in and setting the dial at twenty. At once the visascreen burst into radiance. A succession of beautiful colors floated across. I reached out and pulled a switch marked "Spectroletope," and then a change took place on the screen. The beautiful colors were broken and separated, mingling and intermingling in a bewildering manner, tiny lines forming regularly through the whole. I watched it fascinated for a while, and then turned off the switch, humming a parody on a popular song:

> *"It might mean something to someone*
> *But it don't mean nothing to me."*

Well, Dad was gone and here I was with the laboratory full of marvelous equipment that I only faintly understood. I read his letter over again and tried to reassure myself that he was all right. But how could I convince myself he was safe? What kind of a world had he gone into? How was he going to return? The more I thought about it the more alarmed I became. Why hadn't he allowed me to go exploring this new world so he could stay here in his laboratory among his beloved scientific instruments, where he belonged? He was a marvelous scientist, but outside of his laboratory he was lost; he would always be a child to the world.

After two days of restless and troubled thoughts I determined to get someone to operate the machine and follow him through to that strange world. Acting on this decision I radiophoned my former classmate, Marion Wells, who was already successful in a scientific career. I had not been in personal touch with her for several years but had followed with interest her steady rise to fame. The whole world had her to thank for their clean, easy, and never-failing atomic household heaters.

Marion

After looking up her private wavelength I tuned in and in a few seconds her serious, spectacled face appeared on my television as her clear voice said "Marion Wells on the air." Then as she recognized me on her screen she smiled in friendly greeting. I did not go into detail but explained that I needed desperately the aid of her scientific knowledge and asked her to come to my house.

"Be with you in ten minutes," she promised and signed off.

And in ten minutes as I watched out the window, her autoplane landed in a vertical drop below our driveway, its wings automatically collapsing as it touched the ground. I admired her skilful driving as she came through the gate and taxied under the trees up to the front verandah.

With our greetings over, she asked what the trouble was and after my halting and doubtless inadequate explanation of what had taken place, she said crisply, "Let's go up to your father's laboratory and examine the equipment. Perhaps I can get a better idea of what you are trying to tell me."

In the laboratory Marion showed the greatest interest in the Hewitt Ray; the light-wave receiver in fact seemed to be familiar to her. Then she turned it on and watched the visascreen awhile. Curiously, I asked her if she knew what the colors and lines meant.

"Yes, they are the international wave code system," she nodded. "Slowly but surely this manner of communication is taking the place of the old-fashioned method. The light-wave stations are more simple to construct and much cheaper to operate and the regular service provided is vastly superior to the old telegraph method."

When the wonders of the laboratory had been examined and tried out we sat down and tried to figure out some way of getting Dad back safely. Marion advocated waiting for a definite message from Dad, but I was too worried to consider that. I wanted Marion to stay here and intercept messages, while I went through to get Dad.

"But listen to reason, foolish child," Marion pleaded. "This plane of existence to which your father has gone is without a doubt as big as the world in which you are now living. Perhaps he has gone or been carried thousands of miles away and how do you expect to find him?"

"Well," I answered stubbornly. "If he is over there, perhaps he needs me and if he needs me I am going to him. I'll find him somehow."

"Very well. Tell me how you propose to get back once you find him."

I must have looked crestfallen for Marion reached over and patted my hand. "Don't worry, Lou. I have a plan. We will have to get busy, though, if you expect to go through in the near future."

"Oh! Marion, I knew I could depend on you!"

Briskly she asked me for the manuscript Dad had written, and from it got a detailed description of how to build and operate the new Hewitt Ray machine.

"You see," she explained finally, "we will construct another ray machine and send it on through with you. That is your only chance to get back."

At once I became enthusiastic. So for the next few weeks we worked furiously. I had radioed my company for an extension of leave which was granted. One afternoon it was finished. Five o'clock came and we set the light-wave receiver according to Dad's instructions. Marion watched intently the message shown on the visascreen, then frowned and consulted Dad's notes again.

"I am afraid, Lou, there is something wrong. That certainly isn't your father's private code. Nor is it the international code which I know."

"Perhaps it is the same message that Dad has been receiving," I said.

"Yes, that must be it. For some reason your father is unable to send his message and these beings are trying to get in touch with you."

"Oh! I knew something had happened to him," I wailed. "Let me go through now, Marion. You can finish the other ray machine and send it on later. I'll find it. It will have to arrive at the same place I do, won't it?"

"Hardly," she replied thoughtfully. "But it won't be long now and a few hours cannot make such a difference. You had better play safe and wait for the other machine."

But it was morning before the machine was completed and I was able to start. I had dressed myself in my flying togs and strapped a 45 Colt and cartridges around me. A few clean handkerchiefs and a couple of packages of cigarettes completed my personal luggage.

Worried as I was, I was yet all athrill as I mounted the platform and gave Marion the signal to turn on the ray.

A faint glow surrounded me. I began to tingle from head to toe. Glancing at my hands I noticed that they glowed faintly. I was passing through! "Dear God, please help me find Dad!" I became numb. . . . A sudden gap appeared in my consciousness—then the tingling sensation returned . . . . ceased . . . . and I had passed through.

The New World

For a few seconds I was bewildered. Where was I, and what was I doing here? Then my head cleared, I remembered and began to look about me. I was in an inclosure of some kind. The walls, ceiling and floor were snow white. I stooped and touched the floor. It felt like earth. I touched the walls—they were rock! I was in a cave, a snow white cave!

A cave must have an entrance of some kind, I reasoned, so after packing the Hewitt Ray machine back into a corner, I began to walk along the side of one of the walls. After walking about 500 feet, I came to a turn which I followed. Three times the tunnel through which I was moving turned before I saw an opening. The brightness reflected from the white walls gradually gave place to a pale pink flush which became deeper as I advanced until I came to an opening which was bathed in a rosy glow.

I stepped out cautiously and stood rooted to the spot in amazement. A softly glowing red sun rode high in a pale pink sky. I was on a low hill whose path ran down into a forest of scarlet trees. Hurriedly I ran down the path, the earth of which was as white as the interior of the cave, to get a better look at the scarlet trees. Were they really scarlet or was it just a reflection of the rosy sky?

In a few moments I was among the trees and saw indeed that it was no reflection which colored them. The leaves were bright scarlet, the trunks and branches snow-white like the ground. All around grew scarlet bushes, bursting into bloom with tiny silver-grey and pale amber-colored blossoms. A little farther on, a narrow brook rippled merrily and I decided to follow and see where it would lead me. All about lay peace and quiet. The air was soft and balmy, a direct contrast to the sharp winter winds I had left at home. It was a veritable fairyland, and made me wonder if Dad had come through near here and if so what he thought of the weird scenery.

At first I was a little fearful of meeting some strange animal or person but presently I became bolder and left the shadow of the trees, under which I had been traveling, and walked along the exposed bank of the brook.

Without the least warning, there broke upon the air the most frightful noise imaginable. Grasping my revolver, I fled to the shelter of the trees and from behind a broad, white trunk, I waited breathlessly as the dreadful noise drew near.

Nearer and nearer, and louder and louder came the noise until there burst through the bushes to my right the most astonishing sight.

Two enormous creatures, whether men or animals, I could not at first determine, for they seemed to resemble both, came tumbling into the road before me. That they were engaged in a fight to the death, I did not for a moment doubt. Screeching and yelling, they grappled and fought, broke apart only to rush together again and tear and bite until, in disgust, I turned away. When I looked towards them again, one was on the ground evidently in death agony but the victorious one still kept up the frightful noise, at the same time, tearing his still living opponent apart. The sight so disgusted and infuriated me that I forgot my own precarious position and, lifting my automatic which I still clutched in my hand, I fired at the hideous monster.

At the bark of the gun, the creature stopped his howling and started stupidly about. At last, apparently locating the direction of the strange noise, he started in my direction. Thoroughly frightened now, I lifted the gun again, but before I could bring my trembling fingers to pull the trigger, he suddenly stopped, staggered, and fell with a crash and a long unearthly howl to the ground, where he lay thrashing about. When he finally lay quiet,

I drew near, trembling and fearful at every step; yet my curiosity to see these strange creatures was stronger than any fear.

Upon the ground not very far apart lay the two great bodies. The one who had fallen in the battle was so mangled that I turned away to the one I had shot. The body, fully eight feet in length and weighing, I judged, around four hundred pounds, was covered completely by a short bristly hair. The feet and hands of the creatures were like great huge claws that looked cruel and powerful. But the face! How shall I describe it? If the body, except for the claw-like hands and feet and the short hairs covering it, was human there was nothing human about the face. The monstrous head, looking too heavy even for the enormous and powerful body and neck supporting it, was flat on top and back, coming in front to a blunt point with two open nostrils. The eyes, now fixed with a glassy stare, were small and green, and the mouth, a thick-lipped enormous slit, was drawn back in a snarl, showing a double row of sharp cruel teeth. There was no chin, the lower jaw sloping abruptly to the neck. All in all, he was the most loathsome and fearful object it had ever been my misfortune to encounter.

CHAPTER III

Captured!

With an uncontrollable shudder, I turned away. If this were a specimen of the inhabitants of the fourth dimension I must find my father immediately and take him back to our own world.

I walked on, wondering where my father was. Was he held captive by these creatures? Perhaps I could find their village or city and after dark scout around and see if there was any sign of Dad.

Suddenly a twig cracked sharply in the bushes beside me. I looked about in swift alarm. Was I being stalked? With flying feet I made for the low trees ahead. A long howl came from behind me and the thud-thud-thud of a heavy fast-moving body sounded. Faster and faster I ran but ever behind and dangerously nearer every few seconds came that ominous thud.

Twang! Something flew by my head and to my horror a strange but wicked-looking arrow-like missile buried itself in the soft white earth before me. I ran on until the path abruptly ended at a wide chasm over which it was impossible for me to jump. I came to a halt. What should I do? Drop to certain death or stay and submit to a captivity fraught with untold horrors? "Never! Never!" I fiercely whispered to myself, as my hand quickly flew to the temporarily forgotten automatic at my side. Too late!—My pursuer was right beside me and before I could draw my gun I felt clawlike hands clutching me and saw piggish eyes close to my own.

He picked me up and throwing me over his shoulder like a sack of flour, let out a howl of triumph and started swiftly through the trees. My sensations, then, were brief for with that howl coming so close beside me I sank into a merciful faint.

When I came to, I found myself lying on the ground completely surrounded by these repulsive creatures. No one touched me but all looked at me curiously, gibbering in excited guttural tones. Evidently I was a novel sight to them.

I sat up and there was a startled movement in the crowd. H'm! I thought, they are not quite sure of just how dangerous I might be. No one molested me and I sat there for some time surrounded by my curious audience. I was hungry but no one seemed to think of offering me food. Finally I lit a cigarette. If they were startled when I sat up they were panic-stricken at the sight of the tiny flame and smoke. They fled in all directions and gazed at me from a distance.

"The fools," I said. "Do they think this is some kind of an infernal machine?" I was hungry and cross and their foolish fear did not amuse me as it ordinarily would have. Finally a line of the creatures approached me armed with bows and arrows. The leader courageously came forward and motioned for me to put down my fearful weapon. I ignored the obvious command and calmly blew a cloud of smoke towards him. Immediately a shower of arrows embedded themselves in the ground around me. I do not think they intended to wound me, they were merely wanting me to obey, which I now prudently did. After that I was let alone and I began to stroll about, a group of the creatures following at a safe distance.

It was a curious contrast between the beautiful and fairy-like scenery and these hideous creatures who were oblivious of its beauty.

I walked all around but look as I might I could see no sign of Dad. Deciding to try to get some information from these people, I beckoned to one who seemed to be the leader and by various signs tried to ask him if there were another creature like myself in their midst.

At first he stared at me stupidly, then the little piggy eyes lit up and he turned and motioned me to follow. I did so with a beating heart. Perhaps they had Dad hidden away somewhere in the wilderness! If so, he and I together might find some way of escaping from these beastly people. Surely they were not the ones who had been sending messages to Dad: they were rank savages.

Flight

My guide led me into a thicket and we followed a narrow path through the scarlet growth until we came to a clearing. There before us stood an aircraft of peculiar design and on the ground near it lay a woman. But what a woman! Tall almost as the creature beside me, she was magnificently proportioned. Short, crisp black hair covered her head. Her face was beautiful but the features were set in grim lines. An arrow had pierced her left breast and her clothing, a single blue tunic, was saturated with blood. She was dead, but my heart lightened considerably at the sight of her and her aircraft. These savage beast men were not the only inhabitants of this plane. Another and more intelligent group of people were here also and, no doubt, they were the ones who had been communicating with our world by way of the light-wave machine. Even now, Dad might be with them!

I turned from the figure of the dead woman and scrutinized closely the vehicle beside her. It was an aircraft of the enclosed cabin type. I had never seen one just like it before and I itched to get in and try out the various strange-looking controls I could see through the glass of the cabin door.

By pantomime, I asked permission to enter and investigate the machine. But my guide, hastily placing himself between me and the car, motioned me away.

Waves of fury mounted to my brain. Was I to let a stupid savage keep me prisoner when here was a chance to get away? My hand slid along my belt and I cautiously grasped the butt of my gun, which my captors, not knowing what it was, had not bothered to take away from me.

Not by a flicker of an eye did my guide show that he thought he was in danger, but he kept motioning me to go back the way we had come. Go back and miss this wonderful chance to escape?—Not much!

Quickly I drew and fired pointblank at the creature's leg. What a howl he let out! Between the noise of the shot and his terrible howling, the whole pack would be here soon. I pulled open the door and hastily climbed into the plane.

"Oh God! please let it work!" I grasped a handle and pulled. With a suddenness that took my breath away, I shot vertically upward. Recovering, I pushed the handle back to the first notch and the car ceased its upward flight and shot forward. Well, I didn't know where I was going but I was on my way!

A few manipulations of the dials and switches and the strange-looking knobs on the control board, and I soon learned what they were for. I flew in a straight line, hoping for a sight of civilization, but for mile after mile I could see nothing but the red sun above and the scarlet forests below.

Suddenly, as three tiny bulbs in front of the cabin lit up, the vehicle swerved sharply to the right and I found myself traveling at a right angle to my previous direction. I was alarmed. I had made no change in the controls, yet of its own volition the car turned and traveled in the new direction at terrific speed.

In the distance I made out a tiny speck which gradually, as my car hurled itself forward, became larger and larger until it assumed mountainous proportions. I was headed straight for it and none of my feverish manipulations of the levers or dials would swerve my car one inch!

Suddenly the speed of my car slackened and at an easy pace it glided to a gentle landing on top of what I took to be a flat-topped mountain. With hardly a perceptible jar, the car halted and the tiny globes turned off.

For a few moments I was too astonished to think; then the explanation flashed on me. Remote control! I had been guided here by an unseen force. Did they, whoever controlled the latter part of my trip, know I was coming and in that manner help me along; or had I accidentally come into the field of a control station? If so, then there ought to be some sign of human habitation. But look around as I might all I could see through my window was the flat top of this mountain or plateau.

Mavia

Just as I was wondering what I should do, I felt a sinking sensation and looking out I saw that I was being gently lowered into this mountain! What next, I thought fearfully? But immediately the plane came to a halt and to my amazement I saw that it was in a line with many similar planes.

I opened the door and stepped out into what must have been a huge hangar. Then I heard a low hum and looking up in the direction of the sound I saw the roof open and another flying car gently descending. My own and the other cars moved soundlessly down the line making room for the descending machine, which settled into the place previously occupied by my own plane.

The door opened and out stepped what looked like the counterpart of the dead woman in the scarlet forest! She looked startled at the sight of me for a moment, then gravely held her hand up palm outward in what I took to be a greeting. Just as gravely I returned the salute and the woman smiled and spoke in a strange tongue.

I answered in English. Though neither understood the other we simultaneously laughed, and she companionably linked arms with me and led me to a wall. A row of buttons studded its side, one of which she pressed. After a slight click an opening appeared. Though I expected to step into some kind of elevator there was nothing in front of us but a lighted space. Unhesitatingly, the woman started to step through but I fearfully held back.

We were at a deadlock for a few minutes until another woman came around a corner and the two talked together a moment in their strange language. Then the second woman laughed and without hesitation stepped into the void. I expected to see her crash to the bottom, but instead, she floated gently down.

With grave misgivings, I let my companion lead me through and we too gently sank down through the void. Then our descent became slower and ceased altogether before another door, through which we stepped. We were now, I reasoned, on the second floor from the top.

A long vista of hallways from the great arched doors greeted us. Hurrying past many of them we at last entered one. At that moment, I do not know exactly what I expected, some kind of oriental splendor, I suppose, but what I saw was only a very business-like office of some sort, where many women were busy operating peculiar looking machines. They reminded me of the electro-typists at home.

Passing through this room we reached a private room and my companion motioned me to be seated. She then pushed a button on her desk and another woman from the outer office entered, carrying what looked like a football head-gear with wire attachments.

Following my companion's example, I put the thing on my head, then looked at her. Smiling she spoke, and to my astonishment I understood every word she said.

"Welcome, Visitor, to City 43 of the Second Evolutionary plane. May I introduce myself? I am Mavia, chief factor of this city and in the name of my comrades-in-rule, I welcome you and put ourselves and our city at your service."

It was quite an elaborate speech and as I wasn't exactly sure of what she was talking about I answered hesitatingly.

"Thank you. I feel very strange. I am Lucile and I came here from the third dimension, looking for my father."

"Oh, you are from the third dimension? Really? I had no idea that the beings of the third dimension had evolved to the point of inter-dimensional travel. Very interesting. You said something about another of your world being here?"

"Yes, my father. He was receiving light-wave messages from this world and by using an invention of his he came through. I was worried about him so I followed him through. Have you seen him?"

"No. I am sorry to say I have not. Nor have any of the other Second Evolutionary cities or I would have had a report on it."

My heart sank. Poor Dad. Where was he? Mavia went on speaking.

"You say he was receiving light-wave messages? I think I can explain that. But first let me tell you about ourselves, then you will be able to follow my explanations more easily."

CHAPTER IV

The Three Evolutions

"This world in which you now find yourself is the fourth dimension. In it are the beings of the First, Second, and Third Evolutionary planes. The first plane consists of savages of a very low order—just now they are emerging from the beast stage into the human."

"Yes," I interrupted eagerly. "I have seen them. I was captured and held prisoner by them. They have killed one of your women and I escaped in her airplane."

Mavia seemed unmoved by the accident to her comrade.

"That was Doona, my second in command. Against my advice, she ventured alone in the scarlet forest. I recognized her plane in the hangar and wondered how you came to be using it. So she is dead? Well, we must all die sometime." She shrugged her shoulders.

"The Second Evolutionary plane consists of ourselves. We have seventy-nine cities. Each city is like the one you are now in. They were originally mountains and our cities are built inside the mountains as a means of defense against the first and third planes, who are continually waging wars of extermination against us.

"Our plane consists almost entirely of women. We keep just enough men to maintain the race. These few masculine creatures that we allow to live are kept in luxury and idleness. They are well taken care of and have no complaint. A very long time ago, many centuries in fact, the men were the ruling sex of this plane, but gradually the women demanded equal rights and once we gained a footing, it wasn't long before we were ruling the men. Those were bitter and bloody days. We call them in history 'The Sex War Epoch.'

"Eventually the women won, and we destroyed millions of the despised masculine sex. For untold centuries they had kept women subjugated and we finally got our revenge."

"Oh!" I said. "In our world the women are getting equal rights with the men. For a long time we, too, were held back but now we stand shoulder to shoulder with the men. I hope we won't have any sex war. That would be horrible."

"Time will tell," Mavia answered. "Now, Lucile, are there any questions you are eager to ask, because I know you are hungry and we will continue our conversation after you have eaten and rested."

"First, tell me how it is that we understand each other when we both speak different languages?"

Mavia laughed. "It is very simple. By means of sensitized plates within these caps your spoken thoughts vibrate along those short wires and are received and translated by the wires on my cap and come to me as if spoken in my own language. The same thing happens to my spoken thoughts. In other words, these caps are tiny thought-wave sending and receiving sets. We have had them from the time the men were the ruling sex. At that time each of our cities was a separate nation speaking its own language and making its own laws and warring upon each other. When the women took control of things we internationalized the languages and laws and now each city is a part of one great whole. The Second Evolutionists are not equal to the Thirds in every way. Before, we were beset by outside foes and our strength was being continually used up in civil wars. Now that we are organized we are able to strengthen our forces and in time we expect to be the only evolutionary plane in this dimension."

"How was it," I asked, "that we did not crash when we stepped into that void between floors?"

"Because the minute we stepped off the floor our bodies lost almost all weight with the lessened force of gravity from above the shaft. The fact that we did not stay stationary in the air but floated down was due to a gentle but persistent counter-pull exerted on our bodies, gradually giving them weight until we reached bottom. Now, Lucile, I am going to take you to my apartment where you will rest and eat, for I have much more to tell you and tomorrow is to be a busy day. Come with me."

We left the office and floated down another shaft to the floor below. Mavia explaining, as we went, the general layout of the floors we were traversing. The top floor was devoted entirely to the airplanes. The second floor—that is, the next to the top—was the office floor, and the third to the tenth were devoted to the living quarters of these remarkable women. I was extremely worried about Dad, but felt confident that Mavia would help me to find him.

When we stepped onto the third floor I was startled to see an immense insect crawling towards me and I drew back in alarm. Mavia said:

"Don't be afraid. That is one of our servants. It is of the ant family and by careful breeding we have developed them to this size. They make highly efficient servants, each one trained to its own task. They are perfectly harmless. Countless centuries of selective breeding have eradicated all vicious tendencies."

"Perhaps it has," I quavered, "but they don't look it. Please don't let any of them wait on me."

"Just as you say," Mavia replied, courteously, "but I assure you they are very gentle."

What Happened to Males

I noticed in the center of this hallway, or street as Mavia called it, a wide section in the floor, bisected and moving along in opposite directions while at either side an equally wide strip remained stationary. We now stepped onto the moving roadway and we were carried at a swift pace to our destination.

Mavia's apartment was strictly utilitarian, bare almost to emptiness. Only the most necessary furniture stood about. I expressed a desire for a bath and she ushered me into a room and instructed me to strip except for the thought transferring apparatus and stand under what I took to be a shower. She then turned a wheel and a bright light filtered down on me.

"Where is the soap and water?" I asked.

Mavia said: "This is our method of cleansing and rejuvenating the body. Those radio-active rays cleanse the skin and penetrate the pores, revivifying the body with new life and strength."

It was true. The dust and grime I had collected disappeared and although I had been feeling fatigued I now felt as if I had been resting. Mavia presented me with one of her tunics to wear instead of my cumbersome flying suit.

The tunic on her barely reached below her hips, but I was so much smaller that it came modestly to my knees and after strapping on my automatic I felt quite dressed up.

We went next into the dining room and Mavia, dismissing three giant insect servants, waited on me herself. First she went to the wall and operated a machine that resembled a portable typewriter. Then she opened a section of a wall and pulled out a table with dishes and service on it. By the time she had arranged it, a slight buzzing over the typewriter affair was heard and Mavia removed from a section in the wall a little tray. Strange but delicious foods were placed before me and I ate heartily.

During the course of the meal I asked her where the food came from and she said that on the thirty-first floor were the kitchens where food for the whole city was prepared and on the floors thirty-two to fifty agriculture was successfully carried on by means of artificial sunlight and irrigation.

"Mavia, tell me," I asked finally, "do you think you could help me find my father?"

"If he is where I think he is, perhaps I can."

"Thank you," I replied. "Please go on with your descriptions of the three evolutions of your world. You left off at the sex war of the second evolution."

Mavia complied. "After the war there was complete chaos for a while. Women were not used to their power and it went to their heads. They wanted to kill every male creature in the second evolutionary plane, for they were tired of child-bearing and child-rearing. A few of us who were able to withstand the headiness of our triumph took hold of things and prevented the complete extermination of the males, until we could see whether or not they were necessary to the future of our race."

"I should think," I interrupted, "that with your advanced knowledge of science you would have been able to produce young without the actual help of the male. In our world we have certain low forms of life that do that very thing."

Mavia laughed heartily. "We did try it and you should have seen the results. Perfect monstrosities. We did not want our race to deteriorate, so we went back to the age-old method.

"The males who had escaped extermination were put through rigid physical and mental tests. Those of a high average are all housed on the twelfth floor, as you call it, and these men are called the reproducing males.

"Every woman is required by law to give to the city two children which, by improved scientific methods, she does with a minimum of pain and time.

"The males whose intelligence average was below our mental standard but who had physical beauty were made sterile by a special process and housed on the thirteenth tier."

"But you don't need these sterile men," I said. "Why do you keep them?"

Mavia smiled grimly. "We changed a lot of things but we were unable, without danger to the future of our race, to change the fundamentals of natural instincts. When we women have borne two children to the race we are not allowed to reproduce a third time. Nevertheless the old biological urge returns and then we find use for the sterile male."

"But that is downright immoral," I objected.

Planning the Raid

Mavia frowned. "What is morality? Isn't it living in such a manner that you are able to give the best of yourself to the race to which you belong? What we consider proper would probably be condemned as immoral in your sphere. Yet were I to visit you, no doubt I should be shocked by many of your customs that you people either put up with or ignore. Am I not right?"

"I don't know," I answered, "It still doesn't seem right to me."

"Well, to you with your present standard of morals it isn't right, but to us it is a highly efficient manner of settling our difficulties. But let's get back to our explanations of the three evolutionary planes. We, you understand, are of the second evolution, and there is yet another plane, called the third, whose inhabitants are our deadly enemies.

"They are horrible grotesque creatures with abnormal mental developments. They have tiny weak bodies and enormous heads. Clever machines carry them around to do the physical acts that their little wizened bodies are incapable of performing."

"Why are they your enemies?" I asked, curiously.

"They fear us," Mavia replied. "They are afraid that we will evolve to the point where we shall take their place. But, although they don't know it, we are quite content to remain on our present evolutionary plane with which we are very well satisfied. Nevertheless, we shall probably have to exterminate them for the safety of our own race. Now about those light-wave messages—"

Just then a knock sounded and about fifteen women entered, all wearing the thought-wave caps. They were prepared to meet and converse with me.

Mavia introduced them. They were all fine, intelligent, well-developed, good-looking women and they gazed at me with disguised curiosity. I could easily stand under the arm of any of them. For a time they kept me busy explaining the customs and accomplishments of our dimension until finally Mavia rapped for order.

"Comrades-in-rule," she said, "just as you came in I was explaining something to our visitor which I think will be of interest to you as well. A man whom she calls 'Father" had been receiving light-wave messages from this world. By means of a disintegrating ray this 'Father' has traveled through from the third dimension to this one. Lucile was captured by the First Evolutionists and 'Father' was not with them. We know that he is not with us, therefore he must be with the Thirds.

"As you know, the Thirds are planning a raid upon us and, no doubt, the light-wave messages that 'Father' has been intercepting were calls for reinforcements from those horrible beings of the second dimension."

A murmur of horror came from the women. It amused me to hear Mavia call Dad 'Father', as if that were his given name.

Mavia went on. "My suggestion is this: The Thirds do not know we have this knowledge of their proposed raid, so why not take them unaware by a midnight attack and with our newly-perfected rays, wipe them out of existence?"

A cheer went up and it was quite a few minutes before I could make myself heard. "My Father!" I wailed. "If he is with these Third Evolutionists and you wipe them out—what will happen to him?"

"I'm afraid it is unavoidable, but if he is with them he will have to go too."

Hysterically, I began to cry and beg them to save my father from destruction. They gazed at me in amazement. I suppose such an exhibition of emotion was totally unfamiliar to them. Finally Mavia awkwardly patted my back and said:

"I am sorry if we wounded your sensibilities, but we, of this world, are accustomed to considering the good of the race before individual preferences. Yet, you are our guest and we will make an exception in your favor."

"You mean you will save my father?" I cried joyfully and to everyone's astonishment I threw my arms around Mavia.

"Just a second," she cried. "I do not promise positively that we will be able to save him, but we will endeavor, for your sake, to do so."

"Thank you all," I said quietly. "I feel as if Father were saved already."

"Well, now that that is settled, we will have to get busy and prepare for our midnight attack. You, Calissia, I appoint as guide and instructor to our visitor. Show her over the city. You are both to return here to my apartment and I will assign you your place in tonight's raid."

One of the women rose and saluted and together we left the apartment.

CHAPTER V

Exploring

Calissia I found to be a very pleasant companion and with her I explored the city, descending from floor to floor, or as I should call it, tier to tier.

The first three tiers I had already seen and as the next six were the same as the third, that is, women's apartments, we dropped down an express shaft from the third tier to the eleventh. There the scientists worked. The whole floor was a huge laboratory and I met many women who had heard of my presence and were anxious to meet me. Many of them tried to explain to me the wonders of the various experiments they were conducting, but I am afraid that most was beyond me. But how Dad would have enjoyed it!

On the twelfth floor were the quarters for reproducing men. I will admit I was anxious to see them. We went straight to the recreation section where we found hundreds of men walking around or reclining in comfortable chairs reading. They were not as tall as the women and were dressed almost similarly. I expected to see effeminate creatures simpering about, but instead, I found a group of men, who except for their peculiar shoulder-length hair might have been men of my own world.

On the next floor, however, my expectations were more than justified. Curled and perfumed and elaborately dressed, these unfortunate creatures gazed coyly at us and I urged Calissia to take me away at once. We went on to the fourteenth tier and saw the community shops, where one could get anything from a new tunic to an airplane.

The fifteenth tier held the city nurseries where, cared for by the giant insects, were children of both sexes. Poor little mites! They simply walked gravely around or played sedately with educational toys. There did not seem to be that spontaneous joy of living, characteristic of the children of our own world. The older children were grouped into classrooms where they were being educated for the particular career in life for which they were desired.

The sixteenth tier contained the hospital where feminine doctors and assistants bustled efficiently about. One particular case the doctors insisted on showing me. I protested that I did not know anything about surgery or medicine, but Calissia said: "Do come and see it. It is a perfectly wonderful piece of work and our doctors will be offended, as they are justly proud of themselves for having accomplished it."

Reluctantly I accompanied them to a private room where we found a woman seated at a table busily writing. As we entered she arose and came towards us, evidently pleased at our visit. I was introduced and the doctor in charge said, "We will now show you the triumph of science over the crudities of nature."

The patient took off her tunic and I saw that in her left side was a transparent square that looked like glass but was soft, like flesh, to the touch. Through this I could see her heart beating. Tiny wires connected to the heart came up under the breast and were connected to a small, flat, box-like object fastened under her left arm.

"Very clever, but what is it all about?" I asked. I suppose they thought I was awfully dumb but very courteously they explained:

"In the last raid upon the Thirds, the patient was wounded through the heart. When she was brought to us she was dead. Dead but still warm. As she was in perfect physical condition except for the wounded heart we decided to try out an experiment we had been working on. Her flesh and blood heart was removed and this artificial rubber heart inserted. It worked. Pumping blood through the system it brought back life and now she is just as well off as before the accident."

"Is it possible?" I exclaimed. "What keeps it going?"

The doctor pointed to the flat object under her arm and explained that this tiny box contained stored up electrical energy which operated the rubber heart. The electrical apparatus had to be renewed about every thirty days.

I thanked them for the interesting exhibition and we went on down through the next fourteen floors where factories and centers of manufacture were located.

Tier thirty-one I explored extensively. Food in huge quantities was being prepared and I thought of what a boon such a system would be to many tired housewives. Huge automatic refrigerating systems helped keep the food pure.

We next visited the agriculture tiers. From tier thirty-two to tier fifty inclusive, were acre upon acre of growing crops. Overhead were immense lights that supplied the sunlight needed by all growing things while cleverly arranged sprinklers watered the crops. All about were the giant insects industrially farming.

Tier fifty-one, Calissia informed me, was set aside for the exclusive use of the huge ants, where they had their living, breeding and training quarters. When I declined to visit them, Calissia suggested that we return to Mavia's apartment.

"Are there no more tiers? Have we reached ground level?" I asked.

"Oh, no," Calissia replied, "we haven't reached ground level. There are many more tiers, some even below ground, but they are used mostly as granaries, store houses and burial vaults for the ashes of our dead. And below them are the old, unused prisons."

"What do you do with your prisoners if you do not use the prisons?"

"We do not have any prisoners. If anyone shows criminal tendencies, he is scientifically treated to eradicate such impulses. If the treatments are successful, he is restored to society but, if they are not, then he is painlessly put out of the way."

The Trial

On the way to the upgoing shaft, Calissia showed me ultra-violet artificial sunlight containers that diffused an even health-giving light over the whole city. Nearby were the machines for manufacturing the artificial air which they breathed.

We had by then reached an express shaft going straight up to the third tier. Curious, I asked as we were drawn swiftly upward by an unseen force, how this shaft was operated. Calissia explained that when we stepped into the bottom of the upward going shaft, we kept our proper weight but huge magnetic beams from above drew us irresistibly upward. But for all the reassurance of her explanations I drew a great breath of relief as we stepped out of the shaft onto the solid ground of the third tier.

When we reported to Mavia, she requested Calissia to preside over the trial of an insubordinate reproducing male. When it was suggested that perhaps I would find it interesting to attend, I agreed willingly, and accompanied Calissia back to the twelfth tier.

We found a group of five women, seated comfortably, while before them stood the defendant, his head thrown back and a light of rebellion flashing from his handsome dark eyes.

Calissia took her place and motioned me to a seat beside her. She then requested them all, the man included, to put on the thought-wave caps so that I could follow the trial.

While one of the women procured and distributed the caps, I studied the defendant.

Slightly built but straight as a sapling, he stood before us. He was very good-looking. I suppose, being a woman, it was natural that I should notice his good looks first of all.

Back home I had had no time for the usual run of men, though I was by no means a man hater. Some day, if I ever met the right man, I knew I would marry. But somehow or other the men with whom I came into contact either left me cold or, if they did appeal to me, they usually aroused my antagonism by their airs of superiority. We women knew we were the equal of the men, but it was taking a long time and much hard work to convince men of our equality. I intended to marry no man who did not look upon me as his equal, mentally and physically.

But back to the trial. Calissia was speaking.

"What is the charge against the defendant?"

One of the women arose and said: "He is charged with talking sedition to the other men and of trying to arouse them to a revolt against the present system of government. We have a witness."

Calissia called for the witness and another man was ushered in. His air of cringing subservience disgusted me and I noticed that even the other women looked at him with good-natured contempt.

"Your name and position?" asked Calissia.

"I am Soonta, Section Head, Number Six," the new-comer answered with a sly glance of malice at the defendant. "That man has been a source of trouble ever since he was sent up to us from the training rooms. He always talks of the terrible way we men are treated—those are his words," he hastily explained. The women nodded indulgently and Soonta continued:

"Finally he got so bad that he declared he would die rather than submit to such a life. He refused to meet the women when they came to visit us and sulked in his room. I tried all the known ways of making him conform to custom but it was useless. Nothing was left but to report him as insubordinate."

"Very well, Soonta, I will make a note of your zeal. You may go now. Defendant, what is your name and what have you to say in your defense?"

The defendant spoke and a thrill of sympathy went through me as I listened to his proud reply.

"My name is Joburza and the charges against me are perfectly true. I abhor the present system of government and I hate you women. You are tyrants of the worst sort. I refused to submit to this reproduction. When you condemn me, I will gladly go to the Lethal Chamber. In fact, I prefer annihilation."

"No doubt you do," Calissia sneered. "But I think that with a few treatments in the electro-coma room to reduce your present mentality, and a passage through the bonite-ray sterilizer you will be ready to take your place with the thirteenth tier men."

Joburza visibly wilted. Fear and loathing lent a desperate note to his voice: "I beg you. Grant me the boon of death. Anything, anything, rather than the thirteenth tier!"

The women laughed cruelly and one of them said:

"Once you pass through the mentality-reducing room you won't care very much. We will see that special attention is given to eradicating your pride."

"Won't you have any pity?" Joburza pleaded, gazing at us all as if we were monsters.

A Joke on Someone

I could not stand the cruelty any longer, so presuming on my status as a welcome visitor, I asked permission to speak.

"I have a request to make. I am a woman like yourselves. If it is not offending your customs, I would like you to let me have the prisoner, to do with as I wish."

An astonished silence greeted my request and Joburza gazed at me suspiciously, wondering, I suppose, what particular form of cruel punishment I desired for him.

"Would you mind telling us what you wish to do?" Calissia asked.

"I want to take him back to my dimension with me."

"Why?" The question was asked simultaneously by all the women.

"For—for—" I thought desperately—"For scientific experiments!"

"Well, it is a peculiar request," Calissia stated. "But then, having you here is a peculiar situation. What do you say, comrades-in-rule? Personally, I am in favor of it. At least it is a novel form of punishment."

The other five women agreed, and carefully hiding my elation, I asked to speak to the prisoner alone.

When the others had gone I asked him if he were glad that he was saved from his punishment.

"I do not know," he replied stiffly. "Perhaps the experiments you have in store for me will be more degrading."

"Poor Joburza!" I said. "Cheer up! I have no wish to experiment with you. I only said that because I wanted to have you turned over to me. I want to help you."

"Help me?" he questioned. "You—you—mean—?"

"I mean, Joburza, that I will take you through to my world, where everyone, men and women alike, have a chance to live and work. You will be free, absolutely free, to live your life as you see fit. Do you understand now?"

"Is it possible?" he murmured, gazing earnestly at me. "I can—I—Oh! It seems too good to be true. How can I thank you?"

"You needn't even try. Just show me by your conduct when we reach my world that I have not made a mistake."

"I will! I will!" he promised, tears of gladness coming into his eyes.

Just then Calissia came in and said Mavia wished to see me in her office. "I think she has some good news for you."

Requesting her to see that my prisoner was taken care of, I fairly raced up to Mavia. "Ho!" she jested, "I hear you have a prisoner. I think turning him over to the third dimensioners is a very good joke," she laughed heartily.

"Yes, indeed!" I replied brightly, but I failed to explain whom the joke was on.

"Come over here, please, I have something I want to show you."

On one side of her office was an affair that I had taken to be a radio. Mavia twirled a few dials and the wall above it lit up. I looked and saw waving scarlet trees with the setting sun, now a great lavender ball, sinking slowly behind them. "Oh!" I exclaimed, "It is a window!"

Mavia smiled. "No indeed; even if it were a window we would not see out of doors as my office is centrally located."

"Then it is television. We have that, too, but our screen only records black and white. How beautiful. This seems just like looking out of doors."

"Wait just a second." Mavia set the lower dial and plugged in a short wire. I suddenly had the sensation of traveling at a terrible speed. The scenery flashed by. Huge mountain after mountain was passed in a second.

"Those are our other cities. The bi-focal wave is picking them up, and recording them on the screen as it passes on its way to its focus. Watch closely, I think you will be interested."

The last mountain passed. We came to the end of the scarlet vegetation. Great barren wastes flashed by. In the distance, but rapidly looming large as we seemingly came closer, was a dense purple mist. For a few seconds the screen was clouded. Then it cleared and we were over what looked like a great bee farm.

Down we dropped. Hive after hive passed us. I call them hives as that is exactly what they looked like, but in reality they were houses. We swerved and a hive larger by far than the others completely filled the screen.

CHAPTER VI

Dad Again!

Suddenly the screen changed. We seemed to have penetrated the wall and were traversing an immense corridor. A great metal door barred our path. Through that we went and seemed to stop on the inner side of it, for a complete room was before us.

In the grotesque-looking creatures in the room I recognized, from Mavia's previous description, the beings of the Third Evolution. And in the center of the room, talking earnestly was—

"Dad!" I cried, jumping up, completely forgetting that what I saw was only a photographic reproduction of a scene, actually taking place thousands of miles away.

"Is that 'Father'?" Mavia inquired. "I thought so! We located him about an hour ago and fifty of our best women scouts have gone to rescue him. We would have seen them through the screen, only they are traveling at a higher altitude than our line of vision. Do not worry about 'Father' now. He will be here with you shortly. Do you wish to watch the battle?—No, I believe it would be too harrowing to you," and she switched off the screen.

"You see," she continued, "by sending these scouts to get 'Father' the Thirds will not be looking for another attack tonight and consequently they will be off their guard."

I could see that she was talking to give me time to compose myself and I did my best to appear calm but that one glimpse of Dad among those horrible inhuman looking creatures had almost unnerved me. I asked Mavia to tune in again and see what was happening, but she was firm in her refusal. Instead she began to question me about the Hewitt Ray. I told her all I understood about it and she suggested that while we were waiting we should try to locate the cave in which I had left the second model, so that she could send some one for it.

While she was directing the unseen eye over the countryside I said, "I suppose you are anxious to get rid of us. My father and I are causing you a lot of trouble."

"Not at all," she answered. "We enjoyed having you here. But only as visitors. When your visit is completed you must go back. We are much too busy living our own lives and working out our destinies. We do not care to take on the responsibility of trying to fit in our lives with those of an odd dimension nor to take the time and trouble to fit the odd dimensioners into our life."

"Will you explain something that has been puzzling me, Mavia?" I asked. "I always understood that if a being of one dimension passed through into another dimension, he would find everything appearing to him at odd angles or in cross sections. How is it that everything seems the same to me? I mean that you seem to have the same number of dimensions as I?"

"I know what you mean," Mavia answered. "But here is something that the theorists have not taken into consideration. When the object or person passes from one dimension into another, it, or they, immediately takes on the dimensional proportions of the new plane of existence. For example, you, a three-dimensional being, in passing into the fourth dimension, took on an extra dimension, which you will lose as you pass back into your own plane. That is why we look normal to you and you look normal to me.

"Whereas, if this Hewitt Ray of yours permitted you to remain in the third dimension and gaze through into the fourth, then you would have seen us in what would appear to you as a cross section or, as you say, in peculiar angles."

She had located the cave containing the machine, and after taking the figures denoting the exact spot, she pressed a button and gave the order to a woman who entered to recover it.

We next went to her apartment and she and I both refreshed ourselves with the radio-active bath. While we were resting, a knock was heard, the door opened and dear old Dad and his rescuers came in.

I flew to his arms and could hardly let go of him in my delight.

"Dear me! dear me!—It's you, Lucile?" Dad's eyes were twinkling. "I thought for a minute that one of these strange ladies was hugging me. But now I see it is you, all dressed up in their clothes."

Amid much laughter, Mavia dismissed the scouts and ordered a meal for the three of us. Dad related his experiences. His eyes shone with delight as he told of the new science he had learned by this trip. He did not seem to realize that he had been in grave danger.

What Happened!

"You know," he was saying to Mavia, "those Thirds, as they call themselves, are mighty smart creatures. I tell you their scientific accomplishments nearly had me floored. But I had a few tricks up my sleeve with which they were unfamiliar," he chuckled. "Miss Mavia, do you know I nearly conducted a war against you young ladies? For a fact! I understood from the Thirds that you were a bunch of savages, threatening to pull down their civilization, with its accumulated scientific knowledge. And here you are, a group of pretty ladies playing at politics."

"I think you will find us doing a little more than playing," Mavia said coldly. "And as for scientific knowledge you won't find us far behind the Thirds. Now, Lucile, I am going to be very busy for the next hour or two. We have decided to set the hour of attack ahead and I must go. You and 'Father' have the freedom of the city. All are instructed to treat you courteously. Show 'Father' around, or, if you wish, just rest yourselves. You are at freedom to do just as you please."

"Mavia, before you go I want to—" I began, but she cut me short saying:

"Now, now—No 'Thank You' if you please. You are our guest and it was our duty to help you," and she was gone!

Dad and I looked at each other. He had a heavy frown. "Come! come! young lady. I want to know what you mean by following me around this way?"

I giggled. "Now Dad! Don't play the heavy father role. It isn't becoming to you. I am dying of curiosity to know how you were rescued. Mavia shut off the screen before the excitement started. I saw you standing in a large room talking to those funny-looking people. Then what happened?"

"Why I hardly know myself. I was explaining the use of certain explosives in warfare, to the Chodrom or head Third, when suddenly, the walls of the room began to crumble. Through the openings came beams of light that, when they touched the Thirds caused them to crumble just as had the walls. I stood still, momentarily expecting one of the beams to touch and finish me but to my surprise the beams flashed over everything, leaving me unhurt.

"Then when the walls had given way sufficiently, a bunch of curiously-armored young women rushed into the room, grabbed me, none too gently, hustled me out into the opening where I saw a number of aircrafts surrounding the building and operating the deadly rays that were destroying it. I presume from its action, that the ray is derived from a very low wavelength of the ultra-violet, which after it had passed a wavelength of—"

"Oh, Dad!" I cut in impatiently. "Please forget the wavelengths and go on. What happened next?"

"Well I was hurried into one of the air machines and almost immediately we all took to the air. For a few moments I was scared stiff, I mean literally. As you know I had never gone up in an airplane before but soon there was enough excitement to take my mind from my fright at finding myself in the air.

"From out of the other buildings poured thousands of the Thirds. Huge machines were hastily erected and great beams of light shot out at us. Two of the planes were caught by the beams and crashed in flames, but the remainder climbed to a safe altitude and flew on. As we neared the great purple mists my pilot gave me an insulating suit to put on. Those purple mists you know are the main protection of the Thirds. Heretofore nothing has been able to come through them and live, but these women have found a way to protect themselves.

"The suit I put on, I saw, was a mesh of glass and rubber. The outside of the planes and everything in it were similarly protected. We passed through the mists safely and here we are!"

"I am glad you are here and not with the Thirds, for after tonight there won't be any Thirds," I said, trying to make him realize how extremely dangerous his position had been.

"Yes—yes—I know. It is terrible. Such scientific knowledge these great people have, and they use it to try to annihilate each other. Why, the Thirds have discovered that life is but——"

Anticipating a long scientific discourse, I interrupted. "Dad, you must come down to the eleventh tier and see what these women have done in the way of science."

I left him there, happy in his own environment, and hastened away to find Mavia.

War

As I expected, she was in her office and I begged her to let me accompany her on the raid tonight. She firmly refused me but promised that I could use her viewing screen and see what was happening. While we were talking, a scout entered and made her report.

The Thirds, it seemed, had succeeded in getting into communications with the beings of the second dimension and thousands of them had come through and were inhabitating the purple mists, which had been expanded to completely cover the Third Evolutionists' domain.

"Oh damn!" said Mavia, or whatever its equivalent is in her language. "Just as we have found a way to insulate ourselves and our planes from the purple mists, they succeed in reaching those horrors of the second dimension. We know that they are unable to harm us except as we pass through the mists for they cannot live in this dimension outside of the mist. But how can we pass them safely?"

"May I suggest something?" I asked timidly.

"Yes, of course," Mavia snapped. "If you have a way of helping us, say so."

"By using my father's Hewitt Ray, I could set you and your whole army down in the center of the Thirds. The people of the second dimension could not harm you as you go through the mists because while you are passing them, there will be nothing for them to harm except a ray which they will not even know is passing."

"H'm. That might do, and once we gain an entrance, we will make very short work of the Thirds. But young woman, have you considered that after we have finished with the Thirds we will be practically stranded? There we will be, completely surrounded by the mist and unable to pass it to get home!"

I smiled in triumph. "Mavia, if you take me with you I promise to bring you back, safely, through the mists."

Mavia grinned. "You certainly are a determined young woman, are you not? Very well! You have earned your place in our ranks and you may go with us tonight."

The next few hours were very busy ones for me. Following my instructions, Mavia ordered an extra Hewitt Ray machine to be built, which the scientists, with Dad's help, erected in short order. I was given an insulating suit to put on.

"It will protect you from the rays of the Thirds but, may your deity, whoever he is, help you if you come in contact with the Second Dimensioners."

"What terrible weapon do they use?" I asked.

"That is just it," answered one of the scouts who was putting on her own insulating suit. "We do not know. They are great obnoxious-looking, winged creatures. Nature herself seems to have equipped them with a defensive weapon. Their bodies emit sparks that annihilate all they touch. We have never been able to insulate ourselves against them. For some reason the electrically-charged purple mists seem to be the only place in which they can live in this dimension."

Finally all was in readiness. The two Hewitt Ray machines were brought up to the mountain top and Dad was detailed to operate the one which was to send us forth. Imagine, if you can, the scene. Dad at one end of the mountain top with his Hewitt Ray machine, the other Hewitt Ray machine in the center, a guard of fifty women surrounding it, whose sole duty was to protect it from the rays of the Thirds. Spread out in close formation were the soldier women, not only of our own city but of the other seventy-eight cities as well. Column after column of glittering, armored women . . . .

Mavia, at whose side I was stationed, gave the signal and—one second we were on the mountain top—the next we were inside the surrounding circle of the purple mists!

Then hell broke loose! Our women began to spread out fan-wise, sowing destruction in their wake. The hive-like houses in our immediate vicinity, at the touch of the destructive rays, wielded by our soldiers, crumbled up and disappeared in a puff of smoke. The Thirds in the outlying houses quickly retreated and erected their enormous machines which shot forth beams of light. Their beams had a greater focus than our ray guns but our women in their insulating suits suffered no great damage. A few here and there whose suits, I suppose, were defective, stiffened out and fell to the ground. It was noticeable that the beams of light, shot out by the retreating Thirds acted differently from our rays. Their beams seemed only to strike their victims dead but our rays consumed them entirely.

I looked back to see if any harm had come to the Hewitt Ray machine. The fifty women surrounding it were directing great beams of light in all directions, forming a light barrier, which I later learned was able to stop and deflect any destructive beam which might be directed towards the machine.

A Souvenir

It was all highly exciting, but so entirely different from the bloody carnage that we of our world expect in battle, that it seemed like some great pageant in which I was taking part.

I marched with the rest of the soldiers and directed my ray gun on the Thirds and their houses. They were such inhuman-looking creatures with their thin machine-like bodies and great globular heads, that when they crumbled and disappeared as my ray touched them, I felt no revulsion as I might have had they been more human-looking. Instead, I cheered wildly at each victory.

We marched fanwise as I said, clear to the edge of the purple mists, leaving not a living thing in our paths, except the unfortunate women who had fallen under the beams of the Thirds. Reaching the mist, we directed our ray guns into it, trying to get some of the great creatures inhabiting it.

Now that we were so close to the mist, we could see them plainly, great bodies, with bat-like wings and tiny heads. Their red fiery eyes seemed to occupy the greater part of the small heads. They grimaced and gestured horribly at us and threw out sparks from their bodies.

We retreated to a safe distance and yelled our defiance at them. Tiring of this sport, the victorious army of women returned, singing and shouting, to the Hewitt Ray machine with its guard still surrounding it.

It was my duty now to operate the ray machine and I had no intention of being left behind. I set the automatic controls as Dad had shown me, then stepped in front into my place.

Nothing happened! There was no amber-colored ray to transport us back to safety! For a few moments the morale of the army seemed to be lost. Were we doomed to stay here surrounded by the horrid creatures of the purple mists?

Helplessly the leaders turned to me and I could only bid them wait, explaining that the automatic controls had not yet taken effect, and I advised them all to keep their places.

Suddenly the softly glowing ray shot forth and we all began a sigh of relief which ended on our own mountain top! We had won through. The purple mists were cheated of their prey!

Dad, who had been anxiously watching the battle through Mavia's viewing screen, hurried to greet us on our return.

"Lucile, I did not know you were such a blood-thirsty savage. Why, I watched you through the television and you certainly did your share of destruction and seemed to be enjoying yourself immensely!"

"Well, Dad, if you will go adventuring off into strange worlds you cannot blame your daughter if she follows in your footsteps."

"Just the same," he said, his eyes twinkling in their old familiar manner, "I think we had better go home before you can find any more trouble to get into."

"Yes," I admitted. "I have only three weeks' leave and I must get a little rest before I go back to work."

While Dad readjusted the Hewitt Ray to take us back I sent for Joburza, my prisoner, and introduced him to Dad. I told him of the trial and its results. Dad laughed and said:

"Well! Well! I suppose, Lucile, it is only natural that you should take back a souvenir. I never heard of a woman yet, who did not want to take back some kind of a souvenir from her travels. I suppose I should be thankful you did not collect a whole cart-load of such souvenirs."

"Of course you should," I agreed cheerfully.

Amid the friendliest "goodbyes" from our strange friends and with their hearty invitation to return some day ringing in our ears, Dad and I and our prisoner passed through the ray and after a few seconds found ourselves in Dad's laboratory.

"Wake up," I cried, shaking Marion, who had fallen asleep before the light-wave machine. "We are home!"

Tired as we were, there was no thought of sleep that night. Marion demanded to be told every little bit of our adventures. It took almost all night to completely tell the tale and explain all about the strange things we had found in the other dimension. Marion declared herself to be a member of the party, on the next trip. She was much interested in the women of the fourth dimension.

"I always thought we were emancipated," she said, "but this Mavia and her crowd are emancipated-plus."

While we were eating a very early breakfast I asked Dad: "How was it, Dad, that you and I landed in different places? You landed in the country of the Thirds and I landed with the savage Firsts."

Dad explained. "Due to the curvature of space we did not travel in a straight line. You took off, to use your aerial language, at a different time than I did and consequently landed at the other side of the circle. Understand?"

"Ye-s-s, I think I do." I replied hesitatingly.

Joburza, whom I promptly re-christened John, fitted himself easily into our life. He learned our language quickly but spoke it with a curiously quaint accent. Dad, discovering that he had an aptitude for science, readily took him into his laboratory as a pupil-assistant.

"My son was a daughter, so I have adopted this boy," he explained laughingly to his friends.

I liked John very much but he exasperated me by his air of timidity with women. Poor boy, with his background, I suppose he could not help himself, and I was continually trying to improve him. What woman can resist the temptation to reform a man?

One day about six months later I returned to the house for my three-day leave and found John meekly taking a scolding from our housekeeper. I sharply sent her about her business; then turned to John.

"Why do you do it, John? For the love of Mike! Brace up! Remember you are a *man*. Forget your other life. You are in a different world now. Remember, women aren't anything to be afraid of. They can't hurt you. Why, don't you know that you are in every way superior to a woman?" (May my sisters in feminism forgive the lies. I had to be drastic). "Just say to yourself—'I am a *man*,' and *be* one! If a woman doesn't agree with you, bully her. She will like it. Try it some time and see how it works."

"I believe I will," John said, and grabbing me he kissed me!

"Why, John!" I cried, astonished. "What made you do that?"

My father was standing by the window. I had not noticed him before.

"Haw! Haw!" he laughed. "Poor John was only taking your advice—'Bully them!' Ho! Ho!—'Try it some time!' Haw! Haw!—but seriously, Lucile, I am surprised to hear you, of all women, advise a man to look on himself as a woman's superior. I thought you wanted the men to admit the women's superiority."

"Oh well!" I answered nonchalantly, glancing out of the corner of my eye at John. "It all depends on who the man is!"

"Oh-h-h! I see," smiled Dad and with exaggerated solicitude tip-toed from the room.

THE GREAT BEAST OF KAFUE

Clotilde Graves
(1863–1932)

Clotilde Inez Mary Graves, or "Clo" as she was usually known, was born into a military family, and was the second cousin of the poet and novelist Robert Graves. Her early days were spent drawing cartoons and writing sketches for the comic papers and subsequently for the stage. She had sixteen plays produced in London and New York between 1887 and 1913. She apparently had a temper. The Times' obituarist remarked that rehearsals of her plays were apt "to be marked by unconventional incidents." Alongside her plays she wrote several novels, mostly humorous, such as A Well Meaning Woman *(1896), about the consequences of a busybody's matchmaking plans. Her life was anything but conventional. She frequently dressed as a man and enjoyed smoking in public. In 1910, she suddenly took on a new persona and, as Richard Dehan, she wrote* The Dop Doctor. *The book was a huge bestseller. It portrayed a city under siege during the Boer War and the work of a disgraced London doctor who redeems his honor. Graves wished to keep the identity of Dehan secret, but it soon leaked out. Thereafter she retained the alternate personality.*

The following story has the aftermath of the Boer War as a setting. Kafue is in present day Zambia, which was then Northern Rhodesia. I have added a few footnotes to explain some of the local language.

IT HAPPENED AT our homestead on the border of South-eastern Rhodesia, seventy miles from the Tuli Concession, some three years after the War.

A September storm raged, the green, broad-leaved tobacco-plants tossed like the waves of the ocean I had crossed and re-crossed, journeying to and coming back from my dead mother's wet, sad country of Ireland to this land of my father and his father's father.

The acacias and kameel thorns and the huge cactus-like euphorbia that fringed the water-courses and the irrigation channels had wrung their hands all day without ceasing, like Makalaka women at a native funeral. Night closed in: the wooden shutters were barred, the small-paned windows fastened, yet they shook and rattled as though human beings without were trying to force a way in. Whitewash fell in scales from the big tie-beams and cross-rafters of the farm kitchen, and lay in little powdery drifts of whiteness on the solid table of brown locust-tree wood, and my father's Dutch Bible that lay open there. Upon my father's great black head that was bent over the Book, were many streaks and patches of white that might not be shaken or brushed away.

It had fallen at the beginning of the War, that snow of sorrow streaking the heavy curling locks of coarse black hair. My pretty young mother—an Irishwoman of the North, had been killed in the Women's Laager at Gueldersdorp during the Siege. My father served as Staats gunner during the Investment—and now you know the dreadful doubt that heaped upon those mighty shoulders a bending load, and sprinkled the black hair with white.

You are to see me in my blue drill roundabout and little homespun breeches sitting on a cricket in the shadow of the table-ledge, over against the grim *sterk* figure in the big, thong-seated armchair.

There would be no going to bed that night. The dam was overfull already, and the next spate from the hill sluits might crack the great wall of mud-cemented saw-squared boulders, or overflow it, and lick away the work of years. The farm-house roof had been rebuilt since the shell from the English naval gun had wrecked it, but the work of men to-day is not like that of the men of old. My father shook his head, contemplating the new masonry, and the whitewash fell as though in confirmation of his expressed doubts.

I had begged to stay up rather than lie alone in the big bed in my father's room. Nodding with sleepiness I should have denied, I carved with my two-bladed American knife at a little canoe I meant to swim in the shallower river-pools. And as I shaped the prow I dreamed of something I had heard on the previous night.

A traveller of the better middle-class, overseer of a coal-mine working "up Buluwayo" way, who had stayed with us the previous night and gone on to Tuli that morning, had told the story. What he had failed to tell I had haltingly spelled out of the three-weeks-old English newspaper he had left behind.

So I wrought, and remembered, and my little canoe swelled and grew in my hands. I was carrying it on my back through a forest of tall reeds and high grasses, forcing a painful way between the tough wrist-thick stems, with the salt sweat running down into my eyes . . . Then I was in the canoe, wielding the single paddle, working my frail crank craft through sluggish pools of black water, overgrown with broad spiny leaves of water-plants cradling dowers of marvellous hue. In the canoe bows leaned my grandfather's elephant-gun, the inlaid, browned-steel-barrelled weapon with the diamond-patterned stock and breech that had always seemed to my childish eyes the most utterly desirable, absolutely magnificent possession a grown-up man might call his own.

A *paauw*[1] made a great commotion getting up amongst the reeds; but does a hunter go after *paauw* with his grandfather's elephant-gun? Duck were feeding in the open spaces of sluggish black water. I heard what seemed to be the plop! of a jumping fish, on the other side of a twenty-foot high barrier of reeds and grasses. I looked up then, and saw, glaring down upon me from inconceivable heights of sheer horror, the Thing of which I had heard and read.

At this juncture I dropped the little canoe and clutched my father round the leg.

"What is it, *mijn jongen?*"

He, too, seemed to rouse out of a waking dream. You are to see the wide, burnt-out-looking grey eyes that were staring sorrowfully out of their shadowy caves under the shaggy eyebrows, lighten out of their deep abstraction and drop to the level of my childish face.

"You were thinking of the great beast of Kafue Valley, and you want to ask me if I will lend you my father's elephant-rifle when you are big enough to carry it that you may go and hunt for the beast and kill it; is that so?"

My father grasped his great black beard in one huge knotted brown hand, and made a rope of it, as was his way. He looked from my chubby face to the old-fashioned black-powder 8-bore that hung upon the wall against a leopard kaross, and back again, and something like a smile curved the grim mouth under the shaggy black and white moustache.

---

1. The bustard, a beautiful bird often hunted.

"The gun you shall have, boy, when you are of age to use it, or a 450-Mannlicher or a 600-Mauser, the best that may be bought north of the Transvaal, to shoot explosive or conical bullets from cordite cartridges. But not unless you give me your promise never to kill that beast, shall money of mine go to the buying of such a gun for you. Come now, let me have your word!"

Even to my childish vanity the notion of my solemnly entering into a compact binding my hand against the slaying of the semi-fabulous beast-marvel of the Upper Rhodesian swamps, smacked of the fantastic if not of the absurd. But my father's eyes had no twinkle in them, and I faltered out the promise they commanded.

"Nooit—nooit will I kill that beast! It should kill me, rather!"

"Your mother's son will not be *valsch*[2] to a vow. For so would you, son of my body, make of me, your father, a traitor to an oath that I have sworn!"

The great voice boomed in the rafters of the farm kitchen, vying with the baffled roaring of the wind that was trying to get in, as I had told myself, and lie down, folding wide quivering wings and panting still, upon the sheepskin that was spread before the hearth.

"But—but why did you swear?"

I faltered out the question, staring at the great bearded figure in homespun jacket and tan-cord breeches and *veldschoens,*[3] and thought again that it had the hairy skin of Esau and the haunted face of Saul.

Said my father, grimly—

"Had I questioned my father so at twice your age, he would have skinned my back and I should have deserved it. But I cannot beat your mother's son, though the Lord punish me for my weakness. . . . And you have the spirit of the *jager*[4] in you, even as I. What I saw you may one day see. What I might have killed, that shall you spare, because of me and my oath. Why did I take it upon me, do you ask? Even though I told you, how should a child understand? What is it you are saying? Did I really, really see the beast? Ay, by the Lord!" said my father thoughtfully, "I saw him. And never can a man who has seen, forget that sight. What are you saying?"

---

2. False, or to renege.
3. A shoe made from rawhide.
4. Hunter.

The words tumbled over one another as I stammered in my hurry—

"But—but the English traveller said only one white man besides the Mashona hunter has seen the beast, and the newspaper says so too."

"*Natuurlijk*. And the white man is me," thundered the deep voice.

I hesitated.

"But since the planting of the tobacco you have not left the *plaats*. And the newspaper is of only three weeks back."

"*Dat spreekt*, but the story is older than that, *mijn jongen*. It is the third time it has been dished up in the *Buluwayo Courant* sauced up with lies to change the taste as belly-lovers have their meat. But I am the man who saw the beast of Kafue, and the story that is told is my story, nevertheless!"

I felt my cheeks beginning to burn. Wonderful as were the things I knew to be true of the man, my father, this promised to be the most wonderful of all.

"It was when I was hunting in the Zambezi Country," said my father, "three months after the *Commandaants* of the Forces of the United Republics met at Klerksdorp to arrange conditions of peace—"

"With the English Generals," I put in.

"With the English, as I have said. You had been sent to your— to *her* people in Ireland. I had not then thought of rebuilding the farm. For more than a house of stones had been thrown down for me, and more than so many thousand acres of land laid waste . . .

"Where did I go? *Ik wiet niet*. I wandered *op en neer* like the evil spirit in the Scriptures," the great corded hand shut the Book and reached over and snuffed the tallow-dip that hung over at the top, smoking and smelling, and pitched the black wick-end angrily on the red hearth-embers. "I sought rest and found none, either for the sole of my foot or the soul in my body. There is bitterness in my mouth as though I have eaten the spotted lily-root of the swamps. I cannot taste the food I swallow, and when I lie down at night something lies down with me, and when I rise up, it rises too and goes by my side all day."

I clung to the leg of the table, not daring to clutch my father's. For his eyes did not seem to see me anymore, and a blob of foam quivered on his beard that hung over his great breast in a shadowy cascade dappled with patches of white. He went on, I scarcely daring to breathe—

"For, after all, do I know it is not I who killed her? That accursed day, was I not on duty as ever since the beginning of the investment, and is it not a splinter from a Maxim Nordenfeld fired from an eastern gun-position, that—" Great drops stood on my father's forehead. His huge frame shook. The clenched hand resting on the solid table of locust-beam, shook that also, shaking me, clinging to the table-leg with my heart thumping violently, and a cold, crawling sensation among the roots of my curls.

"At first, I seem to remember there was a man hunting with me. He had many Kaffir servants and four Mashona hunters and wagons drawn by salted tailless spans, fine guns and costly tents, plenty of stores and medicine in little sugar-pills, in bottles with silver tops. But he sickened in spite of all his quinine, and the salted oxen died, just like beasts with tails; and besides, he was afraid of the Makwakwa and the Mashengwa with their slender poisoned spears of reeds. He turned back at last. I pushed on."

There was a pause. The strange, iron-grey, burnt-out eyes looked through me and beyond me, then the deep, trembling voice repeated, once more changing the past into the present tense—

"I push on west. My life is of value to none. The boy—is he not with her people? Shall I live to have him back under my roof and see in his face one day the knowledge that I have killed his mother? Nay, nay, I will push on!"

There was so long a silence after this that I ventured to move. Then my father looked at me, and spoke to me, not as though I were a child, but as if I had been another man.

"I pushed on, crossing the rivers on a blown-up goatskin and some calabashes, keeping my father's elephant-gun and my cartridges dry by holding them above my head. Food! For food there were thorny orange cucumbers with green pulp, and the native women at the kraals gave me cakes of maize and milk. I hunted and killed rhino and elephant and hippo and lion until the headmen of the Mashengwa said the beast was a god of theirs and the slaying of it would bring a pestilence upon their tribe, and so I killed no more. And one day I shot a cow hippo with her calf, and she stood to suckle the ugly little thing while her life was bleeding out of her, and after that I ceased to kill. I needed little, and there were yet the green-fleshed cucumbers, and ground-nuts, and things like those."

He made a rope of his great beard, twisting it with a rasping sound.

"Thus I reached the Upper Kafue Valley where the great grass swamps are. No railway then, running like an iron snake up from Buluwayo to bring the ore down from the silver-mines that are there.

"Six days' *trek* from the mines—I went on foot always, you will understand!—six days' journey from the mines, above where L'uengwe River is wedded to Kafue, as the Badanga say is a big water.

"It is a lake, or rather, two lakes, not round, but shaped like the bowls of two wooden spoons. A shore of black, stone-like baked mud round them, and a bridge of the same stone is between them, so that they make the figure that is for 8."

The big, hairy forefinger of my father's right hand traced the numeral in the powdered whitewash that lay in drifts upon the table.

"That is the shape of the lakes, and the Badanga say that they have no bottom, and that fish taken from their waters remain raw and alive, even on the red-hot embers of their cooking stove. They are a lazy, dirty people who live on snakes and frogs and grubs—tortoise and fish. And they gave me to eat and told me, partly in words of my own mòder Taal they had picked up some-how, partly in sign language, about the Great Beast that lives in the double lake that is haunted by the spirits of their dead."

I waited, my heart pumping at the bottom of my throat, my blood running horribly, delightfully chill, to hear the rest.

"The hunting spirit revives in a man, even at death's door, to hear of an animal the like of which no living hunter has ever brought down. The Badanga tell me of this one, tales, tales, tales! They draw it for me with a pointed stick on a broad green leaf, or in the ashes of their cooking-fires. And I have seen many a great beast, but, *voor den donder!* never a beast such as that!"

I held on to my stool with both hands.

"I ask the Badanga to guide me to the lair of the beast for all the money I have upon me. They care not for gold, but for the old silver hunting-watch I carry they will risk offending the spirits of their dead. The old man who has drawn the creature for me, he will take me. And it is January, the time of year in which he has been before known to rise and bellow—*Maar!*—bellow like twenty buffalo bulls in spring-time, for his mate to rise from those bottomless deeps below and drink the air and sun."

So there are two great beasts! Neither the traveller nor the newspaper nor my father, until this moment, had hinted at that!

"The she-beast is much the smaller and has no horns. This my old man makes clear to me, drawing her with the point of his fish-spear on smooth mud. She is very sick the last time my old man has seen her. Her great moon-eyes are dim, and the stinking spume dribbles from her jaws. She can only float in the trough of the wave that her mate makes with his wallowings, her long scaly neck lying like a dead python on the oily black water. My old man thinks she was then near death. I ask him how long ago that is? Twenty times have the blue lake-lilies blossomed, the lilies with the sweet seeds that the Badanga make bread of—since. And the great bull has twice been heard bellowing, but never has he been seen of man since then."

My father folded his great arms upon the black-and-white cascade of beard that swept down over his shirt of homespun and went on—

"Twenty years. Perhaps, think I, my old man has lied to me! But we are at the end of the last day's journey. The sun has set and night has come. My old man makes me signs we are near the lakes and I climb a high mahogo, holding by the limbs of the wild fig that is hugging the tree to death."

My father spat into the heart of the glowing wood ashes, and said—

"I see the twin lakes lying in the midst of the high grass-swamps, barely a mile away. The black, shining waters cradle the new moon of January in their bosom, and the blue star that hangs beneath her horn, and there is no ripple on the surface, or sign of a beast, big or little. And I despise myself, I, the son of honest Booren, who have been duped by the lies of a black man-ape. I am coming down the tree, when through the night comes a long, hollow, booming, bellowing roar that is not the cry of any beast I know. Thrice it comes, and my old man of the Badanga, squatting among the roots of the mahogo, nods his wrinkled bald skull, and says, squinting up at me, 'Now you have heard, Baas, will you go back or go on?'

"I answer, '*Al recht uit!*'

"For something of the hunting spirit has wakened in me. And I see to the cleaning of the elephant-gun and load it carefully before I sleep that night."

I would have liked to ask a question but the words stuck in my throat.

"By dawn of day we have reached the lakes," went on my father. "The high grass and the tall reeds march out into the black water as far as they may, then the black stone beach shelves off into depths unknown.

"He who has written up the story for the Buluwayo newspaper says that the lake was once a volcano and that the crumbly black stone is lava. It may be so. But volcanoes are holes in the tops of mountains, while the lakes lie in a valley-bottom, and he who wrote cannot have been there, or he would know there are two, and not one.

"All the next night we, camping on the belt of stony shore that divides lake from lake, heard nothing. We ate the parched grain and baked grubs that my old man carried in a little bag. We lighted no fire because of the spirits of the dead Badanga that would come crowding about it to warm themselves, and poison us with their breath. My old man said so, and I humoured him. My dead needed no fire to bring her to me. She was there always . . .

"All the day and the night through we heard and saw nothing. But at windstill dawn of the next day I saw a great curving ripple cross the upper lake that may be a mile and a half wide; and the reeds upon the nearer shore were wetted to the knees as by the wave that is left in the wake of a steamer, and oily patches of scum, each as big as a barn floor, befouled the calm water, and there was a cold, strange smell upon the breeze, but nothing more.

"Until at sunset of the next day, when I stood upon the mid-most belt of shore between lake and lake, with my back to the blood-red wonder of the west and my eyes sheltered by my hand as I looked out to where I had seen the waters divided as a man furrows earth with the plough-share, and felt a shadow fall over me from behind, and turned . . . and saw . . . *Alamachtig!*"[5]

I could not breathe. At last, at last, it was coming!

"I am no coward," said my father, in his deep resounding bass, "but that was a sight of terror. My old man of the Badanga had bolted like a rock-rabbit. I could hear the dry reeds crashing as he broke through. And the horned head of the beast, that was as big as a wagon-trunk shaking about on the top of a python-neck that topped the tallest of the teak-trees or mahogos that grow in the grass-swamps, seemed as if it were looking for the little human creature that was trying to run away.

"*Voor den donder!* how the water rises up in columns of smoke-spray as the great beast lashes it with his crocodile-tail! His head is

---

5. An exclamation, like 'God Almighty!'

crocodile also, with horns of rhino, his body has the bulk of six
hippo bulls together. He is covered with armour of scales, yellow-
white as the scales of leprosy, he has paddles like a tortoise. God of
my fathers, what a beast to see! I forget the gun I hold against my
hip—I can only stand and look, while the cold, thick puffs of
stinking musk are brought to my nostrils and my ear-drums are
well-nigh split with the bellowing of the beast. Ay! and the wave
of his wallowings that wets one to the neck is foul with clammy
ooze and oily scum.

"Why did the thing not see me? I did not try to hide from those
scaly-lidded great eyes, yellow with half-moon-shaped pupils, I
stood like an idol of stone. Perhaps that saved me, or I was too
little a thing to vent a wrath so great upon. He Who in the beginning made herds of beasts like that to move upon the face of the
waters, and let this one live to show the pigmy world of to-day
what creatures were of old, knows. I do not. I was dazed with the
noise of its roarings and the thundering blows of its huge tail upon
the water; I was drenched with the spume of its snortings and
sickened with the stench it gave forth. But I never took my eyes
from it, as it spent its fury, and little by little I came to
understand.

"*Het is jammer*[6] to see anything suffer as that beast was suffering.
Another man in my place would have thought as much, and when
it lay still at last on the frothing black water, a bullet from the
elephant-rifle would have lodged in the little stupid brain behind
the great moon-eye, and there would have been an end. . .

"But I did not shoot!"

It seemed an age before my father spoke again, though the
cuckoo-clock had only ticked eight times.

"No! I would not shoot and spare the beast, dinosaurus or bron-
tosaurus, or whatever the wiseacres who have not seen him may
name him, the anguish that none had spared me. '*Let him go on!*'
said I. '*Let him go on seeking her in the abysses that no lead-line may
ever fathom, without consolation, without hope! Let him rise to the sun
and the breeze of spring through miles of the cold black water, and find her
not, year after year until the ending of the world. Let him call her through
the mateless nights until Day and Night rush together at the sound of the
Trumpet of the Judgment, and Time shall be no more!*'"

Crash!

---

6. 'Too bad', or 'What a shame'.

The great hand came down upon the solid locust-wood table, breaking the spell that had bound my tongue.

"I—do not understand," I heard my own child-voice saying. "Why was the Great Beast so sorry? What was he looking for?"

"His mate who died. Ay, at the lower end of the second lake, where the water shallows, her bones were sticking up like the bleached timbers of a wrecked ship. And He and She being the last of their kind upon the earth, therefore he knows desolation . . . and shall know it till death brings forgetfulness and rest. Boy, the wind is fallen, the rain has spent itself, it is time that you go to bed."

FRIEND ISLAND

Francis Stevens
(1883–1948)

The name of Francis Stevens is almost legendary amongst devotees of early scientific romance as being the first woman writer to contribute such fiction regularly to the pulp magazines. Despite the male spelling of the first name, there were those who believed it was an alias that masked the identity of a woman, but it was years before she was identified. Her real name was Gertrude Barrows Bennett, a secretary and clerk living in Philadelphia at the time she was writing, looking after her widowed invalid mother and young daughter. Her husband had drowned in an accident a few years earlier, and she had turned to writing for additional income. After her mother's death she continued to write for a while, but then returned to secretarial work. She moved to California in 1926 and remarried, became estranged from her daughter, and wrote no more.

Her best remembered work, "The Heads of Cerberus," appeared in one of the rarest pulp magazines, The Thrill Book, *during 1919, and was the first novel to consider variant time streams and alternate worlds. Her work was highly original and proved very popular. She had for a while worked as a secretary for a Professor at the University of Pennsylvania, typing students' papers, and this may have given her ideas for her stories. Although the following is set in a future long after female superiority has been taken for granted, that is almost incidental to a strange story about a hitherto unknown island that is more than it seems.*

IT WAS UPON the waterfront that I first met her, in one of the shabby little tea shops frequented by able sailoresses of the poorer type. The uptown, glittering resorts of the Lady Aviators' Union were not for such as she.

Stern of feature, bronzed by wind and sun, her age could only be guessed, but I surmised at once that in her I beheld a survivor of the age of turbines and oil engines—a true sea-woman of that

152

elder time when woman's superiority to man had not been so long recognized. When, to emphasize their victory, women in all ranks were sterner than today's need demands.

The spruce, smiling young maidens—engine-women and stokers of the great aluminum rollers, but despite their profession, very neat in gold-braided blue knickers and boleros—these looked askance at the hard-faced relic of a harsher day, as they passed in and out of the shop.

I, however, brazenly ignoring similar glances at myself, a mere male intruding on the haunts of the world's ruling sex, drew a chair up beside the veteran. I ordered a full pot of tea, two cups and a plate of macaroons, and put on my most ingratiating air. Possibly my unconcealed admiration and interest were wiles not exercised in vain. Or the macaroons and tea, both excellent, may have loosened the old sea-woman's tongue. At any rate, under cautious questioning, she had soon launched upon a series of reminiscences well beyond my hopes for color and variety.

"When I was a lass," quoth the sea-woman, after a time, "there was none of this high-flying, gilt-edged, leather-stocking luxury about the sea. We sailed by the power of our oil and gasoline. If they failed on us, like as not 'twas the rubber ring and the rolling wave for ours."

She referred to the archaic practice of placing a pneumatic affair called a life-preserver beneath the arms, in case of that dreaded disaster, now so unheard of, shipwreck.

"In them days there was still many a man bold enough to join our crews. And I've knowed cases," she added condescendingly, "where just by the muscle and brawn of such men some poor sailor lass has reached shore alive that would have fed the sharks without 'em. Oh, I ain't so down on men as you might think. It's the spoiling of them that I don't hold with. There's too much preached nowadays that man is fit for nothing but to fetch and carry and do nurse-work in big child-homes. To my mind, a man who hasn't the nerve of a woman ain't fitted to father children, let alone raise 'em. But that's not here nor there. My time's past, and I know it, or I wouldn't be setting here gossipin' to you, my lad, over an empty teapot."

I took the hint, and with our cups replenished, she bit thoughtfully into her fourteenth macaroon and continued.

"There's one voyage I'm not likely to forget, though I live to be as old as Cap'n Mary Barnacle, of the *Shouter*. 'Twas aboard the old *Shouter* that this here voyage occurred, and it was her last and likewise Cap'n Mary's. Cap'n Mary, she was then that decrepit, it seemed a mercy that she should go to her rest, and in good salt water at that.

"I remember the voyage for Cap'n Mary's sake, but most I remember it because 'twas then that I come the nighest in my life to committin' matrimony. For a man, the man had nerve; he was nearer bein' companionable than any other man I ever seed; and if it hadn't been for just one little event that showed up the—the *mannishness* of him, in a way I couldn't abide, I reckon he'd be keepin' house for me this minute."

"We cleared from Frisco with a cargo of silkateen petticoats for Brisbane. Cap'n Mary was always strong on petticoats. Leather breeches or even half-skirts would ha' paid far better, they being more in demand like, but Cap'n Mary was three-quarters owner, and says she, land women should buy petticoats, and if they didn't it wouldn't be the Lord's fault nor hers for not providing 'em.

"We cleared on a fine day, which is an all sign—or was, then when the weather and the seas o' God still counted in the trafficking of the humankind. Not two days out we met a whirling, mucking bouncer of a gale that well nigh threw the old *Shouter* a full point off her course in the first wallop. She was a stout craft, though. None of your featherweight, gas-lightened, paper-thin alloy shells, but toughened aluminum from stern to stern. Her turbine drove her through the combers at a forty-five knot clip, which named her a speedy craft for a freighter in them days.

"But this night, as we tore along through the creaming green billows, something unknown went 'way wrong down below.

"I was forward under the shelter of her long over-sloop, looking for a hairpin I'd dropped somewheres about that afternoon. It was a gold hairpin, and gold still being mighty scarce when I was a girl, a course I valued it. But suddenly I felt the old *Shouter* give a jump under my feet like a plane struck by a shell in full flight. Then she trembled all over for a full second, frightened like. Then, with the crash of doomsday ringing in my ears, I felt myself sailing through the air right into the teeth o' the shrieking gale, as near as I could judge. Down I come in the hollow of a monstrous big wave, and as my ears doused under I thought I heard a splash close by. Coming up, sure enough, there close by me was floating a new, patent, hermetic, thermo-ice-chest. Being as it was empty, and being as it was shut up air-tight, that ice-chest made as sweet a life-preserver as a woman could wish in such an hour. About ten foot by twelve, it floated high in the raging sea. Out on its top I scrambled, and hanging on by a handle I looked expectant for some of my poor fellow-women to come floating by. Which they never did, for the good reason that the *Shouter* had blowed up and went below, petticoats, Cap'n Mary and all."

"What caused the explosion?" I inquired.

"The Lord and Cap'n Mary Barnacle can explain," she answered piously. "Besides the oil for her turbines, she carried a power of gasoline for her alternative engines, and likely 'twas the cause of her ending so sudden like. Anyways, all I ever seen of her again was the empty ice-chest that Providence had well-nigh hove upon my head. On that I sat and floated, and floated and sat some more, till by-and-by the storm sort of blowed itself out, the sun come shining—this was next morning—and I could dry my hair and look about me. I was a young lass, then, and not bad to look upon. I didn't want to die, any more than you that's sitting there this minute. So I up and prays for land. Sure enough toward evening a speck heaves up low down on the horizon. At first I took it for a gas liner, but later found it was just a little island, all alone by itself in the great Pacific Ocean.

"Come, now, here's luck, thinks I, and with that I deserts the ice-chest, which being empty, and me having no ice to put in it, not likely to have in them latitudes, is of no further use to me. Striking out I swum a mile or so and set foot on dry land for the first time in nigh three days.

"Pretty land it were, too, though bare of human life as an iceberg in the Arctic.

"I had landed on a shining white beach that run up to a grove of lovely, waving palm trees. Above them I could see the slopes of a hill so high and green it reminded me of my own old home, up near Couquomgomoc Lake in Maine. The whole place just seemed to smile and smile at me. The palms waved and bowed in the sweet breeze, like they wanted to say, 'Just set right down and make yourself to home. We've been waiting a long time for you to come.' I cried, I was that happy to be made welcome. I was a young lass then, and sensitive-like to how folks treated me. You're laughing now, but wait and see if or not there was sense to the way I felt.

"So I up and dries my clothes and my long, soft hair again, which was well worth drying, for I had far more of it than now.

After that I walked along a piece, until there was a sweet little path meandering away into the wild woods.

"Here, thinks I, this looks like inhabitants. Be they civil or wild, I wonder? But after traveling the path a piece, lo and behold it ended sudden like in a wide circle of green grass, with a little spring of clear water. And the first thing I noticed was a slab of white board nailed to a palm tree close to the spring. Right off I took a long drink, for you better believe I was thirsty, and then I went to look at this board. It had evidently been tore off the side of a wooden packing box, and the letters was roughly printed in lead pencil.

"'Heaven help whoever you be,' I read. 'This island ain't just right. I'm going to swim for it. You better too. Good-by. Nelson Smith.' That's what it said, but the spellin' was simply awful. It all looked quite new and recent, as if Nelson Smith hadn't more than a few hours before he wrote and nailed it there.

"Well, after reading that queer warning I begun to shake all over like in a chill. Yes, I shook like I had the ague, though the hot tropic sun was burning down right on me and that alarming board. What had scared Nelson Smith so much that he had swum to get away? I looked all around real cautious and careful, but not a single frightening thing could I behold. And the palms and the green grass and the flowers still smiled that peaceful and friendly like. 'Just make yourself to home,' was wrote all over the place in plainer letters than those sprawly lead pencil ones on the board.

"Pretty soon, what with the quiet and all, the chill left me. Then I thought, 'Well, to be sure, this Smith person was just an ordinary man, I reckon, and likely he got nervous of being so alone. Likely he just fancied things which was really not. It's a pity he drowned himself before I come, though likely I'd have found him poor company. By his record I judge him a man of but common education.'

"So I decided to make the most of my welcome, and that I did for weeks to come. Right near the spring was a cave, dry as a biscuit box, with a nice floor of white sand. Nelson had lived there too, for there was a litter of stuff—tin cans—empty—scraps of newspapers and the like. I got to calling him Nelson in my mind, and then Nelly, and wondering if he was dark or fair, and how he come to be cast away there all alone, and what was the strange events that drove him to his end. I cleaned out the cave, though. He had devoured all his tin-canned provisions, however he come by them, but this I didn't mind. That there island was a generous body. Green milk-coconuts, sweet berries, turtle eggs and the like was my daily fare.

"For about three weeks the sun shone every day, the birds sang and the monkeys chattered. We was all one big, happy family, and the more I explored that island the better I liked the company I was keeping. The land was about ten miles from beach to beach, and never a foot of it that wasn't sweet and clean as a private park.

"From the top of the hill I could see the ocean, miles and miles of blue water, with never a sign of a gas liner, or even a little government running-boat. Them running-boats used to go most everywhere to keep the seaways clean of derelicts and the like. But I knowed that if this island was no more than a hundred miles off the regular courses of navigation, it might be many a long day before I'd be rescued. The top of the hill, as I found when first I climbed up there, was a wore-out crater. So I knowed that the island was one of them volcanic ones you run across so many of in the seas between Capricorn and Cancer.

"Here and there on the slopes and down through the jungly tree-growth, I would come on great lumps of rock, and these must have came up out of that crater long ago. If there was lava it was so old it had been covered up entire with green growing stuff. You couldn't have found it without a spade, which I didn't have nor want."

"Well, at first I was happy as the hours was long. I wandered and clambered and waded and swum, and combed my long hair on the beach, having fortunately not lost my side-combs nor the rest of my gold hairpins. But by-and-by it begun to get just a bit lonesome. Funny thing, that's a feeling that, once it starts, it gets worse and worser so quick it's perfectly surprising. And right then was when the days begun to get gloomy. We had a long, sickly hot spell, like I never seen before on an ocean island. There was dull clouds across the sun from morn to night. Even the little monkeys and parrakeets, that had seemed so gay, moped and drowsed like they was sick. All one day I cried, and let the rain soak me through and through—that was the first rain we had—and I didn't get thorough dried even during the night, though I slept in my cave. Next morning I got up mad as thunder at myself and all the world.

"When I looked out the black clouds was billowing across the sky. I could hear nothing but great breakers roaring in on the beaches, and the wild wind raving through the lashing palms.

"As I stood there a nasty little wet monkey dropped from a branch almost on my head. I grabbed a pebble and slung it at him real vicious. 'Get away, you dirty little brute!' I shrieks, and with that there come a awful blinding flare of light. There was a long, crackling noise like a bunch of Chinese fireworks, and then a sound as if a whole fleet of *Shouter*s had all went up together.

"When I come to, I found myself 'way in the back of my cave, trying to dig further into the rock with my finger nails. Upon taking thought, it come to me that what had occurred was just a lightning-clap, and going to look, sure enough there lay a big palm tree right across the glade. It was all busted and split open by the lightning, and the little monkey was under it, for I could see his tail and his hind legs sticking out.

"Now, when I set eyes on that poor, crushed little beast I'd been so mean to, I was terrible ashamed. I sat down on the smashed tree and considered and considered. How thankful I had ought to have been. Here I had a lovely, plenteous island, with food and water to my taste, when it might have been a barren, starvation rock that was my lot. And so, thinking, a sort of gradual peaceful feeling stole over me. I got cheerfuller and cheerfuller, till I could have sang and danced for joy.

"Pretty soon I realized that the sun was shining bright for the first time that week. The wind had stopped hollering, and the waves had died to just a singing murmur on the beach. It seemed kind o' strange, this sudden peace, like the cheer in my own heart after its rage and storm. I rose up, feeling sort of queer, and went to look if the little monkey had came alive again, though that was a fool thing, seeing he was laying all crushed up and very dead. I buried him under a tree root, and as I did it a conviction come to me.

"I didn't hardly question that conviction at all. Somehow, living there alone so long, perhaps my natural womanly intuition was stronger than ever before or since, and so I *knowed*. Then I went and pulled poor Nelson Smith's board off from the tree and tossed it away for the tide to carry off. That there board was an insult to my island!"

The sea-woman paused, and her eyes had a far-away look. It seemed as if I and perhaps even the macaroons and tea were quite forgotten.

"Why did you think that?" I asked, to bring her back. "How could an island be insulted?"

She started, passed her hand across her eyes, and hastily poured another cup of tea.

"Because," she said at last, poising a macaroon in mid-air, "because that island—that particular island that I had landed on—had a heart!

"When I was gay, it was bright and cheerful. It was glad when I come, and it treated me right until I got that grouchy it had to mope from sympathy. It loved me like a friend. When I flung a rock at that poor little drenched monkey critter, it backed up my act with an anger like the wrath o' God, and killed its own child to please me! But it got right cheery the minute I seen the wrong-ness of my ways. Nelson Smith had no business to say, 'This island ain't just right,' for it was a righter place than ever I seen elsewhere. When I cast away that lying board, all the birds begun to sing like mad. The green milk-coconuts fell right and left. Only the monkeys seemed kind o' sad like still, and no wonder. You see, their own mother, the island, had rounded on one o' them for my sake!

"After that I was right careful and considerate. I named the island Anita, not knowing her right name, or if she had any. Anita was a pretty name, and it sounded kind of South Sea like. Anita and me got along real well together from that day on. It was some strain to be always gay and singing around like a dear duck of a canary bird, but I done my best. Still, for all the love and gratitude I bore Anita, the company of an island, however sympathetic, ain't quite enough for a human being. I still got lonesome, and there was even days when I couldn't keep the clouds clear out of the sky, though I will say we had no more tornadoes.

"I think the island understood and tried to help me with all the bounty and good cheer the poor thing possessed. None the less my heart give a wonderful big leap when one day I seen a blot on the horizon. It drawed nearer and nearer, until at last I could make out its nature."

"A ship, of course," said I, "and were you rescued?"

"'Tweren't a ship, neither," denied the sea-woman somewhat impatiently. "Can't you let me spin this yarn without no more remarks and fool questions? This thing what was bearing down so fast with the incoming tide was neither more nor less than another island!

"You may well look startled. I was startled myself. Much more so than you, likely. I didn't know then what you, with your book-learning, very likely know now—that islands sometimes float.

Their underparts being a tangled-up mess of roots and old vines that new stuff's growed over, they sometimes break away from the mainland in a brisk gale and go off for a voyage, calm as a old-fashioned, eight-funnel steamer. This one was uncommon large, being as much as two miles, maybe, from shore to shore. It had its palm trees and its live things, just like my own Anita, and I've sometimes wondered if this drifting piece hadn't really been a part of my island once—just its daughter like, as you might say.

"Be that, however, as it might be, no sooner did the floating piece get within hailing distance than I hears a human holler and there was a man dancing up and down on the shore like he was plumb crazy. Next minute he had plunged into the narrow strip of water between us and in a few minutes had swum to where I stood.

"Yes, of course it was none other than Nelson Smith!

"I knowed that the minute I set eyes on him. He had the very look of not having no better sense than the man what wrote that board and then nearly committed suicide trying to get away from the best island in all the oceans. Glad enough he was to get back, though, for the coconuts was running very short on the floater what had rescued him, and the turtle eggs wasn't worth mentioning. Being short of grub is the surest way I know to cure a man's fear of the unknown."

"Well, to make a long story short, Nelson Smith told me he was a aeronauter. In them days to be an aeronauter was not the same as to be an aviatress is now. There was dangers in the air, and dangers in the sea, and he had met with both. His gas tank had leaked and he had dropped into the water close by Anita. A case or two of provisions was all he could save from the total wreck.

"Now, as you might guess, I was crazy enough to find out what had scared this Nelson Smith into trying to swim the Pacific. He told me a story that seemed to fit pretty well with mine, only when it come to the scary part he shut up like a clam, that aggravating way some men have. I give it up at last for just man-foolishness, and we begun to scheme to get away.

"Anita moped some while we talked it over. I realized how she must be feeling, so I explained to her that it was right needful for us to get with our kind again. If we stayed with her we should probably quarrel like cats, and maybe even kill each other out of pure human cussedness. She cheered up considerable after that, and even, I thought, got a little anxious to have us leave. At any rate, when we begun to provision up the little floater, which we had anchored to the big island by a cable of twisted bark, the green nuts fell all over the ground, and Nelson found more turtle nests in a day than I had in weeks.

"During them days I really got fond of Nelson Smith. He was a companionable body, and brave, or he wouldn't have been a professional aeronauter, a job that was rightly thought tough enough for a woman, let alone a man. Though he was not so well educated as me, at least he was quiet and modest about what he did know, not like some men, boasting most where there is least to brag of.

"Indeed, I misdoubt if Nelson and me would not have quit the sea and the air together and set up housekeeping in some quiet little town up in New England, maybe, after we had got away, if it had not been for what happened when we went. I never, let me say, was so deceived in any man before nor since. The thing taught me a lesson and I never was fooled again.

"We was all ready to go, and then one morning, like a parting gift from Anita, come a soft and favoring wind. Nelson and I run down the beach together, for we didn't want our floater to blow off and leave us. As we was running, our arms full of coconuts, Nelson Smith, stubbed his bare toe on a sharp rock, and down he went. I hadn't noticed, and was going on.

"But sudden the ground begun to shake under my feet, and the air was full of a queer, grinding, groaning sound, like the very earth was in pain.

"I turned around sharp. There sat Nelson, holding his bleeding toe in both fists and giving vent to such awful words as no decent sea-going lady would ever speak nor hear to!

"'Stop it, stop it!' I shrieked at him, but 'twas too late.

"Island or no island, Anita was a lady, too! She had a gentle heart, but she knowed how to behave when she was insulted.

"With one terrible, great roar a spout of smoke and flame belched up out o' the heart of Anita's crater hill a full mile into the air!

"I guess Nelson stopped swearing. He couldn't have heard himself, anyways. Anita was talking now with tongues of flame and such roars as would have bespoke the raging protest of a continent.

"I grabbed that fool man by the hand and run him down to the water. We had to swim good and hard to catch up with our only hope, the floater. No bark rope could hold her against the stiff breeze that was now blowing, and she had broke her cable. By the time we scrambled aboard great rocks was falling right and left. We couldn't see each other for a while for the clouds of fine gray ash.

"It seemed like Anita was that mad she was flinging stones after us, and truly I believe that such was her intention. I didn't blame her, neither!

"Lucky for us the wind was strong and we was soon out of range.

"'So!' says I to Nelson, after I'd got most of the ashes out of my mouth, and shook my hair clear of cinders. 'So, that was the reason you up and left sudden when you was there before! You aggravated that island till the poor thing druv you out!'

"'Well,' says he, and not so meek as I'd have admired to see him, 'how could I know the darn island was a lady?'

"'Actions speak louder than words,' says I. 'You should have knowed it by her ladylike behavior!'

"'Is volcanoes and slingin' hot rocks ladylike?' he says. 'Is snakes ladylike? T'other time I cut my thumb on a tin can, I cussed a little bit. Say—just a li'l' bit! An' what comes at me out o' all the caves, and out o' every crack in the rocks, and out o' the very spring o' water where I'd been drinkin'? Why snakes! *Snakes*, if you please, big, little, green, red and sky-blue-scarlet! What'd I do? Jumped in the water, of course. Why wouldn't I? I'd ruther swim and drown than be stung or swallowed to death. But how was I t' know the snakes come outta the rocks because I cussed?'

"'You, couldn't,' I agrees, sarcastic. 'Some folks never knows a lady till she up and whangs 'em over the head with a brick. A real, gentle, kind-like warning, them snakes were, which you would not heed! Take shame to yourself, Nelly,' says I, right stern, 'that a decent little island like Anita can't associate with you peaceable, but you must hurt her sacredest feelings with language no lady would stand by to hear!'

"I never did see Anita again. She may have blew herself right out of the ocean in her just wrath at the vulgar, disgustin' language of Nelson Smith. I don't know. We was took off the floater at last, and I lost track of Nelson just as quick as I could when we was landed at Frisco.

"He had taught me a lesson. A man is just full of mannishness, and the best of 'em ain't good enough for a lady to sacrifice her sensibilities to put up with.

"Nelson Smith, he seemed to feel real bad when he learned I was not for him, and then he apologized. But apologies weren't no use to me. I could never abide him, after the way he went and talked right in the presence of me and my poor, sweet lady friend, Anita!"

Now I am well versed in the lore of the sea in all ages. Through mists of time I have enviously eyed wild voyagings of sea rovers who roved and spun their yarns before the stronger sex came into its own, and ousted man from his heroic pedestal. I have followed—across the printed page—the wanderings of Odysseus. Before Gulliver I have burned the incense of tranced attention; and with reverent awe considered the history of one Munchausen, a baron. But alas, these were only men!

In what field is not woman our subtle superior?

Meekly I bowed my head, and when my eyes dared lift again, the ancient mariness had departed, leaving me to sorrow for my surpassed and outdone idols. Also with a bill for macaroons and tea of such incredible proportions that in comparison therewith I found it easy to believe her story!

THE ARTIFICIAL MAN

Clare Winger Harris
(1891–1968)

Clare Winger Harris has the distinction of being the first woman contributor to the world's first science fiction magazine, Amazing Stories. *She was a housewife raising three children when she sold her first story, "A Runaway World," to* Weird Tales, *where it appeared in July 1926. It was a remarkable debut. It built on the popular idea that a solar system is like an atom with the planets like subatomic particles and that some greater cosmic being starts manipulating the planets. She entered a story contest run by* Amazing Stories *coming in third with "The Fate of the* Poseidonia,*" published in June 1927. A little more down to Earth, so to speak, it dealt with Martians who, needing water, start to draw it away from Earth. Harris would write eleven stories in all during the years 1926 to 1930 before she laid down her pen. All of them were later collected as* Away from the Here and Now *(1947).*

Although it doesn't use the word, the following story is amongst the first to consider the idea of an augmented human, or cyborg.

IN THE ANNALS of surgery no case has ever left quite as horrible an impression upon the public as did that of George Gregory, a student of Austin College. Young Gregory was equally proficient in scholastic and athletic work, having been for two years captain of the football team, and for one year a marked success in intercollegiate debates. No student of the senior class of Austin or Decker will ever forget his masterful arguments as he upheld the affirmative in the question:—"Resolved that bodily perfection is a result of right thinking." Gregory gave every promise of being one of the masterful minds of the age; and if masterful in this instance means dominating, he was that—and more. Alas that his brilliant mentality was destined to degradation through the physical body—but that is my story.

It was the Thanksgiving game that proved the beginning of George's downfall. Warned by friends that he would be wise to desist from the more dangerous physical sports, he laughingly—though with unquestionable sincerity—referred to the context of his famous debate, declaring that a correct mental attitude toward life—he had this point down to a mathematical correctness—rendered physical disasters impossible. His sincerity in believing this was laudable, and so far his credence had stood him in good stead. No one who saw his well-proportioned six-foot figure making its way through the opponents' lines, could doubt that the science of thinking rightly was favorably exemplified in young Gregory.

But can thinking be an exact science? Before the close of that Thanksgiving game George was carried unconscious from the field, and in two days his right leg was amputated just below the hip.

During the days of his convalescence two bedside visitors brightened the weary hours spent upon the hospital cot. They were David Bell, a medical student, and Rosalind Nelson, the girl whom George had loved since his freshman year.

"I say, Rosalind," he ventured one day as she sat by his bedside. "It's too bad to think of you ever being tied up to a cripple. I'm willing to step aside—can't do it gracefully of course with only one leg—but I mean it, my dear girl. You don't want only part of a husband!"

Rosalind smiled affectionately. "George, don't think for a minute that it matters to me. You're still you, and I love you dear. Can't you believe that? The loss of a bodily member doesn't alter your identity."

"That's just what gets me," responded her lover with a puzzled frown. "I have always believed, and do now, that the mental and physical are so closely related as to be inseparable. I think it is Browning who says, 'We know not whether soul helps body more than body helps soul.' They develop together, and if either is injured the other is harmed. Losing part of my body has made me lose part of my soul. I'm not what I was. My mental attitude has changed as a result of this abominable catastrophe. I'm no longer so confident. I feel myself slipping and I—oh it is unbearable!"

Rosalind endeavored to the best of her ability to reassure the unfortunate man, but he sank into a despondent mood, and seeing that her efforts at cheering him were unavailing, she arose and left him.

In the outer hall she met Bell on his way to visit the sick man. He noticed her troubled mien and asked if George were not so well today.

"Yes, David," she replied, a quiver in her voice, "the wound is healing nicely, but he is so morose. He has a notion—oh how can I tell it—a sort of feeling that some of his mental poise and confidence have gone with his lost limb. You will soon be a graduate physician, won't you assure him that his fears are groundless?"

"I don't know but that his case is one for the minister or psychologist rather than the medical man," answered Bell. "His physical wound is healing, but it seems his mental wound is not. However, I will do my best, not only for your sake, Rosalind, but because I am interested in the happiness of my old college chum."

Rosalind smiled her gratitude and turned abruptly away to hide the tears that she had held back as long as possible.

Five months passed, and with the aid of a crutch George made excellent headway in overcoming the difficulties of locomotion. If David and Rosalind noticed a subtle change in the disposition and character of their mutual friend, they made no further reference to it.

A Transformation

At length came a day when in the company of both of these faithful friends George Gregory announced his intention of using an artificial limb instead of a crutch. His sweetheart voiced immediate remonstrance.

"No, George, I'd rather see you walking with the visible aid of a crutch than to think of your using an artificial leg. Somehow it seems like hypocrisy, a kind of appearing to be what you aren't. I know my idea is poorly expressed, but that's the way I feel about it."

A peculiar light came into Gregory's eyes, a light that neither friend had ever seen there before. He straightened visibly, almost without the aid of his crutch.

"I'll walk yet as well as any one and maybe it will give me back my mental confidence. My mind shall triumph over my body as well as it ever did!"

The artificial leg was duly applied to the hip stump, and it really was amazing to observe the rapidity with which Gregory mastered the art of using it proficiently. Anyone unacquainted with his deformity would never have realized that he did not possess two normal legs.

And then came the automobile accident a week before the time set for the Nelson-Gregory nuptials. How George Gregory's car was struck by an on coming truck, reduced to a junk-heap, and George thrown into a ditch, so that one arm was finally caused to be amputated, never will be known, for George had always been a careful driver. Even with his artificial leg he declared he had no difficulty in putting on the brake. The fall had, as was proved later, caused also internal injuries so that some of the bodily organs did not function properly.

The months that followed were to all who were closely concerned with the accident, like a descent into Hades. Dr. Bell, serving as an interne in the Good Samaritan Hospital, devoted himself untiringly to the tragic case of George Gregory. A world famous specialist was summoned in consultation concerning the internal injuries sustained by Gregory. Very little hope was held out for the life of the unfortunate man, although there was one chance; an artificial kidney.* The vigorous constitution of the invalid came to his rescue. He not only survived the operation but seemed to be in the best of health afterward.

And it is not to be wondered that Rosalind began to doubt whether her love for George Gregory could remain the same as before. Thrown constantly as she was in the company of Dr. David Bell, observing his devoted care and interest in George, she began to compare, or rather to contrast, the two men. George's rapid deterioration was no longer a possible flight of the imagination. It was an actuality. It was no longer possible to overlook the meaning behind his words.

"God expresses Himself through the physical world," he said when the three were together at George's apartment on Kenneth Drive. "He is a Spirit, but He makes Himself manifest in the perfection of a physical world. As much of physical perfection as I have lost, that much of God or Goodness has left me and there are no two ways about it."

Remonstrance was useless, so convinced was the invalid that his theories were correct. Also in his mind there grew steadily an ever

---

*Note: An "artificial kidney" has been invented recently, and tried out successfully on dogs. A cylinder of glass contains a number of celloidin tubes which strain the poisons out of the blood.

increasing dislike for the friend of his college days, the doctor. He could no longer be blind to the fact that it was a struggle for Rosalind to be loyal to him. He was also aware of the growing affection that existed between David and Rosalind. From a dislike his feelings gradually changed to those of implacable hatred for his former chum.

The Parting

At length after weary days and nights of indecision Rosalind came to the conclusion that she could not marry George Gregory. She longed to tell David of her feelings, but could not because she was conscious of her love for the young doctor. The subject of marriage had not been mentioned by either George or Rosalind since the second accident, but instinctively the girl felt that her lover's previous offer at the time of his lost leg, to release her from their engagement, was not to be renewed; though he must have known that his qualifications as a husband were now fewer than they could possibly have been before.

The moment that Rosalind had dreaded came at last. They were strolling together one evening toward the outskirts of the town. The moon softened, with its silvery glow, objects that in the glare of noon stood out in too bold relief. As they left the highway for the river-path George said:

"Let us set a day for the wedding. I've waited long enough." As he spoke he put around her waist an arm, not one with which nature had equipped him, but one so cunningly wrought that a casual observer would never have known. But Rosalind knew! She shuddered, and in that act, George Gregory knew that his doom was sealed.

"I can't marry you, George," she pleaded in a hoarse, unnatural voice. "I am sorry that it is so, but I cannot do it."

The man laughed and the tones chilled the heart of the girl. "You said once that my identity remained, no matter what the physical imperfections of my body. Now you deny it!" His voice rose in excitement.

"Listen, oh George," she cried now thoroughly panic-stricken. "You are yourself allowing your mental attitude toward life to be altered. You have admitted it. Had you remained unchanged mentally, I truly believe your physical difference would not have mattered. I loved you for what you were, but, George, you are so changed!"

"Yes I am changed," he shrieked, "but my desires and passions are no different, unless intensification indicates a difference."

He reached toward her, but adept as he was in the use of his two artificial limbs, she eluded his grasp and was off with a bound up the rough river-path and toward the highway. She heard distinctly the sound of pursuit. Could he outrun her handicapped as he was?

Once he fell, and the sound of muttered oaths came to her ears. On and on she flew, not daring to look back though she suspected that he was gaining. Just within the border of the town where the houses were somewhat scattered he caught her and simultaneously she fainted away.

When consciousness returned a dear familiar face was bent near her own. With a sob of joy she put her arms about David's neck, and in a few endearing words they plighted their troth.

David, on his way back from a professional call, where he was substituting for old Dr. Amos who was ill, had witnessed from a distance the two running figures. Before he arrived upon the spot with his car, the pursuing form had overtaken the other.

To rescue a maiden from the arms of her lover seemed a very peculiar service to render—but one look into the eyes of George Gregory proved to the doctor beyond the question of a doubt that he was not dealing with a sane man. The contest was an unequal one, though the agility displayed by the cripple would have done credit to a normal man of more than average prowess. David tried to reason with his antagonist, but the use of logic at that time was unavailing. It was a hard struggle, but George was finally willing to admit himself defeated.

A Man Obsessed

About three months following this incident Dr. Bell (now in possession of the office of the late Dr. Amos) was about to lock up after the afternoon consultations when he heard the approach of a belated visitor in the hall. Looking up he beheld Gregory who passed quickly through the waiting-room and into the inner office, closing the door behind him. The peculiar look of a fanatic, that had become more marked since his second accident, was evident now as he seated himself and turned wild eyes to the doctor.

"Don't be scared, doc," he jeered at sight of Bell's white drawn face. "I didn't come to blame you for winning Rosalind's love, though I confess the thought of your wedding next week goes considerably against the grain. I came for another purpose and I want you to help me."

He rose now and advanced toward the physician. The latter observed the perfect mastery of the artificial limbs, a mastery that proved how well the brain can be trained to control nerves and muscles under unusual conditions. Was all the effort of this brain being turned in that direction to the detriment of a well-balanced reasoning power?

"Here's my proposition, Bell," the words jangled harshly, bringing to a swift conclusion the doctor's thoughts regarding the changed mental status of his one-time friend. "I have decided what I want done. I'll admit that what I'm about to tell you will prove I have a mental quirk which, by the way, corresponds to my physical quirks, but this thing has become an obsession with me."

The speaker leaned forward and held the other's attention with a steady gaze. He then resumed. "I am going to try out an experiment, or rather have it tried out on me, for I shall be a passive factor in this case. I am going to find out how much of this mortal coil I can shuffle off and still maintain my personal identity as a piece of humanity here on earth. In other words, as much of my body as can be removed and substituted by artificial parts, I wish to have done."

During Gregory's recital David's eyes had dilated in horror, and he unconsciously recoiled from his visitor until the width of the room was between them. Not a word could he utter. The seconds ticked away on the little ebony clock on the desk and still the two men regarded each other with unquestionable antagonism.

"Well, will you do it, Bell?" The man pointed significantly to the surgical instruments and the operating table. "I have ample means to pay you handsomely. I'm going to find out about this mortal body and its relation to the soul before I die. You've robbed me of one desire of my heart, but this you shall grant!"

At last Bell spoke, and with the sound of his voice his courage returned. "George, whether you believe it or not, you are a madman and I refuse to comply with your request. If, as you yourself maintain, with the loss of every bodily member, your mental and spiritual powers have waned, what in heaven's name tell me, would you be with only enough of your body left to chain your spirit to earth? I will not aid you in this mad project of yours. Go, or shall I have you taken to the hospital for the insane?"

George Gregory saw that further persuasion was useless. He walked toward the outer office but at the doorway he turned and faced Bell. "There are other surgeons in the world, and mark my words, I shall find out yet by how slender a thread body and soul can hang together."

The Artificial Man

Five years passed. David Bell married Rosalind Nelson and built up a splendid reputation as a surgeon. Nothing had been heard in those years of George Gregory. His memory passed as an evil dream and his name was never mentioned. Then one day (it was shortly after the erection of the new county hospital) David and a young interne by the name of Lucius Stevens were putting away the instruments after an operation, when they felt rather than heard the approach of an individual. Turning they beheld the unfamiliar form of a stranger. He was a little under average height. A cap covered the upper portion of his face and a long loose overcoat concealed most of his figure.

"What can we do for you, stranger?" asked Dr. Bell of the silent figure in the door.

"Stranger!" exclaimed the hollow, metallic voice that issued from somewhere beneath the visor of the cap. "I am no stranger, though possibly you do not recognize me. Do you remember your rival George Gregory, Dr. David Bell? I am he."

"You—it is impossible," exclaimed the amazed doctor. "Gregory was a tall man, altogether different in appearance. You—"

"Nevertheless I tell you I am George Gregory and I have come to settle old accounts with you. Clear out," he shouted to the frightened Stevens. "My trouble is not with you."

Lucius lost no time in following the stranger's suggestion. After his departure the two men in the operating room faced each other for some moments in silence.

"Before I have done with you," came the metallic tones again, "I will explain a few things that may puzzle you."

Here he walked to the office door, locked it and put the key into the overcoat pocket. "Now, sit down, David Bell, don't be in a hurry, for you are not going to leave this room alive. I promise you that and I am accustomed to doing what I promise."

Bell did as he was bade. The curiosity of his analytical mind was aroused and he wished to find out more about this stranger whose identity he could in no way associate with Gregory. Fascinated, he watched while the man removed his cap and overcoat, and then before David's startled gaze the new-comer placed his right hand to his left shoulder and with a slight manipulation removed the left arm which he propped up in the chair nearest him. He then seated himself and proceeded to dismember himself until nought but a torso, head and one arm remained, all of which were scarred with countless incisions. A mirthless laugh jarred to the depths the doctor's overwrought nerves. The features of the intruder were not recognizable as those of his former friend, Gregory. There was no nose, only two nostrils flat upon the surface of the face. The head was bald and earless, the mouth a toothless gap.

A shudder of disgust went through David, and again the dry laugh of this monstrosity echoed through the room.

"I'm not exactly pretty, eh? But I'm finding out what I wanted to know. After I left you five years ago I went to a famous German surgeon and put my plea to him. He was as interested as I in the experiment, and you see the result. The operations required a period of two years in order to give nature a chance to have the body recuperate in the interim between experiments. As you see me now I am without any parts except those absolutely essential to life. One exception to this however, are my eyes. I did not yet wish to be shut off from the outer world by all of the senses. The artificial internal organs I dare not remove as I do my appendages for they are necessary to my life. The crowning operation of all was a pump replacing my heart. This pump is a simple double valve mechanism which circulates the small amount of blood required for my torso, head and arm. Look here!"

As he spoke he proceeded to reattach the artificial members. After he had again thus assumed semblance to human form he called attention to something David had not noticed before, a flat object lying upon his chest.

"This is the control board," he explained. "With the exception of the right arm I now move my body by electricity. The batteries are concealed within a hollow below the hip of my right leg. Behold in me an artificial man who lives and breathes and has his being with a minimum of mortal flesh! My various parts can be mended and replaced as you would repair the parts of your automobile."

During Gregory's recital David had not withdrawn his fascinated but horrified eyes from the mechanical man. Invulnerable and almost immortal, this creature was existing as a menace to mankind, a self-made Frankenstein. When he was again complete he stood before David, a triumphant gleam in the eyes which alone, unchanged physically, were yet scarcely recognizable as Gregory's, for the soul that peered through these windows was transformed.

In the gathering gloom Bell could see the automaton staring at him. He moved slowly toward a window hoping to elude his antagonist by a sudden exit in that direction, but Gregory crept toward him with a clock-like precision in his movements. The doctor noticed that the right hand was kept busy manipulating the control board at his chest. If this were the case, the interloper possessed only one free arm, but little had Bell reckoned on the prowess of that left arm! Like the grip of a vise the metallic fingers clutched at his throat. One thought pervaded his mind. If he could get that right hand away from the control and damage the connections to the various appendages and organs! But he soon realized how futile were his weaponless hands against the invulnerable body of his adversary. Down, down, those relentless claws bore him. The darkness fell about him like a heavy curtain. A throbbing in his temples that sounded like a distant pounding. Then oblivion.

The Thread Snaps

When David Bell regained consciousness he was lying in his bed. The bright sunlight shining through the curtains made delicate traceries across the counterpane. His first thought was that this was heaven by contrast to the events of his last conscious moments. Surely that was an angel hovering above him! No—at least not in the ethereal sense—but an angel nevertheless, for it was Rosalind, her sweet face beaming with love and solicitude.

"Mr. Stevens and I have been watching by your side for hours, David dear," she said as she placed a cool hand upon his brow. "You have him to thank for saving your life, not only at the time of the attack, but during the uncertain hours that have followed."

David turned grateful eyes toward his rescuer.

"Tell me about it, Lucius," he said quietly.

Stevens seated himself in a chair by the bedside and proceeded with this narrative.

"After that demon you called Gregory ordered me from the room, Dr. Bell, I turned over in my mind what had better be done to save you from his vengeance. I thought it advisable to say nothing at the time to Mrs. Bell because I did not wish to alarm her unnecessarily, but I knew that when I forced entrance into the room, it must be with adequate assistance, and within a very short period of time. I made my way to the office as quickly as I could without arousing suspicion. Miss Cullis was at the desk. Knowing I could rely on her natural calmness of demeanor and self-possession, I told her briefly of the danger which threatened you, then I phoned police headquarters. Before ten minutes were over Copeland and Knowles had arrived armed with automatics and crow-bars. I carried an axe. Cautiously we made our way to the door of the operating room and stood without, listening. We heard no sounds of voices and Copeland wanted to force entrance immediately, but I held him in temporary restraint. I wanted to obtain some cue as to conditions on the other side of the door before taking drastic measures. But thanks to Copeland's impatience we broke down the door and saw—I shall never forget the sight till my dying day—that fiend of hell with his talons gripping your throat. He was evidently somewhat deaf for he heard no motion of our approach. We closed in on him from the rear, but he swung around with such force in that left arm that we all went down like ten-pins. Knowles, as soon as he was on his feet again, struck him several times with the bar, but his efforts were wasted, for he might as well have rained blows upon a stone wall. Copeland aimed for his head in which he knew was encased a mortal brain, but that blow was avoided by the monster's ever active legs and arms. I was reserving my axe for a telling stroke, when it came upon me with sudden clarity of understanding, that the man governed his movements by manipulating the fingers of his right hand upon a place of control at his breast. His right arm and the switch board! These were the vulnerable parts. At last I had found the heel of Achilles!

"While Gregory was occupied with his other two antagonists I dealt a sudden stroke with the axe at his right hand, but missed, the weapon falling heavily upon his chest. My first emotion was disappointment at having missed my mark but in another second I realized that the blow had disabled him. The left arm hung useless at his side, but what prowess it lacked was made up in the increased activity of his legs. He ran, and never have I seen such speed. He would have made Atalanta resemble a snail! However, three against one put the odds to heavily in our favor. Between lurches and thrusts at the flying figure I managed to convey to the two policemen my discovery in regard to his mortal points, and we soon had his trusty right arm disabled. The rest was comparatively easy. We dismembered him. We did not want to kill him, but it was soon apparent to us that the damage done to the control board would prove fatal. He wanted to speak, but his voice was faint, and stooping I could barely get the words.

"'Tell David,' he said, 'that I've been wrong, dead wrong ever since I was carried off the field in that football game. I had been right at first. Mental perfection does make the physical harmonious, and with the right mental attitude after that accident, I could have risen above the physical handicap. It was not the physical loss of my leg that brought me to this. *It was the mind that allowed it to do so*. Tell David and Rosalind I am sorry for the past, and I wish them much happiness for the future!' Those were his last words."

David Bell and his wife looked at each other with tear-dimmed eyes.

Next day the "slender thread" which had held George Gregory to this world was laid in its last resting place, but the soul which had realized and repented of its error, who knows whither it went?

CREATURES OF THE LIGHT

Sophie Wenzel Ellis
(1894–1984)

Like Gertrude Bennett and Clare Winger Harris, Sophie Wenzel Ellis, a Southern woman from Memphis, Tennessee, was another regular contributor of strange stories to the early pulp magazines. The first was probably "The Unseen Seventh," a ghost story in The Thrill Book *in 1919 under her maiden name Sophie Louise Wenzel. She married lawyer George E. Ellis in 1922. Most of her fiction was either ghost stories or mysteries, mixed with a few romances, but she had a sudden flourish with science fiction in 1930 when a new magazine,* Astounding Stories of Super Science *appeared and was looking for stories of wild and extravagant scientific adventure. Ellis threw herself into the story with gusto, imagining a scientist seeking to create the perfect human, but the story includes lots of other intriguing ideas, not least the idea of slipping a minute or two into the future in order to be invisible to those around you. It might be over the top, but there's no denying this novelette is a grandiose performance by the author.*

IN A NIGHT club of many lights and much high-pitched laughter, where he had come for an hour of forgetfulness and an execrable dinner, John Northwood was suddenly conscious that Fate had begun shuffling the cards of his destiny for a dramatic game.

First, he was aware that the singularly ugly and deformed man at the next table was gazing at him with an intense, almost excited scrutiny. But, more disturbing than this, was the scowl of hate on the face of another man, as handsome as this other was hideous, who sat in a far corner hidden behind a broad column, with rude elbows on the table, gawking first at Northwood and then at the deformed, almost hideous man.

Northwood's blood chilled over the expression on the handsome, fair-haired stranger's perfectly carved face. If a figure in marble could display a fierce, unnatural passion, it would seem no more eldritch than the hate in the icy blue eyes.

It was not a new experience for Northwood to be stared at: he was not merely a good-looking young fellow of twenty-five, he was scenery, magnificent and compelling. Furthermore, he had been in the public eye for years, first as a precocious child and, later, as a brilliant young scientist. Yet, for all his experience with hero worshippers to put an adamantine crust on his sensibilities, he grew warm-eared under the gaze of these two strangers—this hunchback with a face like a grotesque mask in a Greek play, this other who, even handsomer than himself, chilled the blood queerly with the cold perfection of his godlike masculine beauty.

Northwood sensed something familiar about the hunchback. Somewhere he had seen that huge, round, intelligent face splattered with startling features. The very breadth of the man's massive brow was not altogether unknown to him, nor could Northwood look into the mournful, near-sighted black eyes without trying to recall when and where he had last seen them.

But this other of the marble-perfect nose and jaw, the blond, thick-waved hair, was totally a stranger, whom Northwood fervently hoped he would never know too well.

Trying to analyze the queer repugnance that he felt for this handsome, boldly staring fellow, Northwood decided: "He's like a newly-made wax figure endowed with life."

Shivering over his own fantastic thought, he again glanced swiftly at the hunchback, who he noticed was playing with his coffee, evidently to prolong the meal.

One year of calm-headed scientific teaching in a famous old eastern university had not made him callous to mysteries. Thus, with a feeling of high adventure, he finished his supper and prepared to go. From the corner of his eye, he saw the hunchback leave his seat, while the handsome man behind the column rose furtively, as though he, too, intended to follow.

Northwood was out in the dusky street about thirty seconds, when the hunchback came from the foyer. Without apparently noticing Northwood, he hailed a taxi. For a moment, he stood still, waiting for the taxi to pull up at the curb. Standing thus, with the street light limning every unnatural angle of his twisted body and every queer abnormality of his huge features, he looked almost repulsive.

On his way to the taxi, his thick shoulder jostled the younger man. Northwood felt something strike his foot, and, stooping in the crowded street, picked up a black leather wallet.

"Wait!" he shouted as the hunchback stepped into the waiting taxi.

But the man did not falter. In a moment, Northwood lost sight of him as the taxi moved away.

He debated with himself whether or not he should attempt to follow. And while he stood thus in indecision, the handsome stranger approached him.

"Good evening to you," he said curtly. His rich, musical voice, for all its deepness, held a faint hint of the tremulous, birdlike notes heard in the voice of a young child who has not used his vocal chords long enough for them to have lost their exquisite newness.

"Good evening," echoed Northwood, somewhat uncertainly. A sudden aura of repulsion swept coldly over him. Seen close, with the brilliant light of the street directly on his too perfect face, the man was more sinister than in the café. Yet Northwood, struggling desperately for a reason to explain his violent dislike, could not discover why he shrank from this splendid creature, whose eyes and flesh had a new, fresh appearance rarely seen except in very young boys.

"I want what you picked up," went on the stranger.

"It isn't yours!" Northwood flashed back. Ah! that effluvium of hatred which seemed to weave a tangible net around him!

"Nor is it yours. Give it to me!"

"You're insolent, aren't you?"

"If you don't give it to me, you will be sorry." The man did not raise his voice in anger, yet the words whipped Northwood with almost physical violence. "If he knew that I saw everything that happened in there—that I am talking to you at this moment—he would tremble with fear."

"But you can't intimidate me."

"No?" For a long moment, the cold blue eyes held his contemptuously. "No? I can't frighten you—you worm of the Black Age?"

Before Northwood's horrified sight, he vanished; vanished as though he had turned suddenly to air and floated away.

The street was not crowded at that time, and there was no pressing group of bodies to hide the splendid creature. Northwood gawked stupidly, mouth half open, eyes searching wildly everywhere. The man was gone. He had simply disappeared, in this sane, electric-lighted street.

Suddenly, close to Northwood's ear, grated a derisive laugh. "I can't frighten you?" From nowhere came that singularly young-old voice.

As Northwood jerked his head around to meet blank space, a blow struck the corner of his mouth. He felt the warm blood run over his chin.

"I could take that wallet from you, worm, but you may keep it, and see me later. But remember this—the thing inside never will be yours."

The words fell from empty air.

For several minutes, Northwood waited at the spot, expecting another demonstration of the abnormal, but nothing else occurred. At last, trembling violently, he wiped the thick moisture from his forehead and dabbed at the blood which he still felt on his chin.

But when he looked at his handkerchief, he muttered:

"Well, I'll be jiggered!"

The handkerchief bore not the slightest trace of blood.

Under the light in his bedroom, Northwood examined the wallet. It was made of alligator skin, clasped with a gold signet that bore the initial M. The first pocket was empty; the second yielded an object that sent a warm flush to his face.

It was the photograph of a gloriously beautiful girl, so seductively lovely that the picture seemed almost to be alive. The short, curved upper lip, the full, delicately voluptuous lower, parted slightly in a smile that seemed to linger in every exquisite line of her face. She looked as though she had just spoken passionately, and the spirit of her words had inspired her sweet flesh and eyes.

Northwood turned his head abruptly and groaned, "Good Heavens!"

He had no right to palpitate over the picture of an unknown beauty. Only a month ago, he had become engaged to a young woman whose mind was as brilliant as her face was plain. Always he had vowed that he would never marry a pretty girl, for he detested his own masculine beauty sincerely.

He tried to grasp a mental picture of Mary Burns, who had never stirred in him the emotion that this smiling picture invoked. But, gazing at the picture, he could not remember how his fiancée looked.

Suddenly the picture fell from his fingers and dropped to the floor on its face, revealing an inscription on the back. In a bold, masculine hand, he read: "Your future wife."

"Some lucky fellow is headed for a life of bliss," was his jealous thought.

He frowned at the beautiful face. What was this girl to that hideous hunchback? Why did the handsome stranger warn him, "*The thing inside never will be yours?*"

Again he turned eagerly to the wallet.

In the last flap he found something that gave him another surprise: a plain white card on which a name and address were written by the same hand that had penned the inscription on the picture.

Emil Mundson, Ph.D.,
44-1/2 Indian Court

Emil Mundson, the electrical wizard and distinguished scientific writer, friend of the professor of science at the university where Northwood was an assistant professor; Emil Mundson, whom, a week ago, Northwood had yearned mightily to meet.

Now Northwood knew why the hunchback's intelligent, ugly face was familiar to him. He had seen it pictured as often as enterprising news photographers could steal a likeness from the oversensitive scientist, who would never sit for a formal portrait.

Even before Northwood had graduated from the university where he now taught, he had been avidly interested in Emil Mundson's fantastic articles in scientific journals. Only a week ago, Professor Michael had come to him with the current issue of New Science, shouting excitedly:

"Did you read this, John, this article by Emil Mundson?" His shaking, gnarled old fingers tapped the open magazine.

Northwood seized the magazine and looked avidly at the title of the article, "Creatures of the Light."

"No, I haven't read it," he admitted. "My magazine hasn't come yet."

"Run through it now briefly, will you? And note with especial care the passages I have marked. In fact, you needn't bother with anything else just now. Read this—and this—and this." He pointed out penciled paragraphs.

Northwood read:

Man always has been, always will be a creature of the light. He is forever reaching for some future point of perfected evolution which, even when his most remote ancestor was a fish creature composed of a few cells, was the guiding power that brought him up from the first stinking sea and caused him to create gods in his own image.

It is this yearning for perfection which sets man apart from all other life, which made him *man* even in the rudimentary stages of his development. He was man when he wallowed in the slime of the new world and yearned for the air above. He will still be man when he has evolved into that glorious creature of the future whose body is deathless and whose mind rules the universe.

Professor Michael, looking over Northwood's shoulder, interrupted the reading:

"*Man always has been man,*" he droned emphatically. "That's not original with friend Mundson, of course; yet it is a theory that has not received sufficient investigation." He indicated another marked paragraph. "Read this thoughtfully, John. It's the crux of Mundson's thought."

Northwood continued:

Since the human body is chemical and electrical, increased knowledge of its powers and limitations will enable us to work with Nature in her sublime but infinitely slow processes of human evolution. We need not wait another fifty thousand years to be godlike creatures. Perhaps even now we may be standing at the beginning of the splendid bridge that will take us to that state of perfected evolution when we shall be Creatures who have reached the Light.

Northwood looked questioningly at the professor. "Queer, fantastic thing, isn't it?"

Professor Michael smoothed his thin, gray hair with his dried-out hand. "Fantastic?" His intellectual eyes behind the thick glasses sought the ceiling. "Who can say? Haven't you ever wondered why all parents expect their children to be nearer perfection than themselves, and why is it a natural impulse for them to be willing to sacrifice themselves to better their offspring?" He paused and moistened his pale, wrinkled lips. "Instinct, Northwood. We Creatures of the Light know that our race shall reach that point in evolution when, as perfect creatures, we shall rule all matter and live forever." He punctuated the last words with blows on the table.

Northwood laughed dryly. "How many thousands of years are you looking forward, Professor?"

The professor made an obscure noise that sounded like a smothered sniff. "You and I shall never agree on the point that mental advancement may wipe out physical limitations in the human race, perhaps in a few hundred years. It seems as though your profound admiration for Dr. Mundson would win you over to this pet theory."

"But what sane man can believe that even perfectly developed beings, through mental control, could overcome Nature's fixed laws?"

"We don't know! We don't know!" The professor slapped the magazine with an emphatic hand. "Emil Mundson hasn't written this article for nothing. He's paving the way for some announcement that will startle the scientific world. I know him. In the same manner he gave out veiled hints of his various brilliant discoveries and inventions long before he offered them to the world."

"But Dr. Mundson is an electrical wizard. He would not be delving seriously into the mysteries of evolution, would he?"

"Why not?" The professor's wizened face screwed up wisely. "A year ago, when he was back from one of those mysterious long excursions he takes in that weirdly different aircraft of his, about which he is so secretive, he told me that he was conducting experiments to prove his belief that the human brain generates electric current, and that the electrical impulses in the brain set up radioactive waves that some day, among other miracles, will make thought communication possible. Perfect man, he says, will perform mental feats which will give him complete mental domination over the physical."

Northwood finished reading and turned thoughtfully to the window. His profile in repose had the straight-nosed, full-lipped perfection of a Greek coin. Old, wizened Professor Michael, gazing at him covertly, smothered a sigh.

"I wish you knew Dr. Mundson," he said. "He, the ugliest man in the world, delights in physical perfection. He would revel in your splendid body and brilliant mind."

Northwood blushed hotly. "You'll have to arrange a meeting between us."

"I have." The professor's thin, dry lips pursed comically. "He'll drop in to see you within a few days."

And now John Northwood sat holding Dr. Mundson's card and the wallet which the scientist had so mysteriously dropped at his feet.

Here was high adventure, perhaps, for which he had been singled out by the famous electrical wizard. While excitement mounted in his blood, Northwood again examined the photograph. The girl's strange eyes, odd in expression rather than in size or shape, seemed to hold him. The young man's breath came quicker.

"It's a challenge," he said softly. "It won't hurt to see what it's all about."

His watch showed eleven o'clock. He would return the wallet that night. Into his coat pocket he slipped a revolver. One sometimes needed weapons in Indian Court.

He took a taxi, which soon turned from the well-lighted streets into a section where squalid houses crowded against each other, and dirty children swarmed in the streets in their last games of the day.

Indian Court was little more than an alley, dark and evil smelling.

The chauffeur stopped at the entrance and said:

"If I drive in, I'll have to back out, sir. Number forty-four and a half is the end house, facing the entrance."

"You've been here before?" asked Northwood.

"Last week I drove the queerest bird here—a fellow as good-looking as you, who had me follow the taxi occupied by a hunchback with a face like Old Nick." The man hesitated and went on haltingly: "It might sound goofy, mister, but there was something funny about my fare. He jumped out, asked me the charge, and, in the moment I glanced at my taxi-meter, he disappeared. Yes, sir. Vanished, owing me four dollars, six bits. It was almost ghost-like, mister."

Northwood laughed nervously and dismissed him. He found his number and knocked at the dilapidated door. He heard a sudden movement in the lighted room beyond, and the door opened quickly.

Dr. Mundson faced him.

"I knew you'd come!" he said with a slight Teutonic accent. "Often I'm not wrong in sizing up my man. Come in."

Northwood cleared his throat awkwardly. "You dropped your wallet at my feet, Dr. Mundson. I tried to stop you before you got away, but I guess you did not hear me."

He offered the wallet, but the hunchback waved it aside.

"A ruse, of course," he confessed. "It just was my way of testing what your Professor Michael told about you—that you are extraordinarily intelligent, virile, and imaginative. Had you sent the wallet to me, I should have sought elsewhere for my man. Come in."

Northwood followed him into a living room evidently recently furnished in a somewhat hurried manner. The furniture, although rich, was not placed to best advantage. The new rug was a trifle crooked on the floor, and the lamp shades clashed in color with the other furnishings.

Dr. Mundson's intense eyes swept over Northwood's tall, slim body.

"Ah, you're a man!" he said softly. "You are what all men would be if we followed Nature's plan that only the fit shall survive. But modern science is permitting the unfit to live and to mix their defective beings with the developing race!" His huge fist gesticulated madly. "Fools! Fools! They need me and perfect men like you."

"Why?"

"Because you can help me in my plan to populate the earth with a new race of godlike people. But don't question me too closely now. Even if I should explain, you would call me insane. But watch; gradually I shall unfold the mystery before you, so that you will believe."

He reached for the wallet that Northwood still held, opened it with a monstrous hand, and reached for the photograph. "She shall bring you love. She's more beautiful than a poet's dream."

A warm flush crept over the young man's face.

"I can easily understand," he said, "how a man could love her, but for me she comes too late."

"Pooh!" The scientist snapped his fingers. "This girl was created for you. That other—you will forget her the moment you set eyes on the sweet flesh of this Athalia. She is an houri from Paradise—a maiden of musk and incense." He held the girl's photograph toward the young man. "Keep it. She is yours, if you are strong enough to hold her."

Northwood opened his card case and placed the picture inside, facing Mary's photograph. Again the warning words of the mysterious stranger rang in his memory: "*The thing inside never will be yours.*"

"Where to," he said eagerly; "and when do we start?"

"To the new Garden of Eden," said the scientist, with such a beatific smile that his face was less hideous. "We start immediately. I have arranged with Professor Michael for you to go."

Northwood followed Dr. Mundson to the street and walked with him a few blocks to a garage where the scientist's motor car waited.

"The apartment in Indian Court is just a little eccentricity of mine," explained Dr. Mundson. "I need people in my work, people whom I must select through swift, sure tests. The apartment comes in handy, as to-night."

Northwood scarcely noted where they were going, or how long they had been on the way. He was vaguely aware that they had left the city behind, and were now passing through farms bathed in moonlight.

At last they entered a path that led through a bit of woodland. For half a mile the path continued, and then ended at a small, enclosed field. In the middle of this rested a queer aircraft. Northwood knew it was a flying machine only by the propellers mounted on the top of the huge ball-shaped body. There were no wings, no birdlike hull, no tail.

"It looks almost like a little world ready to fly off into space," he commented.

"It is just about that." The scientist's squat, bunched-out body, settled squarely on long, thin, straddled legs, looked gnomelike in the moonlight. "One cannot copy flesh with steel and wood, but one can make metal perform magic of which flesh is not capable. My sun-ship is not a mechanical reproduction of a bird. It is—but, climb in, young friend."

Northwood followed Dr. Mundson into the aircraft. The moment the scientist closed the metal door behind them, Northwood was instantly aware of some concealed horror that vibrated through his nerves. For one dreadful moment, he expected some terrific agent of the shadows that escaped the electric lights to leap upon him. And this was odd, for nothing could be saner than the globular interior of the aircraft, divided into four wedge-shaped apartments.

Dr. Mundson also paused at the door, puzzled, hesitant.

"Someone has been here!" he exclaimed. "Look, Northwood! The bunk has been occupied—the one in this cabin I had set aside for you."

He pointed to the disarranged bunk, where the impression of a head could still be seen on a pillow.

"A tramp, perhaps."

"No! The door was locked, and, as you saw, the fence around this field was protected with barbed wire. There's something wrong. I felt it on my trip here all the way, like someone watching me in the dark. And don't laugh! I have stopped laughing at all things that seem unnatural. You don't know what is natural."

Northwood shivered. "Maybe someone is concealed about the ship."

"Impossible. Me, I thought so, too. But I looked and looked, and there was nothing."

All evening Northwood had burned to tell the scientist about the handsome stranger in the Mad Hatter Club. But even now he shrank from saying that a man had vanished before his eyes.

Dr. Mundson was working with a succession of buttons and levers. There was a slight jerk, and then the strange craft shot up, straight as a bullet from a gun, with scarcely a sound other than a continuous whistle.

"The vertical rising aircraft perfected," explained Dr. Mundson. "But what would you think if I told you that there is not an ounce of gasoline in my heavier-than-air craft?"

"I shouldn't be surprised. An electrical genius would seek for a less obsolete source of power."

In the bright flare of the electric lights, the scientist's ugly face flushed. "The man who harnesses the sun rules the world. He can make the desert places bloom, the frozen poles balmy and verdant. You, John Northwood, are one of the very few to fly in a machine operated solely by electrical energy from the sun's rays."

"Are you telling me that this airship is operated with power from the sun?"

"Yes. And I cannot take the credit for its invention." He sighed. "The dream was mine, but a greater brain developed it—a brain that may be greater than I suspect." His face grew suddenly graver.

A little later Northwood said: "It seems that we must be making fabulous speed."

"Perhaps!" Dr. Mundson worked with the controls. "Here, I've cut her down to the average speed of the ordinary airplane. Now you can see a bit of the night scenery."

Northwood peeped out the thick glass porthole. Far below, he saw two tiny streaks of light, one smooth and stationary, the other wavering as though it were a reflection in water.

"That can't be a lighthouse!" he cried.

The scientist glanced out. "It is. We're approaching the Florida Keys."

"Impossible! We've been traveling less than an hour."

"But, my young friend, do you realize that my sun-ship has a speed of over one thousand miles an hour, how much over I dare not tell you?"

Throughout the night, Northwood sat beside Dr. Mundson, watching his deft fingers control the simple-looking buttons and levers. So fast was their flight now that, through the portholes, sky and earth looked the same: dark gray films of emptiness. The continuous weird whistle from the hidden mechanism of the sun-ship was like the drone of a monster insect, monotonous and soporific during the long intervals when the scientist was too busy with his controls to engage in conversation.

For some reason that he could not explain, Northwood had an aversion to going into the sleeping apartment behind the control room. Then, towards morning, when the suddenly falling temperature struck a biting chill throughout the sun-ship, Northwood, going into the cabin for fur coats, discovered why his mind and body shrank in horror from the cabin.

After he had procured the fur coats from a closet, he paused a moment, in the privacy of the cabin, to look at Athalia's picture. Every nerve in his body leaped to meet the magnetism of her beautiful eyes. Never had Mary Burns stirred emotion like this in him. He hung over Mary's picture, wistfully, hoping almost prayerfully that he could react to her as he did to Athalia; but her pale, over-intellectual face left him cold.

"Cad!" he ground out between his teeth. "Forgetting her so soon!"

The two pictures were lying side by side on a little table. Suddenly an obscure noise in the room caught his attention. It was more vibration than noise, for small sounds could scarcely be heard above the whistle of the sun-ship. A slight compression of the air against his neck gave him the eery feeling that someone was standing close behind him. He wheeled and looked over his shoulder. Half ashamed of his startled gesture, he again turned to his pictures. Then a sharp cry broke from him.

Athalia's picture was gone.

He searched for it everywhere in the room, in his own pockets, under the furniture. It was nowhere to be found.

In sudden, overpowering horror, he seized the fur coats and returned to the control room.

Dr. Mundson was changing the speed.

"Look out the window!" he called to Northwood.

The young man looked and started violently. Day had come, and now that the sun-ship was flying at a moderate speed, the ocean beneath was plainly visible; and its entire surface was covered with broken floes of ice and small, ragged icebergs. He seized a telescope and focused it below. A typical polar scene met his eyes: penguins strutted about on cakes of ice, a whale blowing in the icy water.

"A part of the Antarctic that has never been explored," said Dr. Mundson; "and there, just showing on the horizon, is the Great Ice Barrier." His characteristic smile lighted the morose black eyes. "I am enough of the dramatist to wish you to be impressed with what I shall show you within less than an hour. Accordingly, I shall make a landing and let you feel polar ice under your feet."

After less than a minute's search, Dr. Mundson found a suitable place on the ice for a landing, and, with a few deft manipulations of the controls, brought the sun-ship swooping down like an eagle on its prey.

For a long moment after the scientist had stepped out on the ice, Northwood paused at the door. His feet were chained by a strange reluctance to enter this white, dead wilderness of ice. But Dr. Mundson's impatient, "Ready?" drew from him one last glance at the cozy interior of the sun-ship before he, too, went out into the frozen stillness.

They left the sun-ship resting on the ice like a fallen silver moon, while they wandered to the edge of the Barrier and looked at the gray, narrow stretch of sea between the ice pack and the high cliffs of the Barrier. The sun of the commencing six-months' Antarctic day was a low, cold ball whose slanted rays struck the ice with blinding whiteness. There were constant falls of ice from the Barrier, which thundered into the ocean amid great clouds of ice smoke that lingered like wraiths around the edge. It was a scene of loneliness and waiting death.

"What's that?" exclaimed the scientist suddenly.

Out of the white silence shrilled a low whistle, a familiar whistle. Both men wheeled toward the sun-ship.

Before their horrified eyes, the great sphere jerked and glided up, and swerved into the heavens.

Up it soared; then, gaining speed, it swung into the blue distance until, in a moment, it was a tiny star that flickered out even as they watched.

Both men screamed and cursed and flung up their arms despairingly. A penguin, attracted by their cries, waddled solemnly over to them and regarded them with manlike curiosity.

"Stranded in the coldest spot on earth!" groaned the scientist.

"Why did it start itself, Dr. Mundson!" Northwood narrowed his eyes as he spoke.

"It didn't!" The scientist's huge face, red from cold, quivered with helpless rage. "Human hands started it."

"What! Whose hands?"

"*Ach!* Do I know?" His Teutonic accent grew more pronounced, as it always did when he was under emotional stress. "Somebody whose brain is better than mine. Somebody who found a way to hide away from our eyes. *Ach, Gott!* Don't let me think!"

His great head sank between his shoulders, giving him, in his fur suit, the grotesque appearance of a friendly brown bear.

"Doctor Mundson," said Northwood suddenly, "did you have an enemy, a man with the face and body of a pagan god—a great, blond creature with eyes as cold and cruel as the ice under our feet?"

"Wait!" The huge round head jerked up. "How do you know about Adam? You have not seen him, won't see him until we arrive at our destination."

"But I have seen him. He was sitting not thirty feet from you in the Mad Hatter's Club last night. Didn't you know? He followed me to the street, spoke to me, and then—" Northwood stopped. How could he let the insane words pass his lips?

"Then, what? Speak up!"

Northwood laughed nervously. "It sounds foolish, but I saw him vanish like that." He snapped his fingers.

"*Ach, Gott!*" All the ruddy color drained from the scientist's face. As though talking to himself, he continued:

"Then it is true, as he said. He has crossed the bridge. He has reached the Light. And now he comes to see the world he will conquer—came unseen when I refused my permission."

He was silent for a long time, pondering. Then he turned passionately to Northwood.

"John Northwood, kill me! I have brought a new horror into the world. From the unborn future, I have snatched a creature who has reached the Light too soon. Kill me!" He bowed his great, shaggy head.

"What do you mean, Dr. Mundson: that this Adam has arrived at a point in evolution beyond this age?"

"Yes. Think of it! I visioned gòdlike creatures with the souls of gods. But, Heaven help us, man always will be man: always will lust for conquest. You and I, Northwood, and all others are barbarians to Adam. He and his kind will do what men always do to barbarians—conquer and kill."

"Are there more like him?" Northwood struggled with a smile of unbelief.

"I don't know. I did not know that Adam had reached a point so near the ultimate. But you have seen. Already he is able to set aside what we call natural laws."

Northwood looked at the scientist closely. The man was surely mad—mad in this desert of white death.

"Come!" he said cheerfully. "Let's build an Eskimo snow house. We can live on penguins for days. And who knows what may rescue us?"

For three hours the two worked at cutting ice blocks. With snow for mortar, they built a crude shelter which enabled them to rest out of the cold breath of the spiral polar winds that blew from the south.

Dr. Mundson was sitting at the door of their hut, moodily pulling at his strong, black pipe. As though a fit had seized him, he leaped up and let his pipe fall to the ice.

"Look!" he shouted. "The sun-ship!"

It seemed but a moment before the tiny speck on the horizon had swept overhead, a silver comet on the grayish-blue polar sky. In another moment it had swooped down, eaglewise, scarcely fifty feet from the ice hut.

Dr. Mundson and Northwood ran forward. From the metal sphere stepped the stranger of the Mad Hatter Club. His tall, straight form, erect and slim, swung toward them over the ice.

"Adam!" shouted Dr. Mundson. "What does this mean? How dare you!"

Adam's laugh was like the happy demonstration of a boy. "So? You think you still are master? You think I returned because I reverenced you yet?" Hate shot viciously through the freezing blue eyes. "You worm of the Black Age!"

Northwood shuddered. He had heard those strange words addressed to himself scarcely more than twelve hours ago.

Adam was still speaking: "With a thought I could annihilate you where you are standing. But I have use for you. Get in." He swept his hand to the sun-ship.

Both men hesitated. Then Northwood strode forward until he was within three feet of Adam. They stood thus, eyeing each other, two splendid beings, one blond as a Viking, the other dark and vital.

"Just what is your game?" demanded Northwood.

The icy eyes shot forth a gleam like lightning. "I needn't tell you, of course, but I may as well let you suffer over the knowledge." He curled his lips with superb scorn. "I have one human weakness. I want Athalia." The icy eyes warmed for a fleeting second. "She is anticipating her meeting with you—bah! The taste of these women of the Black Age! I could kill you, of course; but that would only inflame her. And so I take you to her, thrust you down her throat. When she sees you, she will fly to me." He spread his magnificent chest.

"Adam!" Dr. Mundson's face was dark with anger. "What of Eve?"

"Who are you to question my actions? What a fool you were to let me, whom you forced into life thousands of years too soon, grow more powerful than you! Before I am through with all of you petty creatures of the Black Age, you will call me more terrible than your Jehovah! For see what you have called forth from unborn time."

He vanished.

Before the startled men could recover from the shock of it, the vibrant, too-new voice went on:

"I am sorry for you, Mundson, because, like you, I need specimens for my experiments. What a splendid specimen you will be!" His laugh was ugly with significance. "Get in, worms!"

Unseen hands cuffed and pushed them into the sun-ship.

Inside, Dr. Mundson stumbled to the control room, white and drawn of face, his great brain seemingly paralyzed by the catastrophe.

"You needn't attempt tricks," went on the voice. "I am watching you both. You cannot even hide your thoughts from me."

And thus began the strange continuation of the journey. Not once, in that wild half-hour's rush over the polar ice clouds, did they see Adam. They saw and heard only the weird signs of his presence: a puffing cigar hanging in midair, a glass of water swinging to unseen lips, a ghostly voice hurling threats and insults at them.

Once the scientist whispered: "Don't cross him; it is useless. John Northwood, you'll have to fight a demigod for your woman!"

Because of the terrific speed of the sun-ship, Northwood could distinguish nothing of the topographical details below. At the end of half-an-hour, the scientist slowed enough to point out a tall range of snow-covered mountains, over which hovered a play of colored lights like the *aurora australis*.

"Behind those mountains," he said, "is our destination."

Almost in a moment, the sun-ship had soared over the peaks. Dr. Mundson kept the speed low enough for Northwood to see the splendid view below.

In the giant cup formed by the encircling mountain range was a green valley of tropical luxuriance. Stretches of dense forest swept half up the mountains and filled the valley cup with tangled verdure. In the center, surrounded by a broad field and a narrow ring of woods, towered a group of buildings. From the largest, which was circular, came the auroralike radiance that formed an umbrella of light over the entire valley.

"Do I guess right," said Northwood, "that the light is responsible for this oasis in the ice?"

"Yes," said Dr. Mundson. "In your American slang, it is canned sunshine containing an overabundance of certain rays, especially the Life Ray, which I have isolated." He smiled proudly. "You needn't look startled, my friend. Some of the most common things store sunlight. On very dark nights, if you have sharp eyes, you can see the radiance given off by certain flowers, which many naturalists say is trapped sunshine. The familiar nasturtium and the marigold opened for me the way to hold sunshine against the long polar night, for they taught me how to apply the Einstein theory of bent light. Stated simply, during the polar night, when the sun is hidden over the rim of the world, we steal some of his rays; during the polar day we concentrate the light."

"But could stored sunshine alone give enough warmth for the luxuriant growth of those jungles?"

"An overabundance of the Life Ray is responsible for the miraculous growth of all life in New Eden. The Life Ray is Nature's most powerful force. Yet Nature is often niggardly and paradoxical in her use of her powers. In New Eden, we have forced the powers of creation to take ascendency over the powers of destruction."

At Northwood's sudden start, the scientist laughed and continued: "Is it not a pity that Nature, left alone, requires twenty years to make a man who begins to die in another ten years? Such waste is not tolerated in New Eden, where supermen are younger than babes and—"

"Come, worms; let's land."

It was Adam's voice. Suddenly he materialized, a blond god, whose eyes and flesh were too new.

They were in a world of golden skylight, warmth and tropical vegetation. The field on which they had landed was covered with a velvety green growth of very soft, fine-bladed grass, sprinkled with tiny, star-shaped blue flowers. A balmy, sweet-scented wind, downy as the breeze of a dream, blew gently along the grass and tingled against Northwood's skin refreshingly. Almost instantly he had the sensation of perfect well being, and this feeling of physical perfection was part of the ecstasy that seemed to pervade the entire valley. Grass and breeze and golden skylight were saturated with a strange ether of joyousness.

At one end of the field was a dense jungle, cut through by a road that led to the towering building from which, while above in the sun-ship, they had seen the golden light issue.

From the jungle road came a man and a woman, large, handsome people, whose flesh and eyes had the sinister newness of Adam's. Even before they came close enough to speak, Northwood was aware that while they seemed of Adam's breed, they were yet unlike him. The difference was psychical rather than physical; they lacked the aura of hate and horror that surrounded Adam. The woman drew Adam's head down and kissed him affectionately on both cheeks.

Adam, from his towering height, patted her shoulder impatiently and said: "Run on back to the laboratory, grandmother. We're following soon. You have some new human embryos, I believe you told me this morning."

"Four fine specimens, two of them being your sister's twins."

"Splendid! I was sure that creation had stopped with my generation. I must see them." He turned to the scientist and Northwood. "You needn't try to leave this spot. Of course I shall know instantly and deal with you in my own way. Wait here."

He strode over the emerald grass on the heels of the woman.

Northwood asked: "Why does he call that girl grandmother?"

"Because she is his ancestress." He stirred uneasily. "She is of the first generation brought forth in the laboratory, and is no different

from you or I, except that, at the age of five years, she is the ancestress of twenty generations."

"My God!" muttered Northwood.

"Don't start being horrified, my friend. Forget about so-called
natural laws while you are in New Eden. Remember, here we
have isolated the Life Ray. But look! Here comes your Athalia!"

Northwood gazed covertly at the beautiful girl approaching
them with a rarely graceful walk. She was tall, slender, round-
bosomed, narrow-hipped, and she held her lovely body in the
erect poise of splendid health. Northwood had a confused realization of uncovered bronzy hair, drawn to the back of a white neck
in a bunch of short curls; of immense soft black eyes; lips the color
of blood, and delicate, plump flesh on which the golden skylight
lingered graciously. He was instantly glad to see that while she
possessed the freshness of young girlhood, her skin and eyes did
not have the horrible newness of Adam's.

When she was still twenty feet distant, Northwood met her eyes
and she smiled shyly. The rich, red blood ran through her face; and
he, too, flushed.

She went to Dr. Mundson and, placing her hands on his thick
shoulders, kissed him affectionately.

"I've been worried about you, Daddy Mundson." Her rich
contralto voice matched her exotic beauty. "Since you and Adam
had that quarrel the day you left, I did not see him until this morning, when he landed the sun-ship alone."

"And you pleaded with him to return for us?"

"Yes." Her eyes drooped and a hot flush swept over her face.

Dr. Mundson smiled. "But I'm back now, Athalia, and I've
brought some one whom I hope you will be glad to know."

Reaching for her hand, he placed it simply in Northwood's.

"This is John, Athalia. Isn't he handsomer than the pictures of
him which I televisioned to you? God bless both of you."

He walked ahead and turned his back.

A magical half hour followed for Northwood and Athalia. The girl
told him of her past life, how Dr. Mundson had discovered her
one year ago working in a New York sweat shop, half dead from
consumption. Without friends, she was eager to follow the scientist to New Eden, where he promised she would recover her
health immediately.

"And he was right, John," she said shyly. "The Life Ray, that marvelous energy ray which penetrates to the utmost depths of earth and ocean, giving to the cells of all living bodies the power to grow and remain animate, has been concentrated by Dr. Mundson in his stored sunshine. The Life Ray healed me almost immediately."

Northwood looked down at the glorious girl beside him, whose eyes already fluttered away from his like shy black butterflies. Suddenly he squeezed the soft hand in his and said passionately:

"Athalia! Because Adam wants you and will get you if he can, let us set aside all the artificialities of civilization. I have loved you madly ever since I saw your picture. If you can say the same to me, it will give me courage to face what I know lies before me."

Athalia, her face suddenly tender, came closer to him.

"John Northwood, I love you."

Her red lips came temptingly close; but before he could touch them, Adam suddenly pushed his body between him and Athalia. Adam was pale, and all the iciness was gone from his blue eyes, which were deep and dark and very human. He looked down at Athalia, and she looked up at him, two handsome specimens of perfect manhood and womanhood.

"Fast work, Athalia!" The new vibrant voice was strained. "I was hoping you would be disappointed in him, especially after having been wooed by me this morning. I could take you if I wished, of course; but I prefer to win you in the ancient manner. Dismiss him!" He jerked his thumb over his shoulder in Northwood's direction.

Athalia flushed vividly and looked at him almost compassionately. "I am not great enough for you, Adam. I dare not love you."

Adam laughed, and still oblivious of Northwood and Dr. Mundson, folded his arms over his breast. With the golden skylight on his burnished hair, he was a valiant, magnificent spectacle.

"Since the beginning of time, gods and archangels have looked upon the daughters of men and found them fair. Mate with me, Athalia, and I, fifty thousand years beyond the creature Mundson has selected for you, will make you as I am, the deathless overlord of life and all nature."

He drew her hand to his bosom.

For one dark moment, Northwood felt himself seared by jealousy, for, through the plump, sweet flesh of Athalia's face, he saw the red blood leap again. How could she withhold herself from this splendid superman?

But her answer, given with faltering voice, was the old, simple one: "I have promised him, Adam. I love him." Tears trembled on her thick lashes.

"So! I cannot get you in the ancient manner. Now I'll use my own."

He seized her in his arms crushed her against him, and, laughing over her head at Northwood, bent his glistening head and kissed her on the mouth.

There was a blinding flash of blue electric sparks—and nothing else. Both Adam and Athalia had vanished.

Adam's voice came in a last mocking challenge: "I shall be what no other gods before me have been—a good sport. I'll leave you both to your own devices, until I want you again."

White-lipped and trembling, Northwood groaned: "What has he done now?"

Dr. Mundson's great head drooped. "I don't know. Our bodies are electric and chemical machines; and a super intelligence has discovered new laws of which you and I are ignorant."

"But Athalia. . . ."

"She is safe; he loves her."

"Loves her!" Northwood shivered. "I cannot believe that those freezing eyes could ever look with love on a woman."

"Adam is a man. At heart he is as human as the first man-creature that wallowed in the new earth's slime." His voice dropped as though he were musing aloud. "It might be well to let him have Athalia. She will help to keep vigor in the new race, which would stop reproducing in another few generations without the injection of Black Age blood."

"Do you want to bring more creatures like Adam into the world?" Northwood flung at him. "You have tampered with life enough, Dr. Mundson. But, although Adam has my sympathy, I'm not willing to turn Athalia over to him."

"Well said! Now come to the laboratory for chemical nourishment and rest under the Life Ray."

They went to the great circular building from whose highest tower issued the golden radiance that shamed the light of the sun, hanging low in the northeast.

"John Northwood," said Dr. Mundson, "with that laboratory, which is the center of all life in New Eden, we'll have to whip

Adam. He gave us what he called a 'sporting chance' because he knew that he is able to send us and all mankind to a doom more terrible than hell. Even now we might be entering some hideous trap that he has set for us."

They entered by a side entrance and went immediately to what Dr. Mundson called the Rest Ward. Here, in a large room, were ranged rows of cots, on many of which lay men basking in the deep orange flood of light which poured from individual lamps set above each cot.

"It is the Life Ray!" said Dr. Mundson reverently. "The source of all growth and restoration in Nature. It is the power that bursts open the seed and brings forth the shoot, that increases the shoot into a giant tree. It is the same power that enables the fertilized ovum to develop into an animal. It creates and recreates cells almost instantly; accordingly, it is the perfect substitute for sleep. Stretch out, enjoy its power; and while you rest, eat these nourishing tablets."

Northwood lay on a cot, and Dr. Mundson turned the Life Ray on him. For a few minutes a delicious drowsiness fell upon him, producing a spell of perfect peace which the cells of his being seemed to drink in. For another delirious, fleeting space, every inch of him vibrated with a thrilling sensation of freshness. He took a deep, ecstatic breath and opened his eyes.

"Enough," said Dr. Mundson, switching off the Ray. "After three minutes of rejuvenation, you are commencing again with perfect cells. All ravages from disease and wear have been corrected."

Northwood leaped up joyously. His handsome eyes sparkled, his skin glowed. "I feel great! Never felt so good since I was a kid."

A pleased grin spread over the scientist's homely face. "See what my discovery will mean to the world! In the future we shall all go to the laboratory for recuperation and nourishment. We'll have almost twenty-four hours a day for work and play."

He stretched out on the bed contentedly. "Some day, when my work is nearly done, I shall permit the Life Ray to cure my hump."

"Why not now?"

Dr. Mundson sighed. "If I were perfect, I should cease to be so overwhelmingly conscious of the importance of perfection." He settled back to enjoyment of the Life Ray.

A few minutes later, he jumped up, alert as a boy. "*Ach!* That's fine. Now I'll show you how the Life Ray speeds up development and produces four generations of humans a year."

With restored energy, Northwood began thinking of Athalia. As he followed Dr. Mundson down a long corridor, he yearned to see her again, to be certain that she was safe. Once he imagined he felt a gentle, soft-fleshed touch against his hand, and was disappointed not to see her walking by his side. Was she with him, unseen? The thought was sweet.

Before Dr. Mundson opened the massive bronze door at the end of the corridor, he said:

"Don't be surprised or shocked over anything you see here, John Northwood. This is the Baby Laboratory."

They entered a room which seemed no different from a hospital ward. On little white beds lay naked children of various sizes, perfect, solemn-eyed youngsters and older children as beautiful as animated statues. Above each bed was a small Life Ray projector. A white-capped nurse went from bed to bed.

"They are recuperating from the daily educational period," said the scientist. "After a few minutes of this they will go into the growing room, which I shall have to show you through a window. Should you and I enter, we might be changed in a most extraordinary manner." He laughed mischievously. "But, look, Northwood!"

He slid back a panel in the wall, and Northwood peered in through a thick pane of clear glass. The room was really an immense outdoor arena, its only carpet the fine-bladed grass, its roof the blue sky cut in the middle by an enormous disc from which shot the aurora of trapped sunshine which made a golden umbrella over the valley. Through openings in the bottom of the disc poured a fine rain of rays which fell constantly upon groups of children, youths and young girls, all clad in the merest scraps of clothing. Some were dancing, others were playing games, but all seemed as supremely happy as the birds and butterflies which fluttered about the shrubs and flowers edging the arena.

"I don't expect you to believe," said Dr. Mundson, "that the oldest young man in there is three months old. You cannot see visible changes in a body which grows as slowly as the human being, whose normal period of development is twenty years or more. But I can give you visible proof of how fast growth takes place under the full power of the Life Ray. Plant life, which, even when left to nature, often develops from seed to flower within a few weeks or months, can be seen making its miraculous changes under the Life Ray. Watch those gorgeous purple flowers over which the butterflies are hovering."

Northwood followed his pointing finger. Near the glass window through which they looked grew an enormous bank of resplendent violet colored flowers, which literally enshrouded the entire bush with their royal glory. At first glance it seemed as though a violent wind were snatching at flower and bush, but closer inspection proved that the agitation was part of the plant itself. And then he saw that the movements were the result of perpetual composition and growth.

He fastened his eyes on one huge bud. He saw it swell, burst, spread out its passionate purple velvet, lift the broad flower face to the light for a joyous minute. A few seconds later a butterfly lighted airily to sample its nectar and to brush the pollen from its yellow dusted wings. Scarcely had the winged visitor flown away than the purple petals began to wither and fall away, leaving the seed pod on the stem. The visible change went on in this seed pod. It turned rapidly brown, dried out, and then sent the released seeds in a shower to the rich black earth below. Scarcely had the seeds touched the ground than they sent up tiny green shoots that grew larger each moment. Within ten minutes there was a new plant a foot high. Within half an hour, the plant budded, blossomed, and cast forth its own seed.

"You understand?" asked the scientist. "Development is going on as rapidly among the children. Before the first year has passed, the youngest baby will have grandchildren; that is, if the baby tests out fit to pass its seed down to the new generation. I know it sounds absurd. Yet you saw the plant."

"But Doctor," Northwood rubbed his jaw thoughtfully, "Nature's forces of destruction, of tearing down, are as powerful as her creative powers. You have discovered the ultimate in creation and upbuilding. But perhaps—oh, Lord, it is too awful to think!"

"Speak, Northwood!" The scientist's voice was impatient.

"It is nothing!" The pale young man attempted a smile. "I was only imagining some of the horror that could be thrust on the world if a supermind like Adam's should discover Nature's secret of death and destruction and speed it up as you have sped the life force."

"*Ach, Gott!*" Dr. Mundson's face was white. "He has his own laboratory, where he works every day. Don't talk so loud. He might be listening. And I believe he can do anything he sets out to accomplish."

Close to Northwood's ear fell a faint, triumphant whisper: "Yes, he can do anything. How did you guess, worm?"

It was Adam's voice.

"Now come and see the Leyden jar mothers," said Dr. Mundson. "We do not wait for the child to be born to start our work."

He took Northwood to a laboratory crowded with strange apparatus, where young men and women worked. Northwood knew instantly that these people, although unusually handsome and strong, were not of Adam's generation. None of them had the look of newness which marked those who had grown up under the Life Ray.

"They are the perfect couples whom I combed the world to find," said the scientist. "From their eugenic marriages sprang the first children that passed through the laboratory. I had hoped," he hesitated and looked sideways at Northwood, "I had dreamed of having the children of you and Athalia to help strengthen the New Race."

A wave of sudden disgust passed over Northwood.

"Thanks," he said tartly. "When I marry Athalia, I intend to have an old-fashioned home and a Black Age family. I don't relish having my children turned into—experiments."

"But wait until you see all the wonders of the laboratory! That is why I am showing you all this."

Northwood drew his handkerchief and mopped his brow. "It sickens me, Doctor! The more I see, the more pity I have for Adam—and the less I blame him for his rebellion and his desire to kill and to rule. Heavens! What a terrible thing you have done, experimenting with human life."

"Nonsense! Can you say that all life—all matter—is not the result of scientific experiment? Can you?" His black gaze made Northwood uncomfortable. "Buck up, young friend, for now I am going to show you a marvelous improvement on Nature's bungling ways—the Leyden jar mother." He raised his voice and called, "Lilith!"

The woman whom they had met on the field came forward.

"May we take a peep at Lona's twins?" asked the scientist. "They are about ready to go to the growing dome, are they not?"

"In five more minutes," said the woman. "Come see."

She lifted one of the black velvet curtains that lined an entire side of the laboratory and thereby disclosed a globular jar of glass and metal, connected by wires to a dynamo. Above the jar was a Life Ray projector. Lilith slid aside a metal portion of the jar, disclosing through the glass underneath the squirming, kicking body of a baby, resting on a bed of soft, spongy substance, to which it was connected by the navel cord.

"The Leyden jar mother," said Dr. Mundson. "It is the dream of us scientists realized. The human mother's body does nothing but nourish and protect her unborn child, a job which science can do better. And so, in New Eden, we take the young embryo and place it in the Leyden jar mother, where the Life Ray, electricity, and chemical food shortens the period of gestation to a few days."

At that moment a bell under the Leyden jar began to ring. Dr. Mundson uncovered the jar and lifted out the child, a beautiful, perfectly formed boy, who began to cry lustily.

"Here is one baby who'll never be kissed," he said. "He'll be nourished chemically, and, at the end of the week, will no longer be a baby. If you are patient, you can actually see the processes of development taking place under the Life Ray, for babies develop very fast."

Northwood buried his face in his hands. "Lord! This is awful. No childhood; no mother to mould his mind! No parents to watch over him, to give him their tender care!"

"Awful, fiddlesticks! Come see how children get their education, how they learn to use their hands and feet so they need not pass through the awkwardness of childhood."

He led Northwood to a magnificent building whose façade of white marble was as simply beautiful as a Greek temple. The side walls, built almost entirely of glass, permitted the synthetic sunshine to sweep from end to end. They first entered a library, where youths and young girls poured over books of all kinds. Their manner of reading mystified Northwood. With a single sweep of the eye, they seemed to devour a page, and then turned to the next. He stepped closer to peer over the shoulder of a beautiful girl. She was reading "Euclid's Elements of Geometry," in Latin, and she turned the pages as swiftly as the other girl occupying her table, who was devouring "Paradise Lost."

Dr. Mundson whispered to him: "If you do not believe that Ruth here is getting her Euclid, which she probably never saw before today, examine her from the book; that is, if you are a good enough Latin scholar."

Ruth stopped her reading to talk to him, and, in a few minutes, had completely dumbfounded him with her pedantic replies, which fell from lips as luscious and unformed as an infant's.

"Now," said Dr. Mundson, "test Rachael on her Milton. As far as she has read, she should not misquote a line, and her comments will probably prove her scholarly appreciation of Milton."

Word for word, Rachael was able to give him "Paradise Lost" from memory, except the last four pages, which she had not read. Then, taking the book from him, she swept her eyes over these pages, returned the book to him, and quoted copiously and correctly.

Dr. Mundson gloated triumphantly over his astonishment. "There, my friend. Could you now be satisfied with old-fashioned children who spend long, expensive years in getting an education? Of course, your children will not have the perfect brains of these, yet, developed under the Life Ray, they should have splendid mentality.

"These children, through selective breeding, have brains that make everlasting records instantly. A page in a book, once seen, is indelibly retained by them, and understood. The same is true of a lecture, of an explanation given by a teacher, of even idle conversation. Any man or woman in this room should be able to repeat the most trivial conversation days old."

"But what of the arts, Dr. Mundson? Surely even your supermen and women cannot instantly learn to paint a masterpiece or to guide their fingers and their brains through the intricacies of a difficult musical composition."

"No?" His dark eyes glowed. "Come see!"

Before they entered another wing of the building, they heard a violin being played masterfully.

Dr. Mundson paused at the door.

"So that you may understand what you shall see, let me remind you that the nerve impulses and the coordinating means in the human body are purely electrical. The world has not yet accepted my theory, but it will. Under superman's system of education, the instantaneous records made on the brain give immediate skill to the acting parts of the body. Accordingly, musicians are made over night."

He threw open the door. Under a Life Ray projector, a beautiful, Juno-esque woman was playing a violin. Facing her, and with eyes fastened to hers, stood a young man, whose arms and slender fingers mimicked every motion she made. Presently she stopped playing and handed the violin to him. In her own masterly manner, he repeated the score she had played.

"That is Eve," whispered Dr. Mundson. "I had selected her as Adam's wife. But he does not want her, the most brilliant woman of the New Race."

Northwood gave the woman an appraising look. "Who wants a perfect woman? I don't blame Adam for preferring Athalia. But how is she teaching her pupil?"

"Through thought vibration, which these perfect people have developed until they can record permanently the radioactive waves of the brains of others."

Eve turned, caught Northwood's eyes in her magnetic blue gaze, and smiled as only a goddess can smile upon a mortal she has marked as her own. She came toward him with outflung hands.

"So you have come!" Her vibrant contralto voice, like Adam's, held the birdlike, broken tremulo of a young child's. "I have been waiting for you, John Northwood."

Her eyes, as blue and icy as Adam's, lingered long on him, until he flinched from their steely magnetism. She slipped her arm through his and drew him gently but firmly from the room, while Dr. Mundson stood gaping after them.

They were on a flagged terrace arched with roses of gigantic size, which sent forth billows of sensuous fragrance. Eve led him to a white marble seat piled with silk cushions, on which she reclined her superb body, while she regarded him from narrowed lids.

"I saw your picture that he televisioned to Athalia," she said. "What a botch Dr. Mundson has made of his mating." Her laugh rippled like falling water. "I want you, John Northwood!"

Northwood started and blushed furiously. Smile dimples broke around her red, humid lips.

"Ah, you're old-fashioned!"

Her large, beautiful hand, fleshed more tenderly than any woman's hand he had ever seen, went out to him appealingly. "I can bring you amorous delight that your Athalia never could offer in her few years of youth. And I'll never grow old, John Northwood."

She came closer until he could feel the fragrant warmth of her tawny, ribbon bound hair pulse against his face. In sudden panic he drew back.

"But I am pledged to Athalia!" tumbled from him. "It is all a dreadful mistake, Eve. You and Adam were created for each other."

"Hush!" The lightning that flashed from her blue eyes changed her from seductress to angry goddess. "Created for each other! Who wants a made-to-measure lover?"

The luscious lips trembled slightly, and into the vivid eyes crept a suspicion of moisture. Eternal Eve's weapons! Northwood's handsome face relaxed with pity.

"I want you, John Northwood," she continued shamelessly. "Our love will be sublime." She leaned heavily against him, and her lips were like a blood red flower pressed against white satin. "Come, beloved, kiss me!"

Northwood gasped and turned his head. "Don't, Eve!"

"But a kiss from me will set you apart from all your generation, John Northwood, and you shall understand what no man of the Black Age could possibly fathom."

Her hair had partly fallen from its ribbon bandage and poured its fragrant gold against his shoulder.

"For God's sake, don't tempt me!" he groaned. "What do you mean?"

"That mental and physical and spiritual contact with me will temporarily give you, a three-dimension creature, the power of the new sense, which your race will not have for fifty thousand years."

White-lipped and trembling, he demanded: "Explain!"

Eve smiled. "Have you not guessed that Adam has developed an additional sense? You've seen him vanish. He and I have the sixth sense of Time Perception—the new sense which enables us to penetrate what you of the Black Age call the Fourth Dimension. Even you whose mentalities are framed by three dimensions have this sixth sense instinct. Your very religion is based on it, for you believe that in another life you shall step into Time, or, as you call it, eternity." She leaned closer so that her hair brushed his cheek. "What is eternity, John Northwood? Is it not keeping forever ahead of the Destroyer? The future is eternal, for it is never reached. Adam and I, through our new sense which comprehends Time and Space, can vanish by stepping a few seconds into the future, the Fourth Dimension of Space. Death can never reach us, not even accidental death, unless that which causes death could also slip into the future, which is not yet possible."

"But if the Fourth Dimension is future Time, why can one in the third dimension feel the touch of an unseen presence in the Fourth Dimension—hear his voice, even?"

"Thought vibration. The touch is not really felt nor the voice heard: they are only imagined. The radioactive waves of the brain of even you Black Age people are swift enough to bridge Space and Time. And it is the mind that carries us beyond the third dimension."

Her red mouth reached closer to him, her blue eyes touched hidden forces that slept in remote cells of his being. "You are going into Eternal Time, John Northwood, Eternity without beginning or end. You understand? You feel it? Comprehend it? Now for the contact—kiss me!"

Northwood had seen Athalia vanish under Adam's kiss. Suddenly, in one mad burst of understanding, he leaned over to his magnificent temptress.

For a split second he felt the sweet pressure of baby-soft lips, and then the atoms of his body seemed to fly asunder. Black chaos held him for a frightful moment before he felt sanity return.

He was back on the terrace again, with Eve by his side. They were standing now. The world about him looked the same, yet there was a subtle change in everything.

Eve laughed softly. "It is puzzling, isn't it? You're seeing everything as in a mirror. What was left before is now right. Only you and I are real. All else is but a vision, a dream. For now, you and I are existing one minute in future time, or, more simply, we are in the Fourth Dimension. To everything in the third dimension, we are invisible. Let me show you that Dr. Mundson cannot see you."

They went back to the room beyond the terrace. Dr. Mundson was not present.

"There he goes down the jungle path," said Eve, looking out a window. She laughed. "Poor old fellow. The children of his genius are worrying him."

They were standing in the recess formed by a bay window. Eve picked up his hand and laid it against her face, giving him the full, blasting glory of her smiling blue eyes.

Northwood, looking away miserably, uttered a low cry. Coming over the field beyond were Adam and Athalia. By the trimming on the blue dress she wore, he could see that she was still in the Fourth Dimension, for he did not see her as a mirror image.

A look of fear leaped to Eve's face. She clutched Northwood's arm, trembling.

"I don't want Adam to see that I have passed you beyond," she gasped. "We are existing but one minute in the future. Always Adam and I have feared to pass too far beyond the sweetness of reality. But now, so that Adam may not see us, we shall step five minutes into what-is-yet-to-be. And even he, with all his power, cannot see into a future that is more distant than that in which he exists."

She raised her humid lips to his. "Come, beloved."

Northwood kissed her. Again came the moment of confusion, of the awful vacancy that was like death, and then he found himself and Eve in the laboratory, following Adam and Athalia down a long corridor. Athalia was crying and pleading frantically with Adam. Once she stopped and threw herself at his feet in a gesture of dramatic supplication, arms outflung, streaming eyes wide open with fear.

Adam stooped and lifted her gently and continued on his way, supporting her against his side.

Eve dug her fingers into Northwood's arm. Horror contorted her face, horror mixed with rage.

"My mind hears what he is saying, understands the vile plan he has made, John Northwood. He is on his way to his laboratory to destroy not only you and most of these in New Eden, but me as well. He wants only Athalia."

Striding forward like an avenging goddess, she pulled Northwood after her.

"Hurry!" she whispered. "Remember, you and I are five minutes in the future, and Adam is only one. We are witnessing what will occur four minutes from now. We yet have time to reach the laboratory before him and be ready for him when he enters. And because he will have to go back to Present Time to do his work of destruction, I will be able to destroy him. Ah!"

Fierce joy burned in her flashing blue eyes, and her slender nostrils quivered delicately. Northwood, peeping at her in horror, knew that no mercy could be expected of her. And when she stopped at a certain door and inserted a key, he remembered Athalia. What if she should enter with Adam in Present Time?

They were inside Adam's laboratory, a huge apartment filled with queer apparatus and cages of live animals. The room was a strange paradox. Part of the equipment, the walls, and the floor was glistening with newness, and part was mouldering with extreme age. The powers of disintegration that haunt a tropical forest seemed to be devouring certain spots of the room. Here, in the midst of bright marble, was a section of wall that seemed as old as the pyramids. The surface of the stone had an appalling mouldiness, as though it had been lifted from an ancient graveyard where it had lain in the festering ground for unwhole-some centuries.

Between cracks in this stained and decayed section of stone grew fetid moss that quivered with the microscopic organisms that infest age-rotten places. Sections of the flooring and woodwork also reeked with mustiness. In one dark, webby corner of the room lay a pile of bleached bones, still tinted with the ghastly grays and pinks of putrefaction. Northwood, overwhelmingly nauseated, withdrew his eyes from the bones, only to see, in another corner, a pile of worm-eaten clothing that lay on the floor in the outline of a man.

Faint with the reek of ancient mustiness, Northwood retreated to the door, dizzy and staggering.

"It sickens you," said Eve, "and it sickens me also, for death and decay are not pleasant. Yet Nature, left to herself, reduces all to this. Every grave that has yawned to receive its prey hides corruption no less shocking. Nature's forces of creation and destruction forever work in partnership. Never satisfied with her composition, she destroys and starts again, building, building towards the ultimate of perfection. Thus, it is natural that if Dr. Mundson isolated the Life Ray, Nature's supreme force of compensation, isolation of the Death Ray should closely follow. Adam, thirsting for power, has succeeded. A few sweeps of his unholy ray of decomposition will undo all Dr. Mundson's work in this valley and reduce it to a stink-ing holocaust of destruction. And the time for his striking has come!"

She seized his face and drew it toward her. "Quick!" she said. "We'll have to go back to the third dimension. I could leave you safe in the fourth, but if anything should happen to me, you would be stranded forever in future time."

She kissed his lips. In a moment, he was back in the old familiar world, where right is right and left is left. Again the subtle change wrought by Eve's magic lips had taken place.

Eve went to a machine standing in a corner of the room.

"Come here and get behind me, John Northwood. I want to test it before he enters."

Northwood stood behind her shoulder.

"Now watch!" she ordered. "I shall turn it on one of those cages of guinea pigs over there."

She swung the projector around, pointed it at the cage of small, squealing animals, and threw a lever. Instantly a cone of black mephitis shot forth, a loathsome, bituminous stream of putrefaction that reeked of the grave and the cesspool, of the utmost reaches of decay before the dust accepts the disintegrated atoms. The first touch of seething, pitchy destruction brought screams of sudden agony from the guinea pigs, but the screams were cut short as the little animals fell in shocking, instant decay. The very cage which imprisoned them shriveled and retreated from the hellish, devouring breath that struck its noisome rot into the heart of the wood and the metal, reducing both to revolting ruin.

Eve cut off the frightful power, and the black cone disappeared, leaving the room putrid with its defilement.

"And Adam would do that to the world," she said, her blue eyes like electric-shot icicles. "He would do it to you, John Northwood—and to me!" Her full bosom strained under the passion beneath.

"Listen!" She raised her hand warningly. "He comes! The destroyer comes!"

A hand was at the door. Eve reached for the lever, and, the same moment, Northwood leaned over her imploringly.

"If Athalia is with him!" he gasped. "You will not harm her?"

A wild shriek at the door, a slight scuffle, and then the doorknob was wrenched as though two were fighting over it.

"For God's sake, Eve!" implored Northwood. "Wait! Wait!"

"No! She shall die, too. You love her!"

Icy, cruel eyes cut into him, and a new-fleshed hand tried to push him aside. The door was straining open. A beloved voice shrieked. "John!"

Eve and Northwood both leaped for the lever. Under her tender white flesh she was as strong as a man. In the midst of the struggle, her red, humid lips approached his—closer, closer. Their merest pressure would thrust him into Future Time, where the laboratory and all it contained would be but a shadow, and where he would be helpless to interfere with her terrible will.

He saw the door open and Adam stride into the room. Behind him, lying prone in the hall where she had probably fainted, was Athalia. In a mad burst of strength he touched the lever together with Eve.

The projector, belching forth its stinking breath of corruption swung in a mad arc over the ceiling, over the walls—and then straight at Adam.

Then, quicker than thought, came the accident. Eve, attempting to throw Northwood off, tripped, fell half over the machine, and, with a short scream of despair, dropped into the black path of destruction.

Northwood paused, horrified. The Death Ray was pointed at an inner wall of the room, which, even as he looked, crumbled and disappeared, bringing down upon him dust more foul than any obscenity the bowels of the earth might yield. In an instant the black cone ate through the outer parts of the building, where crashing stone and screams that were more horrible because of their shortness followed the ruin that swept far into the fair reaches of the valley.

The paralyzing odor of decay took his breath, numbed his muscles, until, of all that huge building, the wall behind him and one small section of the room by the doorway alone remained whole. He was trying to nerve himself to reach for the lever close to that quiet formless thing still partly draped over the machine, when a faint sound in the door electrified him. At first, he dared not look, but his own name, spoken almost in a gasp, gave him courage.

Athalia lay on the floor, apparently untouched.

He jerked the lever violently before running to her, exultant with the knowledge that his own efforts to keep the ray from the door had saved her.

"And you're not hurt!" He gathered her close.

"John! I saw it get Adam." She pointed to a new mound of mouldy clothes on the floor. "Oh, it is hideous for me to be so glad, but he was going to destroy everything and everyone except me. He made the ray projector for that one purpose."

Northwood looked over the pile of putrid ruins which a few minutes ago had been a building. There was not a wall left intact.

"His intention is accomplished, Athalia," he said sadly. "Let's get out before more stones fall."

In a moment they were in the open. An ominous stillness seemed to grip the very air—the awful silence of the polar wastes which lay not far beyond the mountains.

"How dark it is, John!" cried Athalia. "Dark and cold!"

"The sunshine projector!" gasped Northwood. "It must have been destroyed. Look, dearest! The golden light has disappeared."

"And the warm air of the valley will lift immediately. That means a polar blizzard." She shuddered and clung closer to him. "I've seen Antarctic storms, John. They're death."

Northwood avoided her eyes. "There's the sun-ship. We'll give the ruins the once over in case there are any survivors; then we'll save ourselves."

Even a cursory examination of the mouldy piles of stone and dust convinced them that there could be no survivors. The ruins looked as though they had lain in those crumbling piles for centuries. Northwood, smothering his repugnance, stepped among them—among the green, slimy stones and the unspeakable revolting débris, staggering back and faint and shocked when he came upon dust that was once human.

"God!" he groaned, hands over eyes. "We're alone, Athalia! Alone in a charnal house. The laboratory housed the entire population, didn't it?"

"Yes. Needing no sleep nor food, we did not need houses. We all worked here, under Dr. Mundson's generalship, and, lately under Adam's, like a little band of soldiers fighting for a great cause."

"Let's go to the sun-ship, dearest."

"But Daddy Mundson was in the library," sobbed Athalia. "Let's look for him a little longer."

Sudden remembrance came to Northwood. "No, Athalia! He left the library. I saw him go down the jungle path several minutes before I and Eve went to Adam's laboratory."

"Then he might be safe!" Her eyes danced. "He might have gone to the sun-ship."

Shivering, she slumped against him. "Oh, John! I'm cold."

Her face was blue. Northwood jerked off his coat and wrapped it around her, taking the intense cold against his unprotected shoulders. The low, gray sky was rapidly darkening, and the feeble light of the sun could scarcely pierce the clouds. It was disturbing to know that even the summer temperature in the Antarctic was far below zero.

"Come, girl," said Northwood gravely. "Hurry! It's snowing."

They started to run down the road through the narrow strip of jungle. The Death Ray had cut huge swathes in the tangle of trees and vines, and now areas of heaped débris, livid with the colors of recent decay, exhaled a mephitic humidity altogether alien to the snow that fell in soft, slow flakes. Each hesitated to voice the new fear: had the sun-ship been destroyed?

By the time they reached the open field, the snow stung their flesh like sharp needles, but it was not yet thick enough to hide from them a hideous fact.

The sun-ship was gone.

It might have occupied one of several black, foul areas on the green grass, where the searching Death Ray had made the very soil putrefy, and the rocks crumble into shocking dust.

Northwood snatched Athalia to him, too full of despair to speak. A sudden terrific flurry of snow whirled around them, and they were almost blown from their feet by the icy wind that tore over the unprotected field.

"It won't be long," said Athalia faintly. "Freezing doesn't hurt, John, dear."

"It isn't fair, Athalia! There never would have been such a marriage as ours. Dr. Mundson searched the world to bring us together."

"For scientific experiment!" she sobbed. "I'd rather die, John. I want an old-fashioned home, a Black Age family. I want to grow old with you and leave the earth to my children. Or else I want to die here now under the kind, white blanket the snow is already spreading over us." She drooped in his arms.

Clinging together, they stood in the howling wind, looking at each other hungrily, as though they would snatch from death this one last picture of the other.

Northwood's freezing lips translated some of the futile words that crowded against them. "I love you because you are not perfect. I hate perfection!"

"Yes. Perfection is the only hopeless state, John. That is why Adam wanted to destroy, so that he might build again."

They were sitting in the snow now, for they were very tired. The storm began whistling louder, as though it were only a few feet above their heads.

"That sounds almost like the sun-ship," said Athalia drowsily.

"It's only the wind. Hold your face down so it won't strike your flesh so cruelly."

"I'm not suffering. I'm getting warm again." She smiled at him sleepily.

Little icicles began to form on their clothing, and the powdery snow frosted their uncovered hair.

Suddenly came a familiar voice: "*Ach, Gott!*"

Dr. Mundson stood before them, covered with snow until he looked like a polar bear.

"Get up!" he shouted. "Quick! To the sun-ship!"

He seized Athalia and jerked her to her feet. She looked at him sleepily for a moment, and then threw herself at him and hugged him frantically.

"You're not dead?"

Taking each by the arm, he half dragged them to the sun-ship, which had landed only a few feet away. In a few minutes he had hot brandy for them.

While they sipped greedily, he talked, between working the sun-ship's controls.

"No, I wouldn't say it was a lucky moment that drew me to the sun-ship. When I saw Eve trying to charm John, I had what you American slangists call a hunch, which sent me to the sun-ship to get it off the ground so that Adam couldn't commandeer it. And what is a hunch but a mental penetration into the Fourth Dimension?" For a long moment, he brooded, absent-minded. "I was in the air when the black ray, which I suppose is Adam's deviltry, began to destroy everything it touched. From a safe elevation I saw it wreck all my work." A sudden spasm crossed his face. "I've flown over the entire valley. We're the only survivors—thank God!"

"And so at last you confess that it is not well to tamper with human life?" Northwood, warmed with hot brandy, was his old self again.

"Oh, I have not altogether wasted my efforts. I went to elaborate pains to bring together a perfect man and a perfect woman of what Adam called our Black Age." He smiled at them whimsically.

"And who can say to what extent you have thus furthered natural evolution?" Northwood slipped his arm around Athalia. "Our children might be more than geniuses, Doctor!"

Dr. Mundson nodded his huge, shaggy head gravely.

"The true instinct of a Creature of the Light," he declared.

THE FLYING TEUTON

Alice Brown
(1857–1948)

The following story is usually treated as supernatural because of its depiction of not just a ghost ship—as per The Flying Dutchman, *hence the title—but an entire fleet. But on closer reading the ships aren't ghosts at all. It's not even that they're just invisible but, rather like the protagonist in the earlier story, "The Ray of Displacement," they seem to be able to pass through solid matter. The public believe it's a curse from God, so no scientific rationale is provided, but that doesn't stop the basic premise from having a science fiction element. What's more, the story is set slightly in the future. It takes place after the conclusion of the First World War, but the story was first published in August 1917, over a year before the armistice and almost two years before the peace treaty was signed. So on two counts the story classifies as science fiction.*

It is perhaps Alice Brown's best-known story, and certainly one of the most discussed in its day, hailed as that year's best short fiction. Brown was born and raised in New Hampshire where, for a while, she was a school teacher until she could escape to Boston and become a staff writer on the Youth's Companion. *She had a long career writing novels, plays and children's books well into her seventies. Much of her work has mystical or supernatural overtones, and the best of it was collected as* The Empire of Death *(2003).*

WE WERE TALKING, that night, about the year after the great war, which was also the year of the great religious awakening. A few of us had dropped into the Neo-Pacifist Club, that assemblage of old-time pacifists who, having been actually immersed in the great war, afterward set humbly about informing themselves on the subject of those passions that make the duty of defensive fighting at times a holy one, and who, having once seen Michael hurl Satan down to the abyss, actually began to suspect you'd got to do more than read

213

Satan the beatitudes if he climbed up again. There never was anything like the eagerness of these after-the-war pacifists to study human nature in other than its sentimental aspects, to learn to predict the great waves of savagery that wreck civilization at intervals—unless there are dykes—and to plumb the heroism of those men who gave their bodies that the soul of nations might securely live. We retraced a good many steps on wide territory that night, took up and looked at things familiar we were all the better for remembering, as a man says his creed, from time to time, no matter how well he knows it; and chiefly we read over, in its different aspects, the pages of the great revival.

This was not, it will be remembered, an increase in the authority of any church, but simply the recognition in all hearts of all peoples that God is, and that the plagues of the world spawn out of our forgetfulness that He is, and our overwhelming desire toward the things of this temporal life. Whence, in our haste, we sacrifice to the devil.

The terms of peace had been as righteous as it is possible for hurt hearts to compass. Evil had been bound and foresight had made the path of justice plain. The nations that had borne the first attack (and with what light limbs they sprang to meet it!), they who had learned to read God in that awful unfurling of the book of life, were wonderfully ready to enter on their task of building up the house of peace.

The United States, which had saved its skin so long that it had almost mislaid its soul, was sitting at the knees of knowledge and plainly asking to be taught.

One amazing detail of the great revival was that there would be no industrial boycott. The men about the peace table came away from it imbued with a desire to save the peoples who had been guilty of the virtue of obedience in following false rulers, and they represented to their governments the barbarity of curbing even the commerce of those nations which had set the world ablaze. So it followed that territory and indemnities were the penalties imposed.

Boundaries had changed—and so had governments!—but every country was to go back to its former freedom of selling goods in all quarters of the earth. In their arguments the peace delegates had used the supreme one that, "Vengeance is mine, saith the Lord." They had fixed the terms of all the vengeance they were sure they were entitled to, fixed it soberly and sternly, too. But they did not quite see, having effectually crippled the powers of evil, that they ought also to cripple the powers of good—the desire of nations to sell their products and the work of their hands abroad. So they said, "Vengeance is mine," but they did not go so far as to note that, judging from the centuries, God Himself would indubitably be on the spot. He would repay.

It was in the spring of that year that a German liner, tied up since 1914, and waiting the will of the English fleet, was released and put into commission again and loaded with goods for the United States. On board her was Frank Drake, a newspaper correspondent who had, after hovering about the Peace Congress, been wandering over Germany, in a desultory fashion, to see what changes had been wrought in her by the war. And it was Drake who sat with us at the Neo-Pacifist Club that night, and was persuaded to tell a story he had, in the year after the great war, got into print, and so done incalculable service to the muse of history and incidentally made his own name to be remembered. For what he had seen hundreds of others confirmed—only he saw it first, and gave his testimony in a manner so direct as well as picturesque that it might as well have been he alone who sang that epic story.

He was a tough, seasoned-looking man, spare, and hard as whipcord, and with an adventurer's face—aquiline, uplifted, looking for horizons, some one said. At this point of his life he was gray-headed—yet he never would be old. We had gathered about him as near as might be, and really filled the room 'way back into the shadows. He had been talking about the supernatural events that had been inextricably mingled with facts of battle and march and countermarch, and owned himself frankly bemused by them.

"It isn't as if I hadn't actually been in the war, you know. I've seen things. So I haven't the slightest doubt the French saw Angels at Mons. I haven't the slightest doubt a fellow blown out of a trench into the next world meets so many of the other fellows that were blown there before him that it gives him that look—I've seen it over and over—of surprise, wonder—oh, and beauty, too, a most awful kind of beauty. Whatever they saw when they went from the trenches to—wherever it is—they were mighty well pleased to be there, and satisfied that the other fellows could get along without them. And, mind you, things lasted, too, after they got over there. I'm as sure of that as I am that I'm sitting here. The love of it all—the *Vive la France*! you know, the grotesque fondness for Old Blighty that made them die for her—those weren't wiped out by getting into another atmosphere. It's all pretty much the same, you know, there and here, only there you apparently see the causes of things and the values. And you absolutely can't hate. You see what a damned shame it was that anybody should ever have been ignorant enough to hate."

"You'd say it was a world of peace?" inquired a rapt-looking saint of a man in the front row.

"Don't talk to me about peace—yet," said Drake. "I'm not 'over there' and I haven't got that perspective. As for Peace, too many crimes were committed in her name those last years of the war—too much cowardice, expediency, the devil and all of people wanting to save their skins and their money. Yes, I know, peace is what they've earned for us, those fellows in Europe, and it's a gorgeous peace. But the word itself does take me back. It sets me swearing.

"Yes, I'll tell you about the ship, the *Treue Königin* and the first sailing from Bremen, if that's what you want. They'd put a good deal of spectacular business into the sailing of that ship because she was the first one after John Bull tied up their navy. There were flags flying and crowds and *Hochs*! and altogether it was an occasion to be remembered. I knew it would be, and that's why I was there. I rather wanted to say I was on the first free ship that sailed out of Bremen, and I hadn't much Teutonophobia any more since *Kultur* had got its medicine. Besides, wasn't the whole world chanting 'Vengeance is mine, saith the Lord'? and I'd begun to be awakened a little, too, in my inward parts, though I didn't talk much about it.

"The voyage began delightfully. I was the only American on board. The rest were merchants going over to take up relations with us again, and a brand-new consul or two.

"Near evening on the second day something queer happened. It was foggy, and I was on deck, talking, in a desultory way, with the first mate, but really wondering if I'd get to sleep to the *obligato* of the fog-horn all night, when suddenly out of the dark came the nose of a great ship. Our engines were reversed, but not in time, and she struck us amidships. I cowered down. Yes, I did. There was no time for life-preservers and lowering boats. I simply cowered, and put my hand over my eyes. But there was no crash, no shock, no grinding of splintered wood and steel. I opened my eyes. The first mate was still there, a foot or two further from me, as if the apparition had started him toward his duty in case of collision. But he was looking off into the fog, and now he turned and looked at me. I have seen men frightened, but never one in such case as this.

"'Did you see it?' he asked. It was as if he implored me to say I did, because otherwise he'd have to doubt his own reason.

"'Did she sheer off?' I asked. My voice sounded queer to me.

"'Sheer off? She struck us amidships and went through us.'

"I began to stare 'round me. I must have looked a fool. It was as if I were trying to find a break in a piece of china. There was the deck unoccupied, except for us two, exactly as it had been when we were struck. There were the smoke-stacks and boats and altogether the familiar outline of the ship.

"'Well!' said I. My voice was a sort of croak now. 'You and I are nutty, that's all. There never was any ship.'

"But he turned and ran up to the lookout, and afterward I heard the wireless zip-zipping away, and later—for I stayed on deck; I couldn't go below—I saw him and the captain standing amidships and talking. They looked pretty serious and really a little sick, just as I felt. And I didn't speak to either of them. Didn't dare. You know when there's a fire in the hold, or any such pleasantry on board ship, you'd better let the great high josses alone. Well, that's what I did. The next day I found the first mate wouldn't notice me. He spoke English perfectly, but all I could get out of him was a *Nein* or a *Was?* and as stupid a grin as I ever saw on a man's face. So I understood the incident was closed. And it began to look a little thin even to me, who'd seen it. But the next night, with no fog at all, the thing happened again. A big British liner came down on us, and we did all in the power of navigation to escape her; but she raked us and passed through us from stem to stern, and I swear I put out a hand and touched her as she cut the length of the deck. For an instant I believed what I know every officer and man on the ship believed at the time—believed madly, for you couldn't reason in the face of that monstrous happening. They believed England had broken the peace, only they cursed 'perfidious Albion', and I knew she'd got wind of some devil's deed we hadn't heard of, and was at her old beneficence of police work on the sea. But it was only an instant we could think that, for there, untouched, unharmed, at her maximum speed went the English liner. And we, too, were untouched. We weren't making our course because we'd manoeuvred so as to avoid her, and now we lay there an instant, trembling, before we swung about again. Yes, it's a fact; the ship did tremble, and though there was her plain mechanical reason for it, it seemed to be out of panic, just as everybody aboard of her was trembling. And that night the ship's doctor, a fat, red haired man whom I'd remembered as waltzing indefatigably and exquisitely on a trip to the West Indies, but who had been turned into a jelly of melancholy by the war, did talk to me. I think he had to. He thought he was dotty and the entire lot were dotty. He had to find out whether a plain American was onto it.

"'A pleasant night, last night,' he said.

"I knew what he was coming at, and I thought there was no need of wasting our time by preambles. 'Yes,' said I, 'till the British liner ran us down.'

"He looked at me—well, I can't tell you how grateful he looked. All melted up, you know, the way those fatties are sometimes. I stepped away a little. I thought he was going to kiss me.

"'You saw it, too. God be thanked!' said he.

"'Saw it!' said I. 'I not only saw her, but I touched her on the elbow as she split the deck. Splendid old lady, wasn't she? But eccentric. Makes nothing of cutting a ship in two, just for fun, I suppose, and not losing speed. Her little joke. That's how I take it, don't you?'

"But I shouldn't have chaffed him. It shut him up. I think he gathered I was in it somehow. But the fact is, I was scared. Well, if you'll believe me (and of course you will, for I've written the thing out in my *Notes on the War*, and it's been quoted over and over till even school children know the text of it), so, as you must believe me and the hundreds that corroborated me, in other cases, the next collision, or ramming—what shall I call it?—happened in broad daylight, ten o'clock in the morning. It was a perfectly clear day and a smooth sea. We were in the track of the freighter *Marlborough* and by George! she didn't make way for us. She ran through us as neat as wax and cut us in two. But we didn't stay cut. We didn't show a crack. And there she went churning off, as gay as you please, and we steamed on our way. Only we weren't gay, mind you. We were scared. And the doctor, ghastly again, came stumping across the deck to me, and I thought he was going to fall into my arms'.

"'*Lieber Gott!*' said he. 'What does it mean? We see them, but they don't see us.'

"That was it. We'd been slow in taking the hint, but we'd got it at last. We were invisible on the seas. We were practically non-existent. And we'd tried wireless. We'd sent out call after call, and finally, desperately, S.O.S., because we knew, if there was a conspiracy against us, no ship but would listen to that. No answer. We were marooned—if you can be marooned on the high seas. Civilization had put us on an island of silence and invisibility. Civilization wasn't going to play with us any more. Though it wasn't civilization at all. It wasn't any punitive device of man. It was something outside.

"For the next two days the doctor hardly left me. I suppose he was forbidden to talk and he had to keep near somebody or die. He wasn't the man he was when he tripped the light fantastic in the West Indies. He'd been through the war, and now he was going through something worse. And he said to me the morning of the day before we were due in New York: 'Now we shall be picking up the pilot. And I sha'n't go back. I've got a married daughter in New York. I shall spend the rest of my life with her.'

"And, as we went on, we sighted ship after ship. It was a great day for ships. You don't know how many there are till they won't notice you. And not one of them would turn out for us or answer our call. And everybody was desperate now on board, though we had learned we were safe enough, even if they did run us down. So we put on all speed and forged ahead and rammed whatever got in our way—and never sunk them. Never seemed to touch them. But with every one we hit and never hurt our panic grew. Desperate panic it was, from the captain down to me.

"Then we came on the pilot-boats, quite a distance out, for of course everybody knew we were coming and there was a little rivalry about it all. Just as I'd wanted to say I'd crossed on the first liner from Germany, every pilot wanted to be the one to take us in. Well, the first one was making for us and we hailed him. But, by God! he didn't slacken speed, but dashed through us. That little bobbing boat ran through our High Mightiness and went careering on in search of us. And we went on in search of another pilot. And we sighted him shortly, several of him; and, though they didn't ram us in that ghostly way they had, they went sliding by us, bowing and ducking to the breeze, and always—that was the awful part of it—looking for us. There we were, and they didn't see us. And we hailed them and they didn't hear. By that time we were all pretty nearly off our nuts, and it took us different ways. The captain was purple with rage and that sense of injured importance the *Deutscher* didn't lose by having to toe the mark after his big war bubble burst.

He swore, and I heard him, that he could take his own ship into New York Harbor as well as any condemned pilot that ever sailed, and he wouldn't even hail another, not even if all the dead in the sea rose up and faced him. I was rather worried over that about the dead in the sea. I couldn't help thinking that if all the dead recently in the sea rose up and combined against any German ship, it would have short shrift. But we were all, I fancy, rather glad of his stand. We had full confidence in him. He was a clever, daring fellow, heavier by the iron cross—for in the last years he'd sent scores of men unwarned to the bottom, and he had been precious to *Kultur*. We much preferred to go in unpiloted to making even one more grisly try at proving; we were living flesh and blood.

"My own particular obsession was to wonder what would happen if, when a ship clove our decks and left them solid, as they'd done so often in the past six days, I put myself in the way of its nose. Would it run through me like a wedge and I close up unhurt? Would it smash me, carry me with it off the deck, to Kingdom Come? I wondered. It didn't smash life-boats or deck-chairs. It—I found I was beginning to call the ramming boats 'it', as if there were but one of them, though really there were all kinds of craft—it would go through a rug on the deck and leave it in its folds. But I hadn't the sand to put myself in its way and find out beyond a peradventure whether it tore me, nerve from nerve. The drama was too absorbing. I wanted to see it through.

"I did once, in my most daring minute, stand at the rail, watching a freighter as it came, head on. And I yelled to the lookout, when we were near enough to pass the time of day, yelled desperately. I can see him now, a small man with a lined face and blue eyes screwed up into a point of light, as if the whole of him concentrated on feeding that one sense, just seeing. And there was a queer-shaped scar on his face, a kind of cornerwise scar, and I wondered how he got it. The freighter was making her maximum, and so were we; but in that fraction of time I waited for her it seemed to be hours, eternities, that I had my eyes on the little man with the scar. It seemed as if he and I alone had the destinies of the world to settle. If I called and he answered me, it would prove our ship was not lost in a loneness of invisibility more terrible than any obvious danger on the unfriending seas. Suppose you were in hell, and you met face to face somebody that had your pardon or your reprieve mysteriously about him, and the pardon and reprieve of all the other millions there—think how you'd fix him with your eyes and signal, call to him for fear he'd pass you by. Well, that was how I signaled and called the little man with the scar. But he stared through me out of those clear lenses of his eyes, and when I yelled the loudest he made up his lips and began whistling a tune. It was a whispering sort of whistle, but I heard it, we were so near. And the tune—well, the tune broke my heart, for it was an old English tune that made me think of the beautiful English country as I had seen it not many weeks before, with the people soberly beginning to till it with unhindered hands. And here were we on a German ship that the world wouldn't even see. The sun himself wouldn't lend his rays for humanity to look at us. And then, as I began to cry—yes, I cried; I'm not ashamed to own it—the freighter passed through us, and I felt the unsteadiness of her wake. The lookout and I had met in hell, and I had hailed and he had not answered me.

"Was I glad to see the Goddess of Liberty and the gay old harbor of New York? I believe you! We went on like a house afire, and once, when I caught a glimpse of the captain's face, I decided he could steer his ship into any harbor against unknown reefs and currents, because there was a fury of revolt in him, a colossal force of will. And as I thought that I exulted with him, for, though nobody knows better than I do the way the Furies ought to be out after *Kultur*—oh yes, they'd have to or lose their job—there was a kind of fighting grit that came up in me, and for that voyage I was conscious that the *Treue Königin* had got to fight, fight, for existence, the mere decency of being visible to other men.

"Did we sail into New York Harbor, invisible or not? You know as well as I. The story's as real as George Washington and Valley Forge, and it'll stay in print, like them, as long as print exists. We stopped short, an instant only, it was, and then against the impetus of the ship and the steering-gear and against the will of her captain and her crew, she turned about and steamed away again. And, by the Lord! it was as graceful a sweep as I ever saw a liner make. I remember thinking afterward that if there were heavenly steersmen on board—the Furies, maybe, taking the wheel by turn—they knew little tricks of the trade we pygmies didn't. At first, of course, this right-about didn't worry us. It didn't worry me, at least. I thought the captain had found it a more difficult matter than he thought, and was going down harbor again, for some mysterious nautical reason, to turn about and make another try. But pretty soon I saw my fat doctor making for me. He was ash-colored by now, and he kept licking his dry lips.

" 'We're going back,' he said.

" 'Ah?' said I. 'They don't find it so easy?'

" 'Why, good God, man!' said he, 'look at the sun. Don't you see your course? We're going back, I tell you!'

" 'Back where?' I asked. But I didn't care. So long as we made New York Harbor within twenty-four hours or more I wasn't going to complain.

" 'Where?' said he. He looked at me now as if he'd got to teach me what he knew, and I thought I'd never seen eyes so full of fear, absolute fear. Nothing in mortal peril calls that look into a man's eyes. It has to be the unknown, the unaccounted for. 'How do I know where? I only know the ship's out of our hands somehow. She won't answer.'

" 'Well,' said I, 'something's the matter with the machinery.'

You see, the bright American air, the gay harbor, the Statue of Liberty—everything had heartened me. For an instant I didn't believe we really were invisible.

" 'The machinery's working like a very devil, but it's working its own way. You can't turn a nut on this ship unless it wants to be turned. You can't change your course unless this devil of a ship wants it changed.'

"I laughed out. 'You've been under too much of a strain,' said I. 'You seem to think the ship's bewitched. Well, if we're not to dock in New York, after this little excursion down the harbor, where is it your impression we're going? Back to Germany?'

" 'God knows!' said he, solemnly. 'Maybe back to Germany. I wish to God we were there now. Or maybe we shall sail the seas—eternally.'

"I laughed again. But he put up his hand and I stopped, his panic was actually so terrible. I was sorry for the beggar.

" 'Wait!' said he. 'I thought that would happen. I wonder it hasn't happened before.'

"A man came running—the quartermaster, I found out afterward—and I had one glimpse of his face as he passed. He covered the deck as if he were sprinting and was near the goal, and suddenly the run seemed only to give him momentum or get his courage up, and he slipped over the rail, with a flying confusion of arms and legs, into the sea. I yelled and grabbed a life-belt and ran to the rail, where I knew there'd be sailors, in an instant, letting down a boat. I threw my life-belt, and kept on yelling. But no one came, no one but the doctor. In an instant I realized he was by my side, his hands in his pockets, his eyes fixed in a dull gaze on the sea. And we hadn't slackened speed, and we hadn't put about, and I saw two other sailors idly at the rail, looking as the doctor looked, into the vacancy of immediate space.

"'For God's sake!' said I, 'aren't they going to do something?'

"'There's nothing to do,' said my doctor. 'He won't come up. They know that.'

"'Won't come up? Why won't he?'

"'Because he doesn't want to.'

"'Didn't you ever hear of the instinct of self-preservation,' I spluttered, 'that steps in and defeats a man, even when he thinks he's done with life? How do you know but that poor devil is back there choking and praying and swallowing salt water, and sane again—sane enough to see he was dotty when he swapped the deck for the sea?'

"'He won't come up,' said the doctor. He turned away and, with his head bent, began to plod along the deck. I couldn't help thinking of the way he used to fly over the planks in the West Indies. But he did turn back again for one word more. 'Did you,' said he—and he looked a little—what shall I say? a little ironic, as if he'd got something now to floor me with—'did you ever happen to hear of the *Flying Dutchman*?'

"Then I understood. They'd understood days and days ago. The words had been whispered round the decks, in the galley even, *Der Fliegende Holländer*. Knowing better than I what *Kultur* had done on the high seas, they had hit sooner on the devilish logic of it. They were more or less prepared. But it struck me right in the center. After they'd once said it I didn't any more doubt it than if I'd been sitting in an orchestra stall, with the score of the old 'Flying Dutchman' and the orchestra's smash-bang, and the fervid conductor with his bald head to divert me for a couple of hours or so. And I went down into my cabin and stretched out in my berth and shut my eyes. And all I remember thinking was that if we were going to sail the seas invisible till doomsday, I'd stay put, and not get dotty seeing the noses of ships cleaving the deck or trying to hail little whistling men with scars on their faces and finding that, so far as they knew, I wasn't in the universe at all. I think I dozed for a matter of two days. The steward brought me grub of a primitive sort—our cuisine wasn't what it had been coming over—and news, whenever I would take it from him. There had been more of the ghastly collisions. We had picked up S.O.S. from an English ship and gone to her rescue, to find we could neither hail her nor, though we launched boats, approach her within twenty feet. Why? The same reason that prevented our going into New York Harbor, if you can tell me what that was. And in the midst of these futile efforts a Brazilian freighter came along and did the salving neatly, and neither ship was any more aware of us than if we had been a ship of air. But my chief news, the only news that mattered, I got from the steward's face. It was yellow-white, and the eyes were full of that same apprehension I had learned to know now—the fear of the unknown. He brought sparse items he dropped in a whisper, as if he had been forbidden to speak and yet must speak or die— about the supply of water, the supply of coal. It was his theory that, when the coal actually gave out and the engines stopped, we should stay everlastingly tossing in the welter of the sea, watching the happy wings of commerce go sailing by and hailed of none. But it proved not to be so, and when he told me that it scared him doubly. For we economized coal to the last point, and it seemed the engines went excellently without it, so long, at least, as we kept our course for Germany. Evidently, so far as we could guess at the designs of those grim powers that had blocked our way, a German ship was to be aided, even by miracle, to sail back to Germany, but not to enter any foreign port.

"And we did go back to Germany, meeting meantime other German ships just out, and we hailed them and they saw us and answered. And the same fear was on the faces of every soul on board, and the news was in every case the same. They were, to all the ships of all the world, invisible.

"We slunk into harbor, and I have never known how the captain met his company or what exporters said to the consignments of merchandise returned untouched in the hold. I only know that the shore officials looked strangely at us, and, since we told the same mad story, seemed to think a whole ship's crew could hardly be incarcerated. You must remember, too, that since the war signs and wonders have had a different value. There have been too many marvels for men to scout them. There was the marvel of the victory, you know. But we won't go into that. I suppose books will be written about it until the end of time. You may be sure of one thing—I didn't let the grass grow under my feet. I made tracks for Holland, and from there I put for England, and sailed from Liverpool, and was in New York in a little over five days. And by that time the whole world knew. German ships were in full possession, as they had been before the war, of the freedom of the seas—except that they mysteriously could not use it. German ships took passengers, as of old, and loaded themselves with merchandise. But there was not a port on the surface of the globe that could receive them. Yet there was a certain beneficence in the power that condemned them to this wandering exile—they could go home. And so strange a thing is hope, and so almost unbreakable a thing is human will, that they would no sooner go home in panic than they would recover and dare the seas again, as if, peradventure, it might be different this time, or as if the wrath of the grim powers might be overpast. And it came out that the shipping rotted in their harbors, and there were many suicides among sailing-men."

When Drake reached this point in his story he almost always got solemn and rhythmic. His book was succinctly and plainly written, but he could never speak of its subject-matter without the rhythm of imagery.

"You know," he said, "it wasn't expected, while the war was going on, that there would be a living being, not of Teutonic birth, who would ever be sorry for a Teuton until near the tail end of time, when some of the penalties had been worked out. But, by George! the countries that had been injured most were the first to be sorry for the poor devils that had prated about the freedom of the seas and now had to keep their own ships tied up in the harbour, tight as in war-time, because the fleet that withstood them, drew the mighty cordon, was the fleet of God. Belgium had prayers for the German fleet. England sent experts over to see what was the matter with their engines. Russia played for the boats, as she had for her four-footed beasties in the war, and France—well, France proposed that she and England should establish a maritime service from Germany to the United States and South American ports, with nominal freight rates, until the world found out what the deuce was the matter or what God actually meant. And it was to begin the week before Christmas, if you remember, and something put it into the clever French brain that maybe a German Christmas ship—a ship full of toys and dolls—might be let to pass. France didn't think it was bamboozling God by swinging a censer of sentiment before Him; but it knew God might be willing to speak our little language with us, encourage us in it, let us think He knew what we were trying to tell Him when we took the toys and dolls.

"And, if you remember, a string of ships went out that day, all with pretty serious men on board, men of an anxious countenance.

And the British and French ships convoyed them like mother birds, and other British and French ships met them, and for a time no Teuton ship dared speak a foreign one for fear it should not be answered. But finally one—it was my old ship the *Treue Königin*, and on her my old captain—couldn't wait any longer and did speak, and every French and English boat answered her, and she knew she and the rest were saved—for the eyes of man could see them and the ears of man were opened to their voice. And that's all. You know the rest—how the German navy slowly and soberly built up its lines and sailed the seas again; but how nobody ceased talking of the wonder of the time when it was under the ban of judgement. And nobody ever will cease, because of all the signs and marvels of these later years this was the greatest."

"I have heard," said the pacifist in the front row—"I hardly like to mention it; these things are best forgotten—that there is one submarine that actually does sail the sea, and never has found rest. But that they say is sometimes visible."

"Yes," said Drake. He looked grim now, and nobody could doubt that he knew whereof he spoke. "She is sometimes visible. She plies back and forth along the Irish coast. I'd heard it over and over, and I'd heard that on the seventh of May she shows her periscope. She is obliged to. And they say she has one passenger— the Man We Do Not Mention."

"Do you suppose—" began the pacifist, and Drake interrupted him.

"Do I suppose that sentence ever will be worked out? Maybe it isn't a sentence. Maybe it's a warning, against pride and cruelty and lust of power; maybe the Man We Do Not Mention is condemned to sail it, and is willing to be hated, so long as he can be the warning to the world—the warning against his sins. Do you know, I've often wondered if he knows one thing—if he knows that, whenever toasts are drunk in Germany, it isn't now *Der Tag*, but it is, since that day when England and France joined hands to help their scared old enemy, 'The Fleet!'"

"He'd think it meant the German navy, anyway," said a younger, unregenerate man, who was no pacifist—only, being young, too quick of tongue and rash of apprehension.

"Oh no, he wouldn't," said Drake, a very warm tone in his voice. It told youth it didn't know what its elders had been through. "He'd know it meant—The Fleet!"

COPYRIGHT ACKNOWLEDGMENTS
AND STORY SOURCES

ALL OF THE stories in this anthology are in the public domain unless otherwise noted. All efforts have been made to trace the authors' estates, and the publisher would welcome hearing from any representative if there has been an inadvertent transgression of copyright.

"Those Fatal Filaments" by Mabel Ernestine Abbott, first published in *Argosy*, January 1903.

"Ely's Automatic Housemaid" by Elizabeth W. Bellamy, first published in *The Black Cat*, December 1899.

"A Divided Republic" by Lillie Devereux Blake, first published in *The Phrenological Journal*, February-March 1887. Included in *A Daring Experiment and Other Stories* (New York: Lovell, Coryell, 1892).

"The Flying Teuton" by Alice Brown, first published in *Harper's Magazine*, August 1917. Included in *The Flying Teuton and Other Stories* (New York: Macmillan, 1918).

"Creatures of the Light" by Sophie Wenzel Ellis, first published in *Astounding Stories of Super-Science*, February 1930. No record of copyright renewal.

"The Great Beast of Kafue" by Clotilde Graves reprinted from *Under the Hermes* (New York: Dodd, Mead, 1917) published under the pseudonym Richard Dehan.

"The Artificial Man" by Clare Winger Harris, first published in *Science Wonder Quarterly*, Fall 1929. Included in *Away from the Here and Now* (Philadelphia: Dorrance & Co., 1947). No record of copyright renewal. Unable to trace author's estate.

"The Automaton Ear" by Florence McLandburgh, first published in *Scribner's Monthly*, May 1873 and included in *The Automaton Ear and Other Stories* (Chicago: Jansen, McClurg, 1876).

"When Time Turned" by Ethel Watts Mumford, first published in *The Black Cat*, January 1901.

"The Third Drug" by Edith Nesbit, first published in *The Strand Magazine*, February 1908 under the name E. Bland.

"Via the Hewitt Ray" by M. F. Rupert, first published in *Science Wonder Quarterly*, Spring 1930. No record of copyright renewal. Unable to trace author's estate.

"The Ray of Displacement" by Harriett Prescott Spofford, first published in *The Metropolitan Magazine*, October 1903.

"Friend Island" by Francis Stevens, first published in *All-Story Weekly*, 7 September 1918.

"The Painter of Dead Women" by Edna W. Underwood, first published in *The Smart Set*, January 1910. Included in *A Book of Dear Dead Women* (Boston: Little, Brown, 1911).